Wideman's Gospel

WIDEMAN'S
GOSPEL

A Novel

David Dayton

BOCA CIEGA
BOOKS
Silver Spring
Maryland

ISBN 978-0-934184-23-6 (epub)

ISBN 978-0-934184-24-3 (trade paperback)

Library of Congress Control Number: 2023938812

The quoted lyrics to "Ripple" are by Robert Hunter, copyright Ice Nine Publishing Company. Used with permission.

The cover was designed and produced by David Dayton using Adobe Express to edit the image from Adobe Stock, which is used under its standard license. The ornamental image at the end of the book is used under the standard license from depositphotos.com. Its creator is the contributor named *weit* (Yulia Buchatskaya).

The title page logo was designed and produced by David Dayton using Adobe Express to edit a public domain photograph from the Art Institute of Chicago used under the terms of Creative Commons Zero (CC0). The image is a plaster sculpture by Auguste Préault, *Silence,* 1842–1843.

Boca Ciega Books is an imprint of Alembic Press.

For my wife Nancy
in memory of my parents
and with gratitude to
my friend Stephen

Chapters & Verses

CHAPTER ONE

Reconciling the World unto Himself

CAL FELT HIS SHOULDER nudged—for the second time, he realized. The stewardess smiled at him and turned away to wake another passenger. Cal uncrumpled himself, sat up, and fastened his seatbelt. He leaned his forehead to the window. The paucity of lights had him thinking they were still downstate. The 747 banked suddenly. The lifted wing revealed a glimmering expanse of lights. They became brighter as they coalesced into an intense rim shining at the edge of Lake Michigan's solid black. Cal stared in amazement.

He sat back and shut his eyes, the better to focus on the floaty sensation of descent. He listened hard to the suddenly tenuous-sounding drone of the engines. He put his nose to the window again to see if he could make out any landmarks. He identified the East-West Tollway where it swerved and snaked northwest toward the Tri-State. Elmore, where he still had a bedroom in his parents' house, was about ten miles south, a Will County farm town that had become, during the White flight of the Sixties, a suburb of both Joliet and Chicago.

Leveling out of another sharp turn, the 747 decelerated into its final approach to O'Hare. He watched the shadowy suburban terrain become relatively clean, orderly, well-lighted neighborhoods, places he'd probably never passed through but recognized as familiar. He couldn't help but recall his recent impressions of Mexico City: motley older neighborhoods and a dusty, chaotic sprawl of newer ramshackle barrios. He felt a twinge of regret that he'd had to leave that foreign city just when he'd begun to feel at home there.

Peering down at the glistening streets of a low-rise apartment complex, he was surprised to see someone out: a White guy with broad shoulders and a big belly striding briskly on a damp sidewalk, swinging a classic black lunch box with a curved top. The mammoth aircraft roared over him at the height of only a few stories, it seemed, and still he didn't look up.

Runway lights stretched out ahead. The thought that in a few minutes he would be walking on the same ground as the guy going to work or just getting home at three in the morning hit Cal with a sudden sense of relief. He sat up straight and shut his eyes, stoically enduring the frantic racing of his heart as the jet engines screeched.

Cal handed his passport to the immigration officer, a youngish-looking Black guy, who listened without looking at him. Cal cut short his spiel about an "educational vacation." The man faintly smiled and carefully placed his rubber stamp. With a perfectly indistinct note of sarcasm as he handed the passport back, he said, "Welcome home."

Cal paused as he entered the Customs area and then went to the farthest inspection counter, which had the shortest line. He unslung the metal-frame backpack and stood it by his side. An odd feeling made him look up to his left. Josh was standing right over him, behind a small section of glass wall on the floor above. His protuberant eyes were fixed in a look of dazed incredulity; his mouth formed a vacuous O. He drew his hand from the pocket of his blue parka, flashed a vampirish Groucho grin, and wiggled his fingers. Cal blushed and looked away, then scratched under his left ear with his extended middle finger.

The Customs officer was only peeking and poking with cursory disdain. The woman in front of Cal, a frazzled-looking Latina whose neon blue eye-shadow appeared to be keeping her false lashes barely open, didn't speak English. The officer questioned her in Spanish pronounced with a flat Midwestern twang and gracelessly conferred permission to move on. He stepped back as Cal hefted the backpack onto the counter. Cal had the impression of penetrating the man's apathetic countenance and glimpsing an inner face pleasurably aroused by contempt. As Cal unbuckled the pack's straps, the officer examined his passport, then leaned over to fake a look inside the pack. "Do you have anything to declare?"

"Just this sweater."

"That's all?"

"Yes. I bought other stuff, but I mailed all of it back to my parents."

"How long have you been out of the country?"

"A little over three months."

"Did you visit countries other than Mexico?"

"Guatemala, for two weeks, and Belize, for a day."

"What is your press-entt occu-*pay*-tion?"

"I was a college student, until recently."

Cal could have sworn the man was gloating behind his mask. "Take everything out and lay it on the counter."

"Sure." He glanced up. Josh shrugged and mimed his Howdy Doody laugh, head and shoulders bobbing.

As Cal stepped off the escalator, Josh greeted him with "Jesus, what an asshole that guy is. Come on, we got a long walk." Wheeling away, he looked genuinely pissed off. Cal caught up and reached for his usual tone of voice for bantering with Josh.

Josh chummily bared his fangs. "So, you short-haired hippie freak, where'd you hide the mary-gee-whah-na?" His bulging eyes looked speedy; his stride was frantic.

Cal flinched a smile that felt all wrong.

"Your beard gave you away," Josh said. "Too bushy."

"Hey, man, this thing is heavy," Cal said. "How about slowing down?"

Josh aped an affronted gape. "You know how much caffeine I've consumed in the past two hours?" He slackened his pace. "It's a good thing you sent me that telegram. Yesterday I got your letter from CheTUmal, in which you say that you are going to the travel agent to see about getting a flight back before Christmas."

"It's ChetuMAL—as if you didn't know."

Keeping his eyes straight ahead, Josh pushed his chin out; his mouth appeared to be full of something he couldn't swallow for wanting to laugh. He prided himself on lexical knowledge and took peculiar delight in mispronouncing all foreign and most highfalutin words. He glanced over, then peered suspiciously.

"Aren't you happy to be back home, boy?"

"Overjoyed."

"You don't look it."

"It's the jet lag."

In his Maxwell Smart voice Josh said, "You can't fool me. You only get jet lag when you fly *across* time zones."

"Believe me, I've changed time zones. I've just come from *tiempo Mexicano*."

"That's not a time zone, you turkey. Take a left."

"It's beyond time zones."

"Beyond time zones," Josh echoed sarcastically.

The Howard Street Gold Coin was packed with the usual nighthawks, almost all of them male—swing-shift insomniacs, truck drivers, winos keeping warm. Cal spotted a foursome of freaks, two couples in a booth back in the corner. He looked squarely at Josh just as Josh looked him in the eyes while tucking a wavy strand of black hair behind his ear.

"Just like old times, eh?" Cal said.

"No-o," Josh said. "We aren't tripping."

"Maybe you aren't."

Josh's thick black eyebrows flexed into peeved position. "I'm really disappointed you didn't take some peyote and turn into a crow like Don Juan."

"A crow-like Don Juan?" Instantly, Cal regretted the quip, seeing the puckish smile it provoked.

"So..." Josh said. "When are you gonna tell me what you obviously didn't want to commit to paper, though you committed practically everything else to paper, if not *on* paper. Is it true what they say about Mexican sin-yerritas?"

"I wouldn't know. What do they say?"

Josh nodded a dubious pucker as he swung a look away and then back, fixing a look that was somewhere between ridicule and pity. "Maybe you should become a priest. You actually told people you'd taken a vow of chastity?"

"It saved my ass that one time."

"As in em-bare-*ass*-ment?"

"Exactly." Cal uneasily chuckled. "They were like the fat whores in a Fellini movie."

Josh aped a look of revulsion then glanced at his watch. "How long do you think we can stretch the Yaqui way of knowledge? I've only got—two hours and fourteen minutes, to be exact."

"You gotta *work* today?"

"Thanks to you Christians, this is my busy season, remember? It's all overtime if I go in today. I plan to take off early Christmas Eve and stay out a couple days—sick."

"Why didn't you get some sleep earlier?"

"I wanna keep in shape for pulling all-nighters."

"Right," Cal said.

"I'm thinking now I'd rather be a psychologist," Josh said. "Get a master's in counseling."

"Career counseling?"

Josh bounced his eyebrows. A proud underachiever, he considered Cal an incurable grade-grubber. Josh had waited until the deadline at the end of sophomore year to declare a major. It came as no surprise to any of his friends that he chose what was reputedly the easiest major at Northwestern. But Josh had fervently insisted that he chose sociology because he wanted to become a social worker. Cal felt vindicated in skepticism when, two months before graduation, Josh took the postal service exam, just to see how he'd do, and nearly aced it.

"So how much you making now?" Cal asked.

"Almost six an hour."

"Damn. When's the next exam."

"Not for a long, long time. By the way, how do you propose to pay your half of the rent, if you don't mind my asking? Especially if we get the two-bedroom on the Near North Side a friend at work is going to vacate in a couple months."

"Really?"

"It's a great location and only fifty dollars more than what I'm paying now. I'm willing to let you have the sofa rent-free until we move."

"I'll take it. That's all I can afford to pay anyway, till I get a job."

Josh's head bobbed like Howdy Doody, mutely laughing. Cal chided with a grumpy look. "I'll start reading the want ads after New Year's. I only need something temporary. I've got some ideas I have to sort out, have to do a little research at the library first and think things through."

"I hate to disillusion you," Josh said, "but finding a job is not like doing a term paper."

"*Tu madre.*"

"Speaking of mod-rays, you're going to call yours first thing you get up tomorrow, meaning *today,* right?"

"Maybe. Don't know if I'll feel up to it."

"What if your dad had a heart attack or something?"

"I bet you my share of the first month's rent on that apartment that it's nothing. She just wants advance notice about whether I'll be there for Christmas Eve—sacred family time. She wouldn't trust you with an 'urgent matter' message—not if it were really urgent."

"Sure she would. Naturally, she wouldn't want me to know what it was about, not before you knew. I don't understand why you aren't more worried about this."

"I know my own *madre*, man. If it were something really urgent, she'd have called the airline and left a message for me to call last night when I checked in."

"She said *urgent family matter*," Josh insisted.

Cal examined him a moment, just to be sure. "And how upset did she sound?"

Josh did his silent fake chuckle, bobbing his head. "Cool as an ice cube. And when I said you were getting in at three-thirty *a.m.*—she said to tell you to call them after church."

"Urgent family matter," Cal muttered, peering upward past the smoke of his cigarette.

Lowering his chin, Josh produced a portentous *basso profundo*: "The return of the prodigal son."

Josh's one-bedroom flat was the remodeled second story of a gabled clapboard house in a lower-middle-class section of Evanston, a few blocks west of neighborhoods adjacent to Northwestern University.

"Holy cannoli," Cal said, "What happened here? You hire a maid?"

Josh threw open the walk-in closet and stepped inside; his voice was thus somewhat muffled when he said, "It's all your fault."

"How's that?" He leaned the backpack against the end of the sofa and turned around, pulling his sweater open. Josh reappeared holding a pillow; he push-passed viciously. Cal caught it and fell back onto the sofa.

"Hey! What did I do?"

Lumbering toward the kitchen, Josh waggled his head and squeakily muttered, "Bitch, bitch, bitch, bitch, bitch."

Cal called after him: "Don't tell me you cleaned this place up just for me." A minute later, as he worked at the knots of the sleeping bag's strings, Josh came back and stood in the doorway to the kitchen, brushing his teeth. "Who cleaned up for you?" Cal asked. "*Tu madre?*"

Josh took the toothbrush from his mouth but found he couldn't comment without leaking. Holding his chin up, he disappeared into the kitchen. He reappeared looking slyly amused. "My mother thought that was real cute, what you said on that postcard you sent them."

"What? Oh, that." (Cal had written that Mexico looked like Josh was in charge of keeping it clean.)

"Thought I wouldn't find out, eh?"

"You know you're a slob. You're proud of it."

"And you know you're anal retentive. This should work out fine, just like in *The Odd Couple*. For starters, tomorrow—I mean today—you can clean the bathtub."

"Oh, crap. You haven't cleaned it yet? And you've been using it?"

Josh widened his Cheshire cat grin. "I bought a can of Bon-ammy, just for you, good friend." He zipped up his parka. "If you want some music to crash out by, use the headphones. The chick downstairs wants to sleep in. She was out late last night."

Cal belabored the effort of getting to his feet. Josh dissembled shrugging off-handedness as he opened the door. "Help yourself to the dope. Or, if you'd prefer, there's some Valium in the bathroom cabinet. However, I don't advise mixing them."

"I don't think I'll have a problem crashing out."

"O-ka-ay. Nighty-night. Don't forget to floss. And call your mom before I get back."

He was in mind of the many times he'd lain awake after tripping all night. It felt the same at the bottom of each breath: a tremulous sweet ache. Sated fatigue overcoming the body's insatiable yearning. Dawn was already leaking into the room. Every object looked alive, softly radiating infinite patience, like plants.

He rolled onto his side and curled up. His eyes played over the coffee table sloppily piled with magazines. He stifled a painfully delicious urge to peruse issues of *Penthouse* and *Playboy*.

He thought again of the sexy chica who'd rubbed her tits slowly across his back as she squeezed past him on a bus in Mexico City yesterday morning. She'd flung him a heavy-lidded glance, her naughty smile opening to a teasing grin.

He sat up. The room seemed remarkably warmer. He glanced at the radiator below the windows and his stare went blank, absorbed by the soft whiteness of the shades. He went to a lot of trouble to smoke a cigarette—balanced a big glass ashtray on the arm of the sofa, carefully sat down, crossed his legs, and pulled the sleeping bag around himself like a blanket. *Chief Weirdman*, he thought, trying to fake contentment.

On one side of the door, the wall was recessed; in the niche thus formed, concrete blocks held up a custom-cut piece of plywood. A stacked turntable and receiver were the center-piece of the makeshift credenza. Around it were scattered bills and bank statements, packs of Viceroy cigarettes, matches, a rolled-up baggie of dope, rolling papers, a small facsimile of a Turkish waterpipe, and a big ceramic ashtray. On the side nearer the door, the *Random House Dictionary* massively re-posed.

Recalling the altars in Mexican homes, usually a little table or bureau displaying a reverently arranged mess of pictures and statuettes, it occurred to Cal that the stereo table was Josh's altar. And that reminded him of the time he had been tempted to buy Josh a picture that would have made a great altarpiece.

Outside a religious paraphernalia shop in Mexico City he had been stopped by a large portrait of Jesus on the cross—head hung atilt, eyes painfully, prayerfully closed. The colors struck him as strange in some way; and then he saw that the colors were fuzzy, it wasn't a painting *per se*—it was made of plastic. The plastic seemed oddly familiar as he leaned closer, and suddenly the thorn-crowned head snapped back and the eyes popped open, directing a deliriously beseeching stare—heavenward, thank God, not right at him.

Idea for Cracker Jack prizes in Mexico: Crucifixion tilt cards.

He drifted into mulling over the discrepancy between his reverence for the religiosity of Mexicans and his cynical opinion of their Church. He admired the cheerful childlike good humor and meek openhearted generosity characteristic of *campesinos*. He had looked forward to praising their natural charitableness to his parents and had savored the thought of declaring that the typical Mexican peasant was a better exemplar of Christ-like virtues than the average American Christian of whatever denomination. He genuinely believed that, but it troubled him to think that his father might be more right than merely prejudiced about Latin America's perpetually struggling economies and paucity of genuine democracies. The root cause of Latin America's underdevelopment, according to Reverend Martin Luther Wideman, was the servility inculcated in the masses at Mass and their predisposition to favor the supreme authority of one man as the divine order of secular as well as religious government.

Cal erased the memory, closing his eyes for a few seconds. They refused to stay shut. His gaze settled on the massive dictionary on the stereo table. *Josh's Bible,* he thought.

He savored a generalized memory of Josh slouched in the somewhat malodorous but comfy wing chair, his chin practically on his chest, bulging eyes searching a page of the dictionary for a word that, to really please him, would have to be whimsically odd, pedantically pleonastic, and preferably punnable. Depending on the quality of a find, he might only chuckle or he might look up and jut out a gloating smile before pronouncing the word and challenging Cal to define it. He almost always got to preface his answer with, "Just as I suspected, you illiterate."

Putting out the cigarette, Cal remembered the Valium and even started for the bathroom, but he changed his mind. He drank a glass of water at the kitchen sink, staring between gulps out the small window at the soft gray light. He remembered that it was Sunday morning.

He pulled the wood crate from under the niche's plywood shelf and hunkered down in front of it. He flipped albums forward quickly, pausing at The Band, but going on to the Grateful Dead's trademark—a grinning skeleton. The title of the album he pulled out—*American Beauty*—was displayed on the jacket in psychedelic cursive writing around a rose. With a willed shift of perception, the title could also be read as *American Reality*.

He adjusted the headphones comfortably over his ears while watching the tonearm descend. He plopped down on the sofa, putting his head back and shutting his eyes as the preludial guitar chords came on, followed by the mellow voice of Jerry Garcia singing the timeless words of Robert Hunter:

> *If my words did glow*
> *with the gold of sunshine*
> *And my tunes were played*
> *on the harp unstrung,*
> *Would you hear my voice*
> *come through the music?*
> *Would you hold it near*
> *as it were your own?*

He hadn't heard his favorite rock song—his secret hymn—in too, too long. After a bit, he shut his teary eyes, whisper singing slightly off-key:

There is a road, no simple highway
Between the dawn and the dark of night
And if you go, no one may follow
That path is for your steps alone

Ripple in still water
When there is no pebble tossed
Nor wind to blow

You who choose to lead must follow
But if you fall you fall alone
If you should stand then who's to guide you?
If I knew the way I would take you home

CHAPTER TWO

Your Young Men Will See Visions

CAL WOKE UP ON Josh's sofa a little before two. He went to the kitchen and had a bowl of Cheerios and a cup of coffee. After a cigarette, he decided it was time for a bath. He'd have preferred a shower, but the bathroom was tucked under the slanting roof, with no headroom for a shower to be installed. He found the can of cleanser and a grungy sponge that Josh had placed in what was surely the dirtiest bathtub in the world. Right after starting, he almost quit, it seemed so pointless. The layer of soap scum only came off with hard scrubbing; it wasn't going to come off in the bathwater, obviously.

After a bit, the scrubbing began to feel therapeutic. Then the sponge began to come apart, a shred here, a chunk there. He was of two minds about it: One was angry and about to order him to get out and look for a better sponge; the other, which had been thinking about Mexico, shrugged. He let the pauses to pick up sponge crumbs become part of the process, random breaks in the rhythm of monotonous motions.

His time in the Yucatán seemed a state of grace. Good things incredibly kept happening and his enjoyment had only increased with awareness that the apogee was also the beginning of the end. The Yucatec charmed him with their Mayan pride and, in the cities, their cultured Old World manners. He had spent many days roaming the ruins of the so-called Second Empire.

Initially, he had professed interest in pre-Columbian cultures to give himself a respectable purpose for straying far from the beaten track into wretchedly primitive areas where he would have been ashamed to admit he was a tourist. In Guatemala City, he bought a map of southern Mexico and Central America showing all the sites of Mayan ruins open to public examination; that map became his basis for improvising an itinerary. Deciding where to go had been a chronic headache up till then.

He cut short his tour of Guatemala, disturbed by the constant signs and rumors of violence and then hassled once too often by soldiers at a check point. He crossed the border to Chiapas, went straight to San Cristóbal de las Casas, and after a pleasant recuperative week in that serenely beautiful mountain town, he went on to the ruins at Palenque. From there he took one of the most difficult backroads bus rides of his entire trip, to see the murals at Bonampak. He lucked out, getting a free plane ride back to Palenque with some professors and graduate students from Penn State.

He zigzagged across the Yucatán from one archeological zone to another. In Cancún, after a day of getting oriented and filling his pack with dried fruit and canned meat, and with a diving mask and snorkel added to his gear, he fled the strip of ritzy hotels chaotically under construction and headed south by local bus. The fellow who took the seat next to him told him about a special beach and instructed the bus driver where to let him off.

The path into the scrub jungle disappeared in undergrowth. Cal unstrapped his machete and hacked his way to a coconut grove. The bay it bordered would have been perfect for filming a tropical paradise flick. He had the wide curving beach to himself that afternoon and the next morning. He moved on, hiking south, constantly looking off at the island of Cozumel blocking most of the horizon. When he came around a point, a Mayan hamlet appeared. The fisherman he bought lunch from offered to take him to an isolated beach on the eastern side of the island; said there was a nice little lagoon there, full of pretty fish.

Cal was so enchanted by the lagoon and nearby beach that he didn't want to leave when the fisherman was ready to go home late that afternoon. The man and his young son were in-credulous—and the man also looked a little suspicious—when Cal said he wanted to stay there alone all night. Cal overcame the man's concerned incomprehension by extemporizing a poetical explanation he thought the guy might readily grasp. He compared the place to Eden. The guy said something like, "Well, as you say, but then where's your Eve?" And Cal said, looking around and throwing up his hands, "Who knows? Probably out looking for an apple tree."

The fisherman guffawed and paid the compliment of re-peating the line to his son. Then he said, "Well, then, you better enjoy the company of God while you can, my friend.

Here in Eden." He waved from the boat, still chuckling and shaking his head.

Lurching from reverie, Cal turned off the vintage porcelain faucet handles, put his head back against the tub and eased down, bending his knees, settling his chin on his chest just under the steaming water.

Closing his eyes, he could almost feel how he'd felt trying to get to sleep that night, slightly drunk on rum-spiked coconut milk, sublimely agape at the Milky Way as he lay on the beach in a ragged sheet sewed up like a sleeping bag. He could almost hear the sloshing rhythm of the waves; he could see the foamy shoreline barely through the star-magnified blackness.

His mind plunged into exquisitely terrifying aloneness again. Abruptly he sat up and grabbed the soap and washcloth.

A memory much older came to mind. As a little boy—second or third grade, he thought—he had discovered while lying in bed waiting to grow tired that if he repeated his name over and over in his mind it would begin to sound strange; if he continued, eventually he would begin to feel himself disconnected from the chant, and suddenly his name would have no meaning to him: He would feel himself unmoored in the dark oceanic space that any mind can fall into at any time if it forget everything all at once.

He had begun to play that scary game with disturbing frequency. Fascination would lure him deeper; dread would urge him back. One night he went too far and got what he thought of now as his first peek at the Void. He had screamed and bawled until his father commanded him back to selfhood, shouting his name. It must have been a bad dream, his mother said. And he'd agreed.

Those intense emotions he'd toyed with as a little boy: Weren't they essentially the same fascination and dread he had experienced while coming up on psychedelic drugs?

Losing my mind. He wondered at the cliché. Wasn't it more like losing yourself *in* your mind?

Arms draped around his parted knees, he stared down at his cock floating in the mess of hair, the tip of the glans protruding from the wrinkled foreskin—looking exactly like an acorn (which, he recalled Josh telling him, is what the word *glans* originally meant in Latin).

He noticed his faint reflection in the water: the exact features of his face seemingly visible, until looked for, and then not quite there.

He stood on the second-story deck of the fire-escape stairway and studied the brambly tree branches and the disheveled brown grass. The familiar bleakness brought mysterious comfort. He pulled his fingers from his front jeans pockets and stuck his fists under his arms. Suddenly jogging in place, he felt the platform move—a slight wobble. Glancing down at his tennis shoes because he could feel the cold through them, he thought of his boots, which were with his wardrobe in a footlocker in the basement.

The basement door was swollen and warped and impossible to shut all the way. He entered cautiously.

A couple hours later, he was discovered sitting on the footlocker under a naked lightbulb, surrounded by boxes crammed with books.

"Knock, knock," Josh said.

The bleary-eyed reader glanced up, blinking, then returned his eyes to the page.

"Knock, knock," Josh repeated.

"I hope this is a new one," Cal said.

"Sam and Janet."

"Wait a second, I know you've done that one before. Sam and Janet...?"

"Now, aren't you glad you don't have a perfect memory? Just think—you'd never want to read a book over again." Josh lowered his chin, spread his arms, and lugubriously crooned: "Sam and Janet evening, you will meet a stranger..."

Cal grinned and tossed the book into a box. "How did you know I was down here?"

"They don't call me Sherlock Shylock for nothing. You left the back door open and all your stuff is down here."

"The apartment's too hot anyway."

"Not anymore. Come on, the Chinese food is getting cold."

Cal stood up and stretched, arching his back. He looked portentously at Josh, said, "Confucius say chow mein in belly better than I Ching in my haht."

"Stealing my puns again, eh? That's plagiarism, boy. Come on, I also broke down and bought a six-pack of Corona."

For dessert, Josh sprinkled his favorite herb into the bowl of the water pipe. "I saw Tamara at the Grace last night," he said, and ducked Cal's look, bending to the pipe stem as he held the flame of the lighter over the bowl.

"I thought she went back to New York, to grad school," Cal said. "She here for a visit? Or she decide to do a master's here?"

Josh shrugged and pushed the pipe across the corner of the small table. "All I know is she's been writing articles on women's issues for the *Reader*."

Wincing, Cal coughed smoke. "Yeah?"

Holding in another hit, Josh said, "Investigative kvetching." When he exhaled his features seemed to deflate, settling into a goofy-puffy expression. "I think you can handle the whole sordid truth. Tamara was getting it on with this guy I've seen her with before, a skinny freak, obviously the intellectual type, and Jewish. He's a new comrade in the collective. That, or he just likes to wash dishes."

Cal shrugged. "What's sordid about that? I was afraid you were going to say she had a new girlfriend."

Josh mimed laughter. "Yeah, that'd be a bitch, wouldn't it? I guess this means we won't be hanging out at the Amazing Grace. In fact, I think you better get out of town before you run into one of your old girlfriends' new boyfriends."

Cal smirked. Josh finished off his beer with a quick chug and stood up. "*Otra?*"

Swirling his can, Cal said, "*Gracias,* no." He lit up a ciga-rette, said, "You know, I did a lot of thinking, the past three months," as Josh sat down with another beer.

"I thought that was against your latest religion-substitute."

"Fuck you."

Josh frowned intently. "Seriously. I thought the whole point of Zen was to stop trying to explain everything, to just go with the flow, live for the moment, let it be—and other choice bits of hippie patois."

Cal simpered and took a swig of beer. Josh waited for eye contact; frowning emphatically, he asked: "What is the an-swer?"

"What is the question?"

"That's right," Josh said, and smugly chugged.

Cal looked at his lifted beer can and shook his head, ruing the day he told Josh that Gertrude Stein's famous last words were "very Zen."

"It's time to call your mother," Josh announced.

"Not tonight. First thing in the morning. If it's so urgent, she would have called by now."

Josh exaggerated the exertion required to get to his feet. Sucking in his gut, which he claimed was due to his being as enlightened as the Happy Buddha, he put on a famous mobster's mask. "You're gonna call yer sweet little ole mother, see. Right now, see. Before I lose my temper, see, and have to call her myself, to tell her about da funeral—*see*?"

"Okay, okay, boss. Ennyting but yer Joshua Levinson em-poysonashun."

Perched on the edge of the bed, he shifted his glum stare back and forth between the phone and the mess in the closet—as many garments piled on the floor as jumbled together on hangers. He spotted a big clump of black hairs covered with feathery dust; he couldn't take his eyes from it. He thought of tumbleweeds, flashed on an image of them bouncing along on a hard-packed desert road, and recalled the verse that begins, *The wind goeth where it listeth.*

Suddenly he was homesick for Mexico, where he had learned the joy of wandering, contentedly homeless, making himself at home wherever he went.

He picked up the phone—and couldn't remember the number for a few seconds, until he stopped trying. He was expecting his mother or his little sister Rachel to answer. The third rolling staccato buzz was cut short and a woman's voice—neither his mother's nor Rachel's but very familiar—answered. He could not speak.

"Hell-o-o?" his older sister repeated. "The Reverend Wideman's residence. Who's calling, please?"

"Hi, hey, Pris. What are you doing there?"

"Calvin? Cal! Where are you?"

"Right here."

"You're back!"

"I'm in Evanston, at Josh's apartment."

"Boy, do we wanna talk to you. Just a sec. Mom's drying her hands. Here she is."

He waited for his mother's voice; after about ten seconds he wondered what was taking so long. He said, "Hello?" Waited some more.

"Hello, Cal? I was just about to call Josh," Sarah said, "to find out if you'd gotten in yet. Did you call earlier? We've been out."

"No, no. This is the first time I've called. I got in around three this morning. I slept all day."

"Well, we thank God you're back safe and sound. There's an urgent matter we need to discuss. Just a minute, your father wants to explain. All right, he's going to get it in the study."

Cal heard his four-year-old niece Naomi whining to go home and Priscilla sweetly—but firmly—explaining that they would have to stay a little bit longer. Sarah said, "Why don't you take off their coats?"

A click preceded his father's resonant voice: "Hello, Cal. Welcome back."

"Hey, Dad. Thanks. What's up?"

"Well, what's up is, we've got a situation that only recently developed, concerning Rachel."

"She's joined a cult!" Sarah interjected on the other line.

"Sarah, please..."

"A cult?" Cal echoed.

"She got a crush on this boy," Sarah rushed to say, "and thought these people were just ordinary Pentecostals."

"I thought we agreed I should be the one to explain this," Martin said.

"I'm sorry, dear, all right, it's just that—I'm so relieved that Cal is here now, to help. I better give Priscilla a hand with the girls. I'll hang up now. Good night, Cal. We'll see you soon."

"Okay. Good night, Mom." When he heard the click, he said, "What cult, Dad?"

"Well," Martin said, "they mostly refer to themselves as True Life Fellowship. Their official name is True Life Fellowship and Biblical Research Association."

A voice interrupted in the background, triggering a contemptuous twinge in Cal. Priscilla's husband Jim spoke rapidly, unctuously excited. Martin started to answer him then apparently muffled the phone. Cal felt the knot in his chest tighten as he tried to make out what they were saying.

"Cal?" Martin said after a few moments.

"I'm here."

"As you heard, Jim is here. He can give you a full report on this cult's travesty of Christian doctrine another time. I expect you'll be as appalled as we are by their deceitful and coercive practices."

"What...exactly...has all of you so upset?"

"Well, yes. You need some context. Your mother mentioned a young man, with whom Rachel has become romantically involved. That is one of this cult's recruiting practices. They go after converts one at a time, using a member of the opposite sex to get them to their meetings.

"Also, as its official name suggests, the cult offers courses in the Bible according to them, their biblical research. They call these spirit power courses. People actually get persuaded to pay to take these courses. Sarah mentioned that Rachel thought this cult was just some Pentecostal group. They fool a lot of people that way because they give a central place to speaking in tongues. However, what they teach as speaking in tongues is not at all what Pentecostals seek—the manifestation of a special grace. They teach that anyone truly indwelt by the Holy Spirit can speak in tongues at any time. At will. In their very first spirit power class—. Just a minute, let me—. Jim is perturbed about something."

During the pause, Cal silently savored that *perturbed*.

"I'm sorry," Martin came back. "I'll leave other specifics about the cult to Jim. I've only just learned all this myself. Where was I? Oh, yes, their way of speaking in tongues. It's about as phony as you can get. In fact, they actually teach it, step-by-step.

"The cult members who teach these spirit power classes get their training in what they call households of faith. Jim calls them high-rent communes. Converts have to donate all their worldly goods to the cult and devote themselves to advanced Bible research, taking these courses they pay for by working in low-skill, fly-by-night businesses. Rachel has moved into the cult's household of—*heresy*, it ought to be called—located in Lake Forest."

"Lake Forest?"

"Right. Not where you'd expect to find a commune. Seems a wealthy convert donated his estate. Jim went up there, hoping to speak with Rachel, but the property is fenced, and their gate is locked. He tried to arrange an appointment to see Rachel, but when he called, they refused to let him speak with her.

"Your mother and I had only the one opportunity to talk with her when she came home this past Monday. We thought, you know, she was going to stay here over the semester break as usual. Well, she had this Mark fellow with her, a complete stranger to us. She told your mother they wanted to speak with her, only her. She told Sarah they were in love, and that she'd found the true meaning of the Holy Spirit. She said she'd taken a leave of absence from Covenant, after completing the semester, thank goodness. She wanted to get some clothes and other things because she had moved into the commune in Lake Forest.

"Well, I—. Imagine our shock! Here she was with this sinister-looking guy, who looks quite a bit older, telling us she was going off with him to a commune. Before I showed up, she informed Sarah that she no longer believed in the divinity of Jesus Christ. She had the gall to say that the Trinity was the *real* heresy.

"Sarah, might have done better not to call me over. But she was beside herself, of course. I was at the church, in a counseling session, which I didn't feel I could just up and leave. But when she called me a second time, I realized it was an emergency. I rushed to the house, but by then Rachel and this guy were getting into a van, about to leave. Regrettably, I lost my temper, and that, of course, only made matters worse."

"It all sounds bizarre, and alarming," Cal said. "I can see why you'd be overwhelmed…at a loss for what to do."

"Cal, you are the only one in the family Rachel will talk to now. We want you to call Rachel and arrange to visit her at the commune. We will provide a car. We are hoping that you will agree to serve as our emissary and be our peacemaker. Please tell her I'm sorry for losing my temper the way I did. Tell her we love her and we want to talk with her. We *need* to speak with her. It's only fair that she give us a chance to understand and make amends. Right now, we're left with this confusion and anger. And guilt. We so want a second chance.

"What we are asking is only fair. If she has discovered the true meaning of the New Testament, as she claimed to your mother, then she should be willing to come here and witness to it in discussion with us."

Cal remained silent for an extended moment. "Well, naturally, I want to visit Rachel for myself, to see what's, what the situation is, and what these people are into. I certainly think she ought to give you and Mom a chance to talk with her, to understand why she would make such a…drastic change…in her life. I'm, I want to know that myself. It seems really out of character that she sprang this on you like that."

Martin tensely sighed. "I knew we could count on you, son. Why don't you invite her to come here for Christmas dinner? You might have to invite this guy Mark, too. I suspect she will only agree if Mark is included. But that's fine. You can assure them that the meal will remain strictly low-key, polite conversation. No sensitive topics. We can use the occasion to learn more about Mark, and after the meal, we'll gather in the living room, each of us with a Bible, and we'll let them present their beliefs—with the understanding that they must allow us to question and challenge their views in a calm, rational discussion."

Cal put his hand over the mouthpiece and deeply sighed, shutting his eyes and bowing his head.

"If you wish, you could act as moderator," Martin said. "In fact, that would be very much appreciated. The thing to stress is: *We* need this discussion, your mother and I. Please impress that upon her. Be sure and tell her that. And that I'm extremely sorry, we both are, for getting so upset and for reacting the way we did."

"All right, Dad, I'll do my best. Of course, I can't guarantee she'll accept the invitation."

"Of course not. We only ask for your sincere best effort."

"I'll do my best, Dad. You have the phone number in Lake Forest?"

"Here, let me turn you over to Jim and talk to your mother about the car."

"No need, I can borrow Josh's."

"That's all right, this will work out fine, we'll get a car to you."

"Borrow Josh's what?" Josh said.

Cal jerked around, putting his hand over the mouthpiece. Just out of the shower, Josh was toweling his hair. "The car, tomorrow?" Cal said. "We got a family crisis here."

Jim came on the line: "Cal, I won't say you know what"—(Praise the Lord!)—"but I'm doing it! Welcome back. Listen: First off, I don't think you ought to call the commune. You should just go out there, and I'll tell you why: You want to catch them with their guard down. We're dealing, in the case of the cult's leaders, with masters of doubletalk and deceit.

"Yesterday I asked around in Lake Forest and found out that the commune's missionaries-in-training slave away in a small business the cult runs. They subcontract on jobs like painting and laying tile and what not—carpeting, you know, that kind of thing. I talked to one contractor who's used them. He said there's a guy named Larry who really knows the business; he's their foreman. He takes crews out each day to do these jobs, and he always comes back to the commune right around six o'clock..."

(Josh slumped down in the armchair by the corner of the bed; he had jeans on, but no shoes, no shirt. His wet hair was combed straight back; he tried to gather it into a pony tail but one strand from each side didn't quite make it. He gave up and combed with his fingers, stood up, and started to pad toward the door. Cal stopped him with an upraised hand.)

"...So there's a good chance she'll be with the group in the van. If she's not, ask them to let you talk to her. I really can't predict how they'll react."

"Hold on, Jim." He covered the mouthpiece tightly and looked at Josh. "It's a long story."

"You want to borrow the car," Josh said matter-of-factly.

"Yeah, tomorrow. Around—four-thirty or five."

"So?"

"So what time—? Oh. You don't drive to work anyway."

Waddling away, Josh said, "He's smar-r-rter than the avvv-er-age goy."

Cal bowed urgently to the mouthpiece. "No problem, Jim, I'm all set. I'll use Josh's car. Why don't you give me directions from where Sheridan Road enters Lake Forest. Wait a sec, let me get something to write with."

Perched on the edge of the armchair, Cal stared into his thoroughly muddled thoughts. Josh lay propped up against pillows like a patient, the blue quilted bedspread up to his armpits. His eyes were closed.

"They must believe in the Holy Spirit, though," Cal continued. "It's supposed to be the Holy Spirit giving you the gibberish, according to Pentecostals. A special blessing. But if Jesus isn't God, there's no Trinity. What do they call their Godhead? The Duality? Doesn't have quite the same ring to it."

He wondered if Josh had dozed off.

Suddenly, Josh said, "I need a beer."

"Really?" Cal stood up. "Well, I could use one. You going to drink it in your dreams?"

"I'm doing out-of-body travel. I've gotten as far as the fridge but I can't open the door."

"Okay, hang on."

Josh had a cigarette ready to light when Cal came back. "Thanks, gaper." He took the beer and held out the pack. Cal took a cigarette and hurried from the room. He came back with another ashtray and sat down. "So," he said, lighting up, "what do you think of my chances for a holly jolly Christmas?"

Josh shrugged and averted his eyes. He said, "You better roll some jays to take with you. And take my Triple-A card."

Josh's queasy look and tone of revulsion struck Cal disagreeably; then he felt contrite for the excitedly glib speculation he'd subjected him to.

Lying awake, Cal felt slightly ashamed of the giddy fascinated excitement he found underneath the numb fog. He was amazed that his parents seemed to have accepted Jim's views uncritically. That was a first. He felt sorry for them though. They'd scared Rachel off with their overreaction, and now she didn't want to talk to them. There was no way she'd trust Jim to mediate. Rachel had never much liked Jim, though Cal figured he and his mother were the only ones who could tell. Rachel, the baby of the family, was Sarah's favorite—everyone knew that.

It took a while of feeling his feelings, figuring them out, to uncover the little boy: sulking. His parents seemed way more upset about Rachel's apostasy than they had ever seemed about his. But then, he'd shed their beliefs gradually, ambiguously, strategically over several years.

During high school, he had read his way to insouciant skepticism, first about the historicity of Adam and Eve—essential to Calvinist doctrine—and from there down the primrose path of ever more skeptical challenges to biblical authority. He had had too much going on—debate club, tennis, girlfriends, drinking on the sly, school politics—to worry about what specifics of his childhood faith he still really and truly believed.

He didn't keep his growing agnosticism secret exactly, but he avoided conversations that might test the limits of his willingness to prevaricate. He had resolved long before he was aware of it that he would play to the general expectations of the adults who could make his daily life and long-term prospects more pleasant. His opinions on most religious and political questions were moderate and flexible, and, in his own mind, entirely provisional—except when he had to express them for adult approval, and then they sounded profoundly sincere even to himself.

In college, however, he cut loose. Christmas break freshman year he went home with a full beard and long hair, half dreading a confrontation, half hoping for one. Sarah and Martin became coldly formal hosts enduring a guest who'd outstayed his welcome due to circumstances beyond anyone's control.

Lying awake in the dark of his bedroom that December four years ago, he had worked on a jeremiad, comparing his parents to the Pharisees and calling down upon them the wrath of the Absurd for their materialism and hard-heartedness. His grand sermon ended—as he figured it must—with a declaration of independence. Total independence.

He calculated, though, that to pay for a degree from Northwestern without their help he would have to get a sizable student loan, an increase in his university grant, and a twenty-hour-a-week job; and he was already working fifteen hours a week in a dorm cafeteria's dish room. Josh came up with the clincher: What if he got a low number in the draft lottery and then had to take a break from school for some reason?

As it turned out, in the draft lottery that summer Cal was lucky and Josh was not. Cal's birthday drew a number over three hundred; Josh's was just below the highest number the Selective Service expected to activate that year. Josh had shocked the Nabobs—what they called themselves, inspired by Vice President Spiro T. Agnew's famous alliteration, "the nattering nabobs of negativism"—when he announced that if his number were activated he would enlist, and not in the Coast Guard either, in the Army. That would be the only morally defensible option, Josh insisted. If he avoided serving after his number came up, even legitimately with a student deferment, the draft would get someone else, someone with the same lousy luck in the draft lottery but much less fortunate in the lottery that decides who can afford to go to college.

Cal threw the sleeping bag open and sat up. He resisted the urge to light another cigarette. He crossed his legs and sat back against the armrest, wondering what time it was. The thought of the Valium in the medicine cabinet crossed his mind. He watched it go.

The lazy Buddha, he thought. *No-o-o...the academic Buddha*, the voice of Josh rejoined. *But-uh...let me think about that...maybe do some research...*

He did deep breathing for a while and erased every thought. But before he knew it he was thinking about Josh's calling Zen his latest religion substitute. He tried to congeal a notion of what it would take for him to get seriously into Zen. His mind remained blissfully empty—for at least half a minute.

Of all that he had read about Buddhism, Cal had only assimilated the anecdotes and sayings from the literature of Zen that supported, however indirectly, teachings attributed to certain disciples of Gautama Buddha a few hundred years after his death: One cannot will the ultimate awakening to one's Buddha nature; to seek it is futile because it is not lost; everyone's natural mind is already enlightened.

To Cal's natural way of thinking, if not to his natural mind, the way to seek without seeking that which, found, would be discovered to have really never been lost was to keep the search unconscious, and every now and again wonder if you were getting closer. He had been content to hope that he would ultimately awaken eventually, unexpectedly all at once, or so gradually he might not notice until moments before flatlining.

The last month of his trip he had felt closer to his natural mind than he'd felt since childhood. That night on Cozumel, he had felt so close to unspeakable experience of nirvana that he had feared he would lose consciousness of it by reason of insanity. He had begun to feel like he was coming up on some strong LSD. More alone than he'd ever been in his life, physically as well as psychologically, he had panicked, certain that he would lose himself in his mind if he followed the mystical compulsion to its end and let go of the fear that he would not find himself again.

After a run along the beach, furiously crying, he had turned around—and immediately regretted the melodrama. His campfire had been swallowed up by the darkness. Animal dread seized him. But after the initial paralyzing moment, he found the visceral charge of primal fear grimly comforting as he walked back the way he'd come.

He had sat down in the sand beside the glowing embers and after stargazing awhile had cried some more, from joy, feeling lucky to be still among the unenlightened.

It seemed damnation-by-cowardice now. He thought of himself as a little boy—the insomniac in training—and began to repeat his full name monotonously in his mind: Calvin Thomas Wideman...

It reminded him of his special conception of hell.

While evolving an ever more liberal faith during high school, he had gladly argued away the patently sadistic notion of fire and brimstone. He had redefined sin as alienation from God's love in the here and now and hell as the eternal separation from divine love in the hereafter. During his first year of college, he had rejoiced over Dostoyevsky's definition of hell in *The Brothers Karamazov*—the inability to love. When he came upon Sartre's definition in *No Exit*, "Hell, that's others"—he had fallen into a funk and had tried to conceive of a hell that would make Sartre's *L'enfer* seem like a relatively comfy cell in purgatory. Josh had said it showed he was still a Christian at heart.

For souls refusing to value love above all else, Cal had prescribed temporary confinement in the vacuity of thoughtless self-reflective awareness; to each, his own. Replacing flames: hopeless panic in the grip of unendurable unending loneliness.

The Valium was a prescription that Josh's mom had gotten. Cal gave one sympathetic thought to wondering why. Death dread was sickeningly strong in his solar plexus. He sneered at it, carefully, and hammed it up, lifting the glass to himself in the toothpaste-splattered mirror before putting the little yellow pill on his tongue. Back on the sofa, he decided another cigarette would help, though it would put him over his aspirational limit of half a pack a day.

He had lived that first semester of freshman year feeling like Zorba the Greek, laughing off the fear of death after swallowing a pill or capsule or licking a little dot off a piece of wax paper. And recently in Mexico he had reacquired the knack for insouciant fatalism. He had smiled serenely at grinning death any number of times while careening down a mountain road in a rickety bus. And just last night he'd felt more thrill than fear as the jet hurtled down the runway, taking off. He had been ready to die.

So why did he feel like such a lonely coward now? How could he lose that fearlessness from one day to the next?

Welcome home...

As he ground out the cigarette, he had a flashback—the mnemonic kind, but related to drugs.

Sitting across from Tamara at a booth in the student union's vending-machine room. They'd been to a Sly and the Family Stone concert, the big event for Spring Thing weekend. It was the only time he and Tamara ever tripped by themselves—together, that is, and with no one else. He'd flashed just now on the exultant certitude that came over him as he ground out a cigarette in an ashtray on the table between them.

With an enigmatic grin he had drawn Tamara's look and announced: "I'm there."

"What?" Frowning confusedly, she shook her marvelous nimbus of limp coppery curls. But he saw that she suspected what *there* he was referring to. Zen was her trip. He had always made fun of it, suggesting that he possessed intuitive insight into *koans* and anecdotes which she treated like sacred texts. She thought that only fools would pretend to understand them, and that only Zen masters really did.

"I'm there," he repeated.

She stared at him over a wincing grin, miming laughter, but unable to hide the hurt in her green eyes.

"Where?" she asked again, as though she really had no idea what he was talking about.

He couldn't remember the rest clearly. He seemed to recall teasing her about her refusal to admit that she understood what he was saying but didn't know what to make of it or how to respond. He hadn't known what to make of his giving in to the urge to say it. He had known that he was shitting on her holy ground, but that's how he felt about holy ground, and the holier the better. Unless it was his very own.

He had done a hell of a lot of thinking the past three months. He had seen how during their sophomore year he'd begun to cast himself as St. Paul's believer unequally yoked to an unbeliever, only the categories were optimist and pessimist.

Tamara became seriously unhappy that fall. She said she couldn't take Northwestern's rah-rah Midwestern ruling class culture. She began to collect the catalogs of small liberal arts colleges—Bard, Bates, Reed, Antioch. He felt compelled to act disinterestedly supportive while hiding a hurt he couldn't very well confess, lest it belie his doctrine of love as a giving of yourself without regard for what you got in return, and, conversely, as a taking of another's love without incurring a debt.

He might have shocked himself and her both into a committed relationship if he'd stopped insisting he was a superior being because his happiness was not dependent on her companionship or anyone else's. To thine own self be sufficient, was his credo.

What a lot of pride he'd have had to swallow to really love Tamara. He thought that she secretly believed herself superior to him—by virtue of greater empathy and vulnerability. She didn't want his stupid narcissistic happiness, his cheerfully cynical insularity. If you have a mind, you suffer, and if you're a woman you're twice damned. How could she go on loving a man who not only didn't need her but mocked her for needing him?

Only after he forced her to break up with him was he able to experience a respectably dark night of the soul. At its nadir, he took comfort in the contemplation of nonbeing. He read the short stories of Camus. He discovered the poetry of John Berryman and consoled himself with the bitter laughs and salacious laments of *The Dream Songs*.

He remembered a poem he'd written in an attempt to capture the mystical certitude that had prompted him to say to Tamara, "I'm there."

ETERNAL DELIGHT?
suddenly body and mind
one in what
they bind
this energy
always wanting
ha
heedless of why
just to be whatever
it is

He had shared the poem in the only creative writing class he took. His classmates quibbled over details like the *ha* and then zeroed in for the kill on the logic in the first three lines. Didn't he have it backwards? Wasn't it energy that bound the body and mind? He had not managed to reconstruct for his classmates the reasoning that had convinced him of the rhyme's mystical rightness, and he didn't even try now, shrugging it off.

He wondered if the numbness spreading in his limbs was similar to what amputees felt—ghost pains: severed nerves remembering limbs no longer there. What if an immaterial pattern of the body-mind did survive death, if only momentarily? Wouldn't the fading patterned energy constitute a brief soul? Disembodied mind given a final timeless time to face the Void as it dissipates into it. Maybe feeling its former body as one big ghost pain.

A slowly growing awareness of nausea brought him back. He tried to ward it off and it seemed to subside. But then the wave of awful feeling resurfaced in his bowels. *Damn Valium,* he thought.

Woozily ensconced on the toilet, he tried to think of something clever to say in case Josh got up. Stabbed by another gut pain, he bowed his head and groaned, "Oh, Gawd."

In the empty-minded moment after, he spasmed a bitter-tasting laugh.

Get me a faith healer, quick! I'm being tempted to start believing again.

CHAPTER THREE

Blessed Are the Peacemakers

THE ROAD GLEAMED MALEVOLENTLY. Northbound traffic was heavy, a double file of tailgating vehicles. Floppy wet snowflakes floated down in slow motion, fuzzing up the cold gray twilight. He stayed in the right lane, thankful for the extra cautious pace, feeling like he was learning to drive all over again. He'd forgotten rush hour would be getting underway but figured he'd get to Lake Forest by quarter to six, if Jim's directions were accurate.

Passing a wide driveway between frat houses on Northwestern's campus, he took his eyes off the road to catch a glimpse of the dorm he lived in freshman year. Still there, looking exactly the same. He remembered walking into Joe and Hank's room: those two perched on one bed, Josh and Kevin across on the other; the haze of sweet smoke between. He waved away the joint—it was late, they had to get going. (They worked in the dish room and had to eat early, before everyone else.) Injun Joe did a great Cheech or Chong impersonation: "Hey, mahn, it's rush hour. Slow down and take a fuckin' hit."

About five minutes later, the Baha'i temple loomed ahead in Wilmette: dazzlingly white, Taj-Mahal-like, rising from a somewhat circular island in the midst of an ordinary upscale suburb. At night, the temple was a breathtaking spectacle—especially if you happened to be high. One time they hiked to it from campus while they were coming up on LSD. They peaked out inside the domed cylinder of luminous white cement, rapturously watching the intricately intertwined ornamental designs rhythmically slithering in place.

With desperately intense glances at the temple, Cal steered through the curve skirting the meticulously landscaped park surrounding it. Tension rubbed his stomach raw. It occurred to him the discomfort was a healthy sign: hunger. He hadn't eaten much all day. He felt okay now; a little weak. He planned to stop for a burger on the way back if the meetup with Rachel was brief—or didn't come off. If he did talk with her and the commune seemed like an okay group, he thought he might get himself invited to dinner.

This morning, when Cal reviewed his impressions of what Martin and Jim had told him, he found himself decidedly skeptical. He and Rachel had never been close, but when he came home from college "looking like a hippie"—his family couldn't believe that he'd actually become one—he had detected in Rachel a secret sympathy and even admiration. During the summers he had lived at home, following his sophomore and junior years, he and Rachel had nurtured an edgy unspoken affinity. He had felt sorry for her. He blamed Sarah's doting dominance for stunting Rachel's personality. She seemed always to be watching herself be demure and ingenuous, the very model of a righteous young woman. However, she gave him what he took to be hints that she harbored a rebellious streak beneath her family persona.

He tried to draw her out in a few late-night conversations. He gave up on that after it became clear that she wasn't really interested to know about the writers and philosophers and poets who had most influenced his views about life, the universe, and everything. Her interest was evangelistic, which aggravated him because he thought it might mean she was secretly moving away from their parents' Reformed Christianity and toward the free-will Southern Baptist doctrines of Priscilla and Jim. Her attitude seemed to be that it was too bad, a real shame actually, that Cal had been blessed with so much intelligence and intellectual curiosity. It meant he'd likely have to suffer many grievous experiences before he would be able to humble himself, repent, and be born again, *again*—for real this time.

He felt now that he could have predicted this turnabout in Rachel's life. In her second year of college, living away from home, she meets an attractive soulful guy attracted to her; he takes her home to his brothers and sisters in Christ; they welcome her into their family of like minds and loving hearts, living together in ideal Christian harmony. He couldn't believe that Rachel could be conned by fast-talking charlatans pushing an ersatz "charismatic" experience. Meek childlikeness was her façade, but like many subservient church-going women—her mother for instance—Rachel was stubborn, strong-willed, and savvy about people: wise to their ways so she could get her way. He was betting that she hadn't been taken in; that she'd joined with her eyes and her heart wide open, and that her new brothers and sisters in Christ were not a bunch of paranoid zealots either. How could they be, with a name like True Life Fellowship and Biblical Research Association?

Not all cults were crazies. He expected to meet a Gethsemane variety of Jesus freak at this commune of Bible-researching Pentecostal heretics. Kindly souls whose apostasy, by the standards of his parents' theology, was on a par with Jehovah's Witnesses, say. Nevertheless, all that day he had run through various scenarios, and he felt ready for anything. He was even prepared to play potential convert if these people were as wacko as Jim made them out to be. Conning them like that might be the only way to find out for sure what Rachel had gotten herself into.

The penultimate turn of Jim's directions put him on a narrow road winding through a thickly wooded neighborhood of houses he would have called mansions. Twice he stopped in front of driveways, mistaking them for intersecting roads. Expecting another driveway as he approached a third curbless intersection, he spotted the post of a street sign all but hidden by a spruce tree. The car slid some when he braked.

Friar's Lantern Lane was barely two cars wide. Magnificently tall blue spruce loomed on both sides. Coming out of an S-curve he saw the piled slate pillars Jim had described; they supported a black ironwork arch and gate. Jutting from each pillar, old-timey lamp fixtures cast faint light.

He pulled the car halfway off the road and stopped shy of the portion of driveway in front of the gate. Peering through the snow, he searched the pillars for a phone or intercom. Jim had said there was no way to contact the house from here. It was about ten minutes to six by his watch. He decided he would wait till a quarter after. Who, he wondered, told Jim that this van came back here every night at six on the dot?

The snow was getting worrisome. Peering through the window, he spotted something on the decorative arch over the gate. At the crest of the arch was a round blue plaque displaying a streamlined Holy Spirit dove diving straight down. It made him think of the Descending God, whose temple he had visited at the ruins of Tulum on the Caribbean coast. Both temple and God were named for the figure of a deity in the frieze over the doorway to the sanctum sanctorum; the god appeared to be doing a clownish dive. No one knew for sure which of the hundreds of Mayan gods the figure represented; the currently prevailing educated guess identified him as the bee god.

Pulling himself from reverie, he dismissed a reminder of his intention to find out which schools had the best programs in Mayan studies. In the car's outside mirror the falling snow gave spooky depth to the blackness. The road was completely covered now. He switched off the ignition, got out, and went up to each pillar, closely inspecting. He peered through the gate: The driveway disappeared into woods. He spotted an aura of light over some trees. Skills he'd honed as a caddy kicked in. The driveway went straight for about a hundred and fifty yards then dog-legged sharply left.

He considered climbing over the gate, which lacked the fence's fancy spear-points capping each black metal bar. He nixed the idea of upping the ante of this adventure and felt warmed by the realization that he was content to stay right where he was. The chill was bracing; the snow, magical. He was glad he'd come even if he had to turn around now and go back with his unpleasant mission unaccomplished. At least he'd tried.

Throwing his head back, he inspected the impenetrable dark, in mind of the night sky of tropical Mexico. He willed himself to be content with what he was seeing instead of stars: Clumped snowflakes, heavy and wet, plummeting from the blackness.

Light flashed through the woods. He jogged stiffly to the car, shutting the door just as headlight beams swung out of the S-curve.

A white van drew up beside the Pinto and slid to a stop. Cal fixed a coolly curious expression as he rolled down the window. A guy leaned out of the van's front passenger seat and peered back. He shouted, "Praise the Lord if you're lost, brother! You've been led to the right place."

"You with True Life Fellowship?" Cal called back.

"What can we do for you?"

"My name's Cal Wideman. I'm here to visit my sister Rachel. Rachel Wideman."

The guy ducked back into the van. After suspiciously many seconds had passed, Cal grabbed his door handle, thinking it might help if he walked over to the van's open window. But just then another head poked out of that window, in a nearly horizontal position, long hair hanging.

"Cal? What are you doing here?" Rachel said excitedly.

"Hey, Rache. I'm back. I came by to see you."

"Just a sec. I'll get out." She drew inside and a moment later the front passenger door jerked open and the guy jumped out. He swung open one side of the van's double doors and helped Rachel climb down. "Praise the Lord for family reunions," he said. "Hallelujah," a male voice flatly rejoined from inside the van.

"Oh, you guys," Rachel said.

Cal extracted himself from the car, took a few steps, and stood awkwardly as Rachel stepped toward him; she hesitated, effusively confessing self-consciousness without saying a word. "It's so good to see you," she said. "I'm really glad you came."

He stepped closer. "I just got back. They told me you were here, when I called them last night."

She stunned him with a lunging hug. His arms went around her. He focused on the cushiony crush of their parkas and then on the cold silky feel of her hair against his cheek. He recognized the smell of her shampoo: Herbal Essence. Catching a wary look from the guy behind her, he asked, in a grim low voice, "Are you okay?"

"Only happier than I've ever been in my life." She whirled away, and he felt her giddy energy. "I guess you've heard about this cradle robber here. Cal, this is Mark Connor."

"Praise the Lord," Mark said, thrusting out his bare hand. Cal stuck out his gloved paw. Mark's grip jolted him; he responded with stepped-up force in his own, and Mark let go. They looked awkwardly at Rachel and back at each other.

Cal felt self-conscious about his bushy beard; Mark's goatee was meticulously trimmed. It seemed of a piece with his eyebrows—one continuous bold black stroke that dipped only slightly over the bridge of his hooked nose.

"Yo, Mark," the driver of the van called, and through the open side door Cal saw another reformed freak. The driver had a Fu-Manchu mustache and skimpy long blond hair stiffly skirting his head. Like Mark, he wore an Army field jacket. Cal had worn one freshman year, the winter coat of his hippie uniform. He had the feeling these field jackets, by contrast, were genuine government issue, and he confirmed the guess, spotting the tag on the right side of Mark's chest: CONNOR displayed in blocky black all caps.

"Hang on, Larry," Mark said. Rachel glanced at him as though seeking a cue. Mark avoided eye contact.

"We're late for dinner," she said, looking at Cal. "Have you eaten yet? You're welcome to join us."

"Thanks, I'd like to, if it's not imposing or anything. I was going to eat on the way, but then I thought I'd better hurry up and get here on account of the snow." Mark's wary glance as he uttered this lie put genuine regret into Cal's voice when he added, "I should have called first, I guess."

"Oh, it's all right," she said. "If you're here, it's God's will." She turned to Mark. "I'll show him where to park."

Mark ducked and shot a hard look into the car, then turned to the van. "You guys go on ahead. I'll ride along with them."

Rachel stepped mincingly around the front of the Pinto, and Cal leaned across to unlock the door. She ducked into the skimpy back seat. Mark climbed into the front passenger seat and pulled the door shut. They watched the two wings of the automatic gate silently swing open in front of the van.

"Did you talk to someone in the house?" Rachel asked.

"What do you mean? How?"

"The intercom—on the left-hand side over there."

"I didn't see it. I got out and looked."

"It's kind of camouflaged," she said. "You have to open this cover that's painted the same gray as the slate."

"How about that," Mark said. "You showed up at just the right time."

"It *is* the right time," Rachel piped up, dispelling the insinuation.

They watched the van wheel carefully through the gate, leaving firm tracks. "Good snowball snow," Cal said. "Here we go." He let the clutch out too carefully, then gave it too much gas. He tried to make the turn without braking but the car slid diagonally backwards anyway. Spruce boughs slapped the rear window as the Pinto rolled into and up a shallow ditch; when it rolled forward, his right foot had the good sense to hit the gas pedal. The tires whirred briefly; abruptly grabbed.

"These aren't snow tires," he felt obliged to explain. "It wasn't sticking when I left. I didn't think it'd get this bad. The forecast said there'd only be flurries."

"You can always stay the night," Rachel said. "We have several guest rooms. They're really nice."

"I'd like to get back tonight," he said. "If I can. I'm staying with Josh in Evanston. This is his car."

The Hotel Holy Spirit was the name he later gave to the Tudor-style mansion. They drove in front of it on a grandly curving driveway and turned sharply, curling steeply downhill to a small parking area outside a basement-level multicar garage.

Rachel warned him that they were late and would have to make an entrance before the entire household in the dining hall. They climbed steps to a service entrance. Passing an open door in the hallway, Cal got a glimpse of the kitchen. It reminded him of the one he'd worked in at Northwestern—stainless steel tables, giant-size pots and pans.

Mark slowed as he drew near the open door at the end of the hall. Cal and Rachel reflexively copied his caution. Mark and Rachel stood still and bowed their heads. Cal heard a man praying and bowed his head, too; then—because not to would have seemed an infringement of their privacy—he shut his eyes. The voice was resonant and warm; the prayer, a standard grace composed of formulaic phrases. He heard nothing re-motely heretical in the prayer, and something amusing: Several of the stock phrases were also favored by Jim, a Southern Baptist minister.

Following the "Amen," the somber cleric became a suavely cheerful Master of Ceremonies, exhorting appreciation for Annie and her kitchen crew. They had cooked up a storm in preparation for the great feast but still managed to get the regular evening meal together.

"Leftovers again?!" someone shouted, evoking a number of jovial retorts amid general laughter.

Mark moved carefully through the doorway and motioned them to stay put. The MC said, "Well, I still think it's a wonder they didn't tell us to forget about dinner and send out for pizza. Let's show them we appreciate the extra effort. Hip, hip—." The group answered with "Hallelujah!" the first two times and "Praise the Lord!" to end the cheer.

A modest chandelier sparkled above the open square of tables: heavy-duty banquet tables that could be folded up. The chairs were basic metal folding chairs, some gray, some Army-green. Mark came up behind the MC, who had the center chair at the nearest table, and bent to his ear.

"That's Bob, the head of our household," Rachel said. When Cal nodded, she added, "We call this a household of faith." Cal went shy, aware of many eyes shifting their way. Mark moved aside and Bob turned with an amiably curious expression. He motioned for them to come over.

Bob was obviously the senior member of the group. Tall and portly, he ate and talked with an air of graciously informal privilege and listened with the blankly earnest intensity of a man who is hard of hearing. With more gray than black in his hair and mustache, he was the only one Cal would have guessed was middle aged. Most of the forty or so White people, about evenly divided by gender, looked to be in their twenties, and Rachel was not the youngest-looking among the women.

Bob won Cal's approval right off by diplomatically pulling rank on Mark, who had suggested Cal sit next to him, putting himself between Cal and Rachel. With deferential aplomb, Bob decreed otherwise, jovially declaring that Rachel and Cal had a lot of catching up to do so Cal should sit on Rachel's other side. Larry wouldn't mind, would he?

With Mark occasionally leaning forward to look past her, Rachel peppered Cal with questions about Mexico. Cal gave a facile, sanitized version of his travelogue. Rachel frowned every now and then but seemed distracted, as though intent on coming up with the next question to keep Cal talking. The beef stew, hearty but bland, inspired him to blabber about how much he missed the spiciness of Mexican food. He dropped in the mellifluous names of street food just to impress them: *tacos, tamales, gorditas, molotes, quesadillas, chicharrón.*

Annie of kitchen crew fame served them dessert, and Cal welcomed the opportunity to praise the meal as he appraised the chef, whom Rachel introduced as Bob's daughter. A tall, freckled redhead, she was not so young-looking close-up: maybe in her thirties. She seemed more mature in her manner, too—or manners. She wore baggy brown corduroys, a lumberjack shirt over a black leotard, and a white apron over that; finishing-school poise still showed through.

When she left them, Rachel revealed that Annie had been a "True Lifer" longer than her father; in fact, it was through her that God reached Bob for Jesus Christ after his wife, Annie's stepmother, died of cancer. Cal did not ask, though he was tempted to, whether the death of the presumably unsaved woman was also part of God's plan for Bob's conversion.

"Bob made a fortune as a commodities broker," Rachel said. "He was a millionaire. Now he likes to say he's almost as poor as a church mouse."

"Was he the one who donated this place?"

"Who said it was donated?"

"Guess."

"What other b.s. did Jim tell you?"

"Well, you know Jim. That's why I'm here—to determine the extent of Jim's misinformation so I can try to undo at least some of the damage." He took a sip of coffee to wash down the peach cobbler, which was undercooked and slightly glutinous.

"True Life bought this property on the open market," she said. "This is our state headquarters. It's the only household of faith in Illinois so far. We're thinking of splitting up, half of us moving to some place near Normal."

He grinned. She twinkled. "Actually, it's closer to Bloomington, the farm we want to buy. I don't know where Jim got the idea this house was donated. All he had to do was ask us. We're not hiding anything—we couldn't even if we wanted to. Not like churches can. You know the IRS can't even audit churches? But they can audit us: We're a nonprofit corporation. We could call ourselves a church if we wanted to, but we think churches are a big part of the problem of what's wrong with Christianity."

"On that, I couldn't agree with you more," Cal said, and settled a candidly affectionate look on her.

She blushed. "Did Jim tell you that I'm learning Greek."

"Greek?"

"New Testament Greek. You can't really know what the Scriptures say unless you know what they say in the languages of the original texts."

"I like that," he said. "Because I've had the exact same thought myself. So how long have you been into this?"

"From the very beginning, about three months. Mostly as a weekend thing. I only moved in here last weekend."

One warm afternoon back in September she and a classmate crossing the small Christian college's park-like "commons" were drawn to a cluster of students. A crowd had gathered in front of the statue of the young school's primary benefactor. Two young men were debating, in loud voices, but respectfully, taking turns to speak. It seemed totally staged. When Rachel understood that one of them, who turned out to be Mark, was quoting from the Scriptures to dispute Christ's divinity, she assumed they were staging the debate as a provocative educational stunt.

"You know, right there on campus and all, that's the only way I could believe it was happening. But then, the guy debating Mark really lost his cool. He got really angry and started yelling at Mark that he was defending the Arian heresy. That's when I realized maybe it was actually a real debate.

"Mark was incredible, just so calm—and brave. He waited till the guy let him speak and then explained how it was only because Emperor Constantine wanted to give the Western churches more power through the Council of Nicaea that Arius was ever considered a heretic in the first place; that what Arius and most of the bishops believed, especially in the Eastern churches, was exactly the way Paul and the First Century Christians believed."

Cal said, "Well..."

"Jesus Christ is the Son of God. But that didn't make him God the Son—that phrase isn't anywhere in the Bible, and the few verses that seem to say that Christ is literally one and the same as God have been misinterpreted, or they were changed after the Trinity got developed as a doctrine. Like the Baptismal formula at the end of Matthew? That was added, which is so obvious because if Jesus said to baptize in the name of the Father and the Son and the Holy Spirit, then why does it always say in Acts that the Apostles just baptized in the name of Jesus?

"Really, Cal, there's just so much that's obvious, even if you don't know Greek."

"I won't argue with you there," he said. He wanted to smoke but had noted the absence of ashtrays. Bob and Larry had excused themselves a few minutes before; others were now carrying stacked plates toward the kitchen. Smiling wryly, Cal lowered his eyes and sighed a chuckle. "Why was it requisite that the Mediator be God?"

"It wasn't requisite." She waggled her head. "Just the opposite was required—that our Savior be fully human and freely choose to do his Father's will, and succeed when he could have failed. Otherwise how could he really atone for Adam's freely choosing not to obey God? The way we were taught, Jesus could have chosen not to do what he did, but he couldn't have failed once he decided to go through with it—because he was God. Right?"

Mark walked up. "I happen to agree with you," Cal said, "that the Trinity was read into the Bible. But what I believe about the Trinity, or the Bible in general, or about what you believe...is irrelevant to why I'm here, which is to"—he involuntarily glanced at Mark—"be a go-between. To get you and Mom and Dad at least speaking to each other again.

"Jim has really got them worked up. They asked me to come out here, mainly to get a second opinion, I guess. I came because I want to understand what you guys are all about, so I can explain it to them, and try to counteract the b.s. they've heard from Jim."

Rachel looked up at Mark, who looked at Cal and said, "You can use the library if you want. There's more privacy there. And it would probably be more comfortable."

"Sounds good," Cal said. "Thanks."

"Will you join us?" Rachel asked Mark. "I'm sure Cal's going to have questions you can answer better than I can."

Mark looked at Cal. "It's up to you."

"Fine with me," Cal said, forthrightly answering the challenge he saw in Mark's eyes.

For those not assigned clean-up chores, the household schedule allotted an hour and a half of free time after dinner. Rachel said the "residents" usually passed the time in study and prayer, to prepare for their Bible study classes. Mark went on ahead to the library while Rachel gave Cal a tour of the ground floor. Large rooms at one end of the house had been divided by walls of wood paneling into small classrooms, each furnished with a freestanding blackboard and a table surrounded by more of the drab folding chairs.

They stopped in at the coat room off the vestibule of the main entrance, a large walk-in closet hung wall-to-wall with outerwear. Plastic collars originally marked with sizes on clothes-store racks divided the hangers; the collars bore names printed with magic marker. Rachel hung up their parkas in her assigned space.

"Why the look?" she asked.

"Oh, just seems odd," he said, "that a commune would be so meticulous about keeping everybody's private property separated like this."

"Commune?! We're not a commune."

They found Mark in the library, a snug room between Bob's spacious office and a greenhouse patio closed off by a sliding glass door.

"You won't believe what else my brother-in-law said about us," Rachel declared as they stepped into the room.

Mark was sitting on a couch staring morosely into a fireless fireplace, a lovely small hearth that seemed merely decorative, a tasteful way to display some marble amid the mahogany bookshelves, which were almost entirely bare. Rachel sat down and snuggled next to Mark. Their joined hands, fingers interlaced, settled limply in the crevice of their contiguous thighs. Cal sat down in an armchair. "Great place you've got here," he said, and thought: *except for this furniture.* The couch and chairs were cheap institutional pieces upholstered in black vinyl.

"You should tell your brother-in-law to get his facts straight," Mark said.

"Won't do any good. I've been telling him that for years."

"Jim called here a couple days ago," Rachel said, "but I didn't want to talk to him."

Cal shifted in the chair, put one leg up on the other knee. "I don't blame you. But you shouldn't let him stand between your talking to Mom and Dad. They really don't know how to deal with this. Couldn't you have tried to soften the blow somehow? Break it to them a little less suddenly?"

Rachel bowed her head ruefully; her mouth fleered. "I wish you'd been here. I couldn't see any way to avoid a bad scene, once I told them I don't believe Jesus is God anymore. That's what really got Mom hysterical. And that's one of the first things I felt I had to tell them."

"Well, they're sorry they got so upset." He wanted to keep his eyes from Mark but kept looking at his boxer's nose, run-on eyebrow, and devilish goatee, trying to see him as unattractive or as a caricature; he could, but he couldn't shake the impression that he was powerfully attractive to women, and possessed formidable intelligence. He figured Sarah and Martin had seen him as a Charles Manson look-alike. "So tell me," he said. "How did TLF get started?"

Mark jabbed a glance at him. "Jim didn't know?"

"I've only talked to him and my parents on the phone. Last night. I just got back yesterday morning, in the wee hours."

Mark's look resentfully challenged Cal's claim. Rachel looked up at him, and he swallowed and squeezed her hand. "Dr. Philip Lewten, who has a master's in theology from Princeton, founded True Life Fellowship almost thirty years ago."

Cal raised his eyebrows. "Princeton, eh?" He gestured to Rachel. "Dad should be impressed."

She didn't seem to know if he was being sarcastic. She looked up at Mark and lifted their hands affectionately. "Dad always talked about how good Princeton seminary used to be—before it got infected with modernism."

"What denomination was Dr. Lewten," Cal asked, "before he founded True Life?"

"German Reformed Church, originally," Mark said. "They're part of the United Church of Christ now."

"Interesting," Cal said. "Reformed—so Calvinism in his past, Lewten's, at least to some extent."

Mark seemed to relax as he talked about Dr. Lewten's life story. His first pastorate was a church in Hopewell, Tennessee, right after World War II. The congregation was small, elderly, and apathetic, but as the young men of the area returned after the war, their energy sparked several years of rapid growth, an exciting time for Lewten.

"It was the pastoral counseling that burned him out," Mark said, "once he'd built up the church membership, and was taking care of their needs as a pastor, not doing as much community outreach. He discovered he wasn't good at counseling. He felt inadequate. He'd begun to have problems of his own, having to do with his walk in Christ. He decided the problem was, he didn't really have a firm grasp on how to walk in the spirit, as a pastor, and as a husband and father, and here he was trying to guide others in working through their problems, through prayer and seeking guidance in the Scriptures, preparing their hearts to receive what the Holy Spirit was telling them.

"He began to think there was something missing in the orthodox understanding of the *pneumatikos*—the *spiritual things* Paul writes about. He prayed about it, for a long time, and God told him, finally, that if he would commit himself one hundred percent to the study of His Word, He'd show him the way to the victorious life through spiritual power, the abundant life that Jesus promised to believers in him.

"He went back to studying the Scriptures in Koine Greek, and God led him to concentrate on a study of The Acts of the Apostles. When God determined that he was ready, he was able to see that the key to the New Testament teachings about leading a spiritual life in Christ Jesus is right in plain sight in the critical Greek texts."

Mark let go of Rachel's hand, to have both of his free for gesturing. "*Pneuma hagion,*" he said, leaning forward. "*Pneuma hagion* is Koine Greek for *holy spirit*. Now, you're thinking *Holy Spirit* with capital letters, right? But *pneuma hagion* is not capitalized in the critical Greek texts."

Cal frowned. "But the earliest manuscripts are written entirely in uncials, which are capital letters, right?"

"That's correct," Mark said. "That's why it's an interpretation to capitalize the words *holy spirit* in translating them into English."

"But then it's also an interpretation *not* to capitalize them. Don't you capitalize any words, the way you translate it?"

"Of course: when it's appropriate to the meaning. But capitalizing holy spirit every time the Greek has *pneuma hagion,* or just *pneuma,* without a definite article, that's just wrong, that's changing the meaning of the original words of God.

"We teach people to study the critical texts and decide for themselves how they should be interpreted. To be absolutely certain of the Word and Will of God, you have to learn to read Koine Greek and Hebrew and, for really advanced study, Aramaic."

Cal was dumbstruck. Mark and Rachel waited patiently for him to respond. "That's...kind of...asking a lot, isn't it? Certainly doesn't sound like a religion for the masses."

"That's an elitist attitude," Mark said. "If a person can read English, he can learn to read the other languages. Given enough desire and discipline and help—which is freely provided to all believers in Christ, simply for the asking."

"Everyone goes at their own pace," Rachel said. "And it's not like anybody's under any pressure or anything. There aren't any grades. Learning the languages as we study the Scriptures is just part of our routine. It's Bible study on a higher level."

Cal raised his eyebrows. "I'll say. All right, so you're saying *holy spirit* shouldn't be capitalized. Meaning what?"

"That's not what we're saying," Mark said. "Sometimes it should be capitalized. But in more than fifty verses in the New Testament *pneuma hagion* appears without the article *the*. To translate it as *the Holy Ghost* or *the Holy Spirit* in those verses is not a correct translation; it's an incorrect interpretation.

"What *the* Holy Spirit—capitalized—showed Dr. Lewten was that there are different meanings to the uses of the words *pneuma hagion* in the New Testament. The forms used with an article, *the pneuma* or *the hagion pneuma* or *the pneuma, the hagion*—all those simply refer to God. They are other names for God.

"For example, John 3:6: *That which is born of the pneuma is pneuma.* The first *pneuma*, which has the definite article, should be translated *Spirit* with a big *S*. Obviously, it refers to God. The second *pneuma,* no article, is *spirit* with a little *s*, referring to holy spirit in us, which is God's gift to us when we believe in His Son Jesus Christ. God, the Holy Spirit, when we believe in His Son Jesus Christ, gives us some of what He, God, is: holy spirit—small *h*, small *s*."

Mark sat back, obviously satisfied with his explanation and not expecting Cal to be. "Even the King James," he added, "admits there's a distinction in that verse. The King James capitalizes the first instance of Spirit but not the second."

Cal asked for another example and received several. He was mortified to be impressed as the reasoning began to make sense to him. Once he'd absorbed an inkling of the ramifications, the whole idea seemed familiar, and thinking aloud about it, after showing them he was favorably intrigued, he became voluble.

"You know, I remember wondering why liberal theologians avoided using 'the Holy Spirit'—the name, I mean. They always refer to 'the Spirit of God' or 'the Spirit of Christ,' and I got the idea that—this was, I guess, when I was a junior in high school—I got the idea that my Dad was right: They wanted to do away with the Trinity by making Jesus more human and the Holy Spirit simply the spirit of compassionate self-sacrificing love. *Caritas,* right? If I speak with the tongues of men and of angels, and have not—*charity*, in the King James. Most people prefer to just call it *love*, but *charity* is closer to the Greek, isn't it? *Caritas*."

Rachel bowed an embarrassed look of self-satisfaction.

"Caritas is Latin," Mark said. "And it's a bad translation of the word Paul used. There's no one word in Latin or English that can give the meaning of the Greek accurately. There are two words for *love* that occur in the Greek New Testament: *phileo*, which is brotherly love, and *agapao*, which is the word Paul used in the thirteenth chapter of First Corinthians.

Agapao is not limited to caritas, though charity is bound to be one result of achieving *agapao*. *Agapao* is the divine love that only believers in Christ who have received holy spirit into manifestation can experience."

Beginning to feel hyper, Cal reached for his cigarettes. "I guess that leaves me out, then. Of course, I can't judge for myself if your interpretation is valid, since obviously I don't know Greek or Latin. You mind if I smoke?"

"Of course not," Rachel said. "I'll get an ashtray."

When she'd gone through the door to the office, Mark looked at his watch and said, "We don't have much time for this tonight. We have classes in ten minutes. We should be getting ready."

Cal bounced the cigarette on the arm of the chair; and then, more effectively, on the face of his watch. "Could I sit in on a class?"

"I'm afraid that's not allowed. Anyone is welcome to attend our introductory half-day course, which we offer at least once a month, but in private homes around the metro area, not here. The courses here are intensive seminars. An outsider guest would throw off the group dynamics, if you know what I mean."

"Oh, yeah, sure. I understand."

Rachel breezed back bearing a green glass ashtray. Cal nodded as he lit up and sat back. "I wanted to smoke after dinner, but I didn't see anyone else and there were no ashtrays. I take it you don't approve of defiling the temple of *pneuma hagion*."

"We don't think it's expedient, but we don't have a dogma against it," Mark said, and Cal chalked it up as hypocrisy, judging by Mark's sternly disapproving vibes.

"At home, Daddy always said it was a waste of time and money," Rachel said. "But when he preached he didn't dare say anything like that, and he never preached about the body being the temple of the Holy Spirit, because half the adults in the congregation smoked."

"Yeah," Cal said, "I told him he should make it a selling point, put it on the letter board sign outside the church: *Holy Smokers Welcomed Here.*"

Rachel kind of smiled. Mark didn't. Embarrassed, Cal changed his tone: "So tell me about this business you guys run. The money-making one I mean, with the van."

"There's nothing much to tell," Rachel said. "It's a business. A small business—to make money."

"He who will not work, neither let him eat," Mark said.

Smiling, Cal said, "So how do you reconcile that to Jesus' command in Matthew to feed anyone who's hungry?"

"Levinson's Home for Prodigal Sons, may I help you?"

"Hey, Josh, it's me."

"You mean, It is I. Where have you been, you illiterate?"

"Right where I said I'd be—visiting the state headquarters of True Life Fellowship and Biblical Research Association."

"Hmmm...T(i)LFABRA?"

"T-L-F, for short. They prefer just True Life."

"I bet they do. I thought you said it was a commune. What's this state headquarters bullshit?"

"It's kind of communal but definitely not a commune. They're set up as a nonprofit corporation—that's P-R-O-F-I-T. Rachel and her fellow fanatics work for a legally separate business."

"Wait a minute," Josh said. "I know this scam. They work for the business and donate all their money to the tax-shelter corporation."

"Almost. They don't donate it. They use it to pay room and board and tuition for their Bible research classes. Pretty nifty setup, huh?"

"A sucker born every minute," Josh said, sounding faintly like W.C. Fields. "Well, well, well, who would have guessed? I look forward to speaking with you further, my good man, but now if you'll excuse me, duty calls. At what hour shall I expect your reappearance?"

A woman giggled. Josh shushed her.

"I suspected as much," Cal said. "Who's the dame?"

"That's for me to know, in the biblical sense, and for you not to find out."

❖

"There's nothing you can say that I haven't already thought about," Rachel said. "I had lots of doubts at first. Really, the

Holy Spirit led me to the truth against my will, I was so blind because of everything we were taught about the Bible."

She and Cal sat cross-legged at the edge of the carpet in front of the fireplace, which Cal had insisted they put to good use, bringing wood from the pile by the big hearth in the dining room. He listened uncritically, mellowed out by the crackling flames.

"The problem was I'd never been taught how to activate *dunamis*—the spiritual ability that believing in Christ automatically gives you. I'd never been taught that to have the abundant life Jesus promised you have to *lambano*—receive into manifestation—and not just receive passively, *dechomai,* which is all most born-again Christians ever do because they're never taught, never shown that they automatically have this power as soon as they believe in Jesus Christ as their Lord and Savior.

"Remember in Acts chapter eight? Peter and John go to Samaria to help the new believers there, who'd been baptized by Philip in the name of Jesus, but Philip didn't tell them about receiving the spirit into manifestation. So Peter and John went and told them and laid their hands on them, and they all started speaking in tongues."

She beamed *agapao* at the fire. And shot a glance of it Cal's way. "The truth is so simple, it's hard for us to accept ahead of time, just hearing about it, but that's the catch—you have to accept it to have it, that's what faith is all about. Once you accept Christ as your savior, you have to activate the power that's in you by receiving the holy spirit into manifestation.

And to do that, all you have to do is trust that you have it and let yourself go. Believing equals receiving."

Cal suspected the *pneuma hagion* business was holy chutzpah, but he hoped there might be something to it, philologically speaking; and that he could satisfy his curiosity on the matter without having to master that wickedly difficult Greek alphabet. He wondered if Lewten's "discovery" was actually Lewten's. It seemed consistent with a lot of modernist theology, and yet Lewten spouted the fundamentalist rule of rules: Scripture must always be interpreted as literally as possible.

He had deeper misgivings about the "language of the spirit" he'd witnessed during the worship service, but Rachel's body language declared that the changes in her life were all to the good; he was impressed to the point of discomfort by how physically at ease she'd become. She seemed as radiantly content and confident as a Degas ballerina. The last time he saw her, three-and-a-half months ago, he'd mocked her ridiculous concern about eating too much: She had been Twiggy-thin. Now he couldn't even tease her about being flat-chested: Wholesome mounds pushed out the blue and red snowflakes of her ski-sweater.

"Praying in tongues is just so far out," she said. "You feel holy spirit in you communing with God, renewing your mind in love and knowledge, the knowledge that God is in you in power, power to control the things that happen to you, the power to make you more creative and energetic and—just victorious in everything. That word sums it up: the victorious life.

"The operation of tongues is just basic, it's the sign that you've received the baptism of the Spirit, which is what John the Baptist said Jesus came to do, remember? *I, indeed, have baptized you with water, but he shall baptize you with the Holy Spirit.*"

Cal stared at the black marble slab in front of the hearth, fascinatingly reflecting the dance of the flames. Something about the scriptural citation seemed off, but he was focused on another thought. *Pneuma* also means *wind*, right?"

"And *breath*," Rachel said.

"Right, okay, now it's coming back. In the Nicodemus story Jesus was punning, comparing the Spirit to the wind, since the word for both was the same in Greek."

"No, no," Rachel said, her glow turned up high. "Jesus was, it was like when he spoke in parables, so that hearing, Nicodemus wouldn't understand. The *pneuma* shouldn't be translated *wind* in those verses, because the wind doesn't have a will, and we can see where the wind is coming from and where it goes. Jesus was talking about the holy spirit in the believer.

"If you translate it correctly it comes out, where he said, *and thou hearest the sound thereof*, supposedly meaning the wind, that what Jesus was really saying there was *and thou hearest his voice*—the voice of the spirit in the believer speaking the language of the spirit, which is what speaking in tongues is."

Cal seemed to play it back, mulling it over. "I'll have to read it over again. But, seems to me, the way you guys interpret it then—or rather, translating it your way makes it sound like gnostic propaganda. So maybe you're right. You know, the opening verses of John were plagiarized from a gnostic hymn."

Her inner light dimmed, her mouth fleering disappointedly as she bowed her head away.

"I think you've got a valid argument though," he said. "I'm honestly intrigued by all this."

"Praise the Lord," she said softly.

He felt the urging of common sense, pointing out an appropriate moment to make the pitch he'd been holding back. "I just wish you'd talk to Mom and Dad the way you've talked to me tonight. They're hurting, Rache. It'd be so great if you could show them that Jim has fed them a lot of misinformation about you guys."

Her facial expression didn't encourage him; he sighed. "They'd like you to come home Christmas Day. For dinner. With a nice friendly discussion after dessert. Don't worry, Jim and Pris won't be there—just you and me, and Mark if he wants to come along. Though I think it would go better if he didn't. But if he comes with you, fine. The plan is that we all make polite conversation during the meal and sit down afterwards, everybody with a Bible—even me. I'll act as moderator—"

She was slowly shaking her head.

"Why not?"

"We're having a feast. Like the one in the parable—the Great Feast. We're going to set up a big tent on this vacant lot on the South Side and have a huge buffet and invite people to come from off the street, just like in the parable. I don't want to miss it."

"Oh. Well—? How about tomorrow night, then? One more Christmas Eve with the family, for old time's sake?"

"I know Mark wouldn't do it. And I just couldn't. If it were just Mom, I'd do it, but—. You can hold your own against Dad, but even when I know I'm right, I can't argue with him. Someday I'll be able to. But I'm not ready yet."

"Not so long ago, you looked up to Dad the way you look up to Mark."

"So? That's natural. But I wasn't really as respectful of Dad as I seemed. I respected his intelligence, and how much he knew about the Bible, how logical he is all the time. But I also know how cold and unsympathetic he can be—even with his own wife.

"Jesus Christ is my Lord, not Mark. Mark was the means God used to reach me, but he isn't the reason I'm here. Though I believe He wants us to be together, as man and wife, to work as a team. But please don't tell Mom and Dad that. We plan to get married."

"You're actually engaged?"

"Yes."

"Wow. Well, congratulations."

"We won't be getting married till next summer. Bob thought we should wait a whole year. But we talked him into just six months."

"And you don't want me tell Mom and Dad?"

"Please—don't. Mark won't be happy I told you."

"I don't think he likes me."

"I don't think you like him."

"Probably can't be avoided. I respect him though."

"You know, I wish we'd gotten to know each other better, before now."

"Might have been nice."

"We should have—that first summer you came home. But I wasn't ready to open up to anybody then. I was crazy. I was like two people, this secret me and the one I had to act like all the time."

"I know what you mean."

"That summer was the first time you started letting it all hang out. And I wanted to, but I couldn't. You could, because—you're a man, for one thing. And you could argue with Dad. You really rubbed it in, how much you despised them because of their conservatism and everything, their materialism; how they say they believe in the love of Christ but don't care about the poor. And they think Blacks are inferior. They're so prejudiced, it makes me sick.

"That summer I began to see why you were so critical of them. But, you know, it bothered me that you were always hiding what you believed. Even in high school you were like that. You'd praise the Sojourners and LaSalle Street Church, any Christians who were working for social justice, but you didn't join them and try to help. You talked like you were all for the Social Gospel, but you weren't about to go work in a slum yourself. Just like, later, when you put Nixon down so bad—Dad was right: Why didn't you go out and work for McGovern if you felt that way?

"I never understood how you could praise do-gooders and talk about how most Christians are really only looking out for Number One and then you weren't looking out for anybody but yourself."

She tucked a strand of hair behind her ear as she lifted her face.

"What do you believe in, Cal?"

He stalled by lighting up a cigarette. "What do I believe in?" He wanted to be Zen about it, wanted to say something whimsically irrelevant or nothing at all, or do something comically enigmatic and refuse to explain. "Believe in," he said, frowning. "That *in* bothers me."

"What are you living for?"

"I don't like that *for* much either. I haven't identified an ultimate purpose to my life. I don't think. If I have, it's a mystery to me. I try to be content to live for the sake of living. Life for life's sake, you know?"

"You're living only for yourself then?"

"Well, for starters, yeah."

"You only believe in yourself, then. Isn't that what you're saying? Or do you have a lover? Like John Lennon. He only believes in himself and Yoko now."

"No, I don't have a girlfriend. And I'm not looking for one at the moment. Precisely because I don't believe only in myself, the way you mean it. It can mean something a lot more complex. Let's just say I believe in living my life the way I see fit, and in letting others live theirs the way they see fit."

He lowered his eyes to his cigarette. She frowned over a handful of hair. She'd never liked its color: variegated browns with auburn highlights. He'd always liked it; it went nicely with her freckles.

"Have you decided whether you're going to go to law school?" she asked. "Mom and Dad are afraid you might end up like Josh, trying to stay a hippie the rest of your life."

"I hope I'll always be a hippie at heart," he said, "whatever I ultimately decide to do with my life. I don't think I'll be going to law school though."

"Must be nice, to be able to do just about anything you want." He let it pass, and she repented with a switch in tone: "So what are you planning to do now?"

"Get a job. I'm about two hundred bucks from being flat broke. But I haven't really given that much thought yet, and right now I'm trying to patch things up between you and Mom, and Dad. You know, you really have to search your heart about this, Rache. Mom especially is torturing herself with guilt, and you could relieve her of that, if you'd just talk to them. They have to see for themselves that you haven't been coerced or brainwashed."

She sulked for a moment. Then said, "I feel so sorry for Mom. She and Dad don't really share much anymore. There's been something wrong in their relationship for a long time. It has to do with sex."

"What makes you think that?" he asked, a little too carefully.

"Oh, things Mom says. She's really uptight you know. Now, more than before, because of her age. Did you know she and Prissy had a big fight over that *Total Woman* book? Did you hear about that book?"

"I've read about it."

"Mom and Dad both read it. Dad didn't like it, but it was, you know—the usual put-down of whatever Jim and Pris think is so great. But Mom really got upset about it."

He said nothing, and pointedly, by shifting his legs.

"I could probably handle talking to Mom," she said. "If Mom can talk to me about it without treating me like a little girl, or like I'm crazy, or both—which is how she acted when I told them I'd decided to live here."

Turning her head but not meeting his eyes, she said, "Tell Mom *that*. Tell her I'm willing to talk to *her*. But not with Dad. And not, not for at least a month. I need more time to get it together."

She tossed her hair over her shoulder. "We should get to bed. It's later than I said we'd be."

She stood up and simpered affectionately, extending her hand; he let her pull him to his feet. Self-consciously inspired when she bowed her head to avoid meeting his eyes, he kissed her on the forehead. She blushed and looked up as he stepped back.

"I just remembered when you did that," she said, "when we were little. You hit me and I ran crying to Mom, and she made you kiss me."

He had hobbled over to the fire screen; as he put it in front of the hearth, he said, "And that, sad to say, was probably the last time I kissed you."

When he turned, she solemnly approached; he saw her intent and turned his cheek. She kissed it and pressed her face to his chest as she wrapped him in her arms.

He was given the guest suite. It didn't surprise him to find the rooms elegantly appointed with mahogany pilasters and plush pile carpeting—and sparsely furnished with secondhand goods. The bed was a king-size. On the wall above the rough-hewn headboard was a blue ceramic plate, bearing the same holy spirit dove he had seen over the front gate—its upswept wings even more flame-like. As he leaned to look at it, his legs pressed into the edge of the bed. He stepped back, confounded, and pulled up the bedspread, revealing a waterbed in a raised box-frame. He marveled: Maybe this group wasn't as puritanical as he'd assumed.

The gently sloshy buoyance, he decided, actually was quite relaxing. He thought he might have been stoned the few times he'd tried out Josh's waterbed. Josh always looked a little queasy when he lay on it—one paw limply curled on his belly like an otter, the other under his head. He claimed it was the only way to sleep. Cal had never believed him. The waterbed had embarrassed him from the first and still did. He saw it as blatantly symbolic of the Nattering Nabobs' delusions of horny grandeur that summer after freshman year.

The Nabobs, minus Hank, who had the good sense to go back to Idaho, sublet an apartment in Evanston. Josh and Kevin found the four of them a uniquely attractive job. It allowed them to be together much of the day; to work without supervision, taking off pretty much whenever they pleased; and to take home more money than they would have from most other summer jobs.

The gig was to go door-to-door in the suburbs making a pitch for concern about pollution and offering a little decal of the ecology symbol in exchange for a "donation" of a buck. For each dollar turned in, the nonprofit organization paid the fund-raiser thirty cents and his crew boss seven. Josh dipped into his bar mitzvah money to buy the Pinto so he could be a crew boss. He paid for gas out of the bonus seven percent and divvied up the rest. They averaged about twenty dollars a day, pay, but it wasn't enough for Kevin. He ripped off some decals from headquarters and when one of the guys had an exceptionally good day he had the option of paying himself a higher percentage, turning in decals from the purloined extras.

Because he was the least larcenous in the group, Cal could have made a lot more money caddying at the Elmore Country Club, as he had done during high school and would do the next two summers. He only decided to go along with the Nabobs because he thought he'd be able to keep his beard and shoulder-length hair. After three days of going door-to-door in the suburbs, constantly getting mean, suspicious, or ridiculing vibes, and several times getting yelled off somebody's property, he visited a barbershop: He entered a hippie and came out hip.

With sardonic pity he recalled that the only female they had succeeded in luring into the apartment all summer was Seymour-the-pusher's girlfriend, who'd been left to fend for herself that summer. She stopped by at Josh's invitation, issued in passing when they bumped into each other on the walkway along Sheridan Road. She was going to summer school. She was a short, plump, voluptuous blonde with a high-pitched voice made raspy from marijuana smoke. He remembered the four of them getting her stoned and giving her the tour of the apartment; he brought up the rear. Amazing: When she looked into Josh's room and remarked the waterbed, she did not say, "Hey, great, let's have an orgy."

Pulled from the edge of sleep by faint erotic stimulation, conscious of keeping the good feeling amorphous and away from his cock, he focused on the warmth his body was imparting to the sheets. Was an aura the same thing as the astral body? He'd always been curious about the occult and ESP, reports on the afterlife, but he'd never allowed himself to get seriously interested in any of that stuff. He was afraid of his innate desire to believe in paranormal phenomena.

Concentrating on the mental image of his body heat, he imagined himself an aura. For a few minutes he managed to merge observer and observed; mind and body; ego and glow.

He spread out his arms deliciously, making waves in the bed and ripples in his nerves. He realized he was in a relaxed crucifixion pose and thought of the dove on the cover of Lewten's book—spread wings forming a cross with the fuzzy vertical bar of light behind its body. The cross, transcended.

Intensely pleasurable emotion fountained in his chest, filling his eyes: so many nights the same night, the same peak moments of soul-suffering provoked by a TV documentary on the concentration camps or devastation scenes from Hiroshima and Nagasaki; "specials" on the civil rights movement or the war in South Vietnam; talk of the Russian missiles that might rain H-Bombs down at any time or headlines numbering the dead from an earthquake or flood—the so-called acts of God reminding God's Elect that Nature after the Fall became more blithely murderous even than the most evil monsters of the human race.

Why did God create such a terrible world?

Time and again as a child he had resurrected that question from the sepulcher of the catechism. He thought he saw why now. After banging his mind against the idea of God-Hidden-in-Mystery and the world of incessant suffering He had created, he would imitate Jehovah's rage for righteousness and justice; he would make like Job, in effect, and call the Creator of the Universe to account. All to the end that he, Calvin Thomas Wideman, might once again come crying to Jesus, and feel the peace that passeth understanding in the mystery of his redeeming love.

In the afterglow of spiritual self-gratification, he would feel so very sorry for the unsaved masses of mankind: unable to know the joy and peace and love that he knew. He didn't deserve to be saved, but he was; his shameful unworthiness was crucial to the mystical absurdity of his specialness. The hidden soft spot of Calvinism was: "There but for the grace of God, go I."

Rachel, Rachel, Rachel.

What was the song? On the Plastic Ono Band album. He didn't know the title. He could almost hear Lennon's voice, though, singing that he didn't believe in miracles. He only believed in himself.

It came out during his freshman year. He didn't like where Lennon was at, man; didn't know the dream was already seen through by the firstborn of the LSD generation. He didn't convert to radical cynicism until sophomore year: wise fool. He came across a line in his French text by Anatole France and made it his credo: "*Chacun fait son salut comme il peut.*" Each one makes his salvation however he can.

Sophomore year he resigned himself to believing only in himself. But it sure shamed him to have sunk so low. He took refuge in books, became monkish in his studies. Josh accused him of harboring the hope that he would find The Answer, not just an answer that would make do for him. He always denied it, angrily at times—because, of course, it was true.

Not anymore. He now thought he knew where Lennon was at when he came out of Primal Scream therapy—feeling, well, yes: born again. But not exactly filled with smiley Christian love.

Meanwhile, George Harrison stayed on the highway to heaven through meditation and chanting. Hare Krishna.

While Ringo and Paul traveled first-class on the Epicurean Express.

Each makes his salvation—*salut* could also be translated *health*—however he can. It was a first-rate epigram. It was Nietzschean, he thought. And then: No. Nietzsche was into power, not health. Nietzsche was a true believer in himself—until he suffered his own personal apocalypse.

In Turin, not long after he finished writing *The Antichrist,* Nietzsche came upon a coachman mercilessly flogging his exhausted horse. The preacher of the will to power and prophet of the Superman became so distraught by this cruelty that he ran and collapsed with his arms around the horse's neck, shielding it from further blows. He was carried unconscious to his lodgings and woke up insane.

Nietzsche's friends were alerted to his madness by letters he wrote shortly after the incident. One of the first letters said, in its entirety, "Sing me a new song: The world is transfigured and all the heavens are full of joy."

It was signed: "The Crucified."

You can run but you can't hide. Like Gauguin slinking over the hedgerow way down low in The Yellow Christ. *Tahiti on his mind. Or any other paradise-now.*

The more I claimed I wasn't a Christian, the more I felt like I had to imitate Jesus. Even looked like him.

Another member in good standing of the Church of Jesus Christ without Jesus Christ.

I wanted to be crucified by joy. Repeatedly.

My antichrist was me, on LSD.

He had to stop. He felt a speedy achiness in his chest and tightness in the root of his tongue. He opened his mouth and took two deep slow breaths; inhaled more slowly through his nose as he shut his eyes. He had never actually had an honest-to-freak-out flashback, but his fear of having one had brought him occasionally to the edge of a panic attack. He sensed that he had just dodged another one. He pressed his hands into the waterbed to create some slight wave motion and the sensation of floating. He visualized again the diving god of the Mayans as his mind sank into sleep.

CHAPTER FOUR

Flashback: Jesus-Tripping at the Kentucky Derby

MAY 1971, NORTHWESTERN UNIVERSITY

"I thought the Kentucky Derby was the only race they ran on Derby Day. Stupid. I didn't really think about it, I guess. I'd read somewhere that there was always a really wild scene in the infield at Churchill Downs and when I mentioned it, Hank said, oh yeah, he'd heard it was a blast. So Injun Joe tells this hilarious story about the time he went there with some buddies in high school.

"He made it sound like a Woodstock for everybody. All sorts of weird authentic Americans overdoing their favorite form of intoxication and watching everybody else enjoy theirs. He claimed that tipsy women with hardly any clothes on were ubiquitous at this bacchanal—'all over the place' is how he phrased it, I believe."

Tamara grinned. Cal blushed and took a drag of his cigarette. He was seated, left leg outstretched, right knee raised, on a slightly inclined surface—one of the breakwater's jumble of humongous concrete blocks. She had chosen a nearly level perch on an adjacent block. She hunched over her crossed legs, gazing at the viscously shimmery lake and the darkening sky, and glancing at him.

"But he didn't go with you, did he?"

Cal snorted. "No. He's got a job in the city on weekends. I'm not convinced he ever went to the Derby. Anyway, so we had these big pink capsules that the pusher at Phi Si swore were organic mesc. I think we have bought mesc about a dozen times and have actually been sold mescaline twice—this time and once before. Well, we bought enough for several trips, just in case. Kevin was in charge of the stash and he brought along two caps apiece. He didn't say anything about taking two, though, until he was handing them out in the car. Big deal, right?"

His voice shifted to an off-key falsetto as he sang to the tune of the chewing-gum jingle: "Double your pleasure, double your fun, with double mesc, double mesc, double mesc fun."

She grinned again and bobbed her head, making her massive halo of coppery curls bounce around. He took another drag, stabbed out his cigarette, and continued his story.

"When it comes to deranging the senses, Kevin can't be out-stoned by anybody. The weekend back in—February, I think—he wanted to celebrate because he'd switched to being an artsie-fartsie, couldn't keep his GPA above a C in Tech, being stoned half the time, which he has to do or lose his scholarship. So that Friday afternoon he drank an entire case of beer, smoked a gram of hash, by himself—and then he decides to drop acid. Suicidal, right? About an hour after peaking out he says that he's tired and he's going to bed. Five minutes after he lies down with the lights off, he's fast asleep.

"Now, that is not normal, to fall asleep on acid. He's got that wacky grin and those big baby-blue eyes. And with that fuzzy blond hair he looks like a Swedish angel who's been through hell and loved every minute of it.

"So he wanted to take two hits, naturally, because he didn't get very high the last time when he only took one. Stands to reason. And Hank has been feeling disappointed by the tripping lately, he says, and doesn't hesitate a bit when Kevin holds out two caps. Josh and I, though, had ve-er-ry serious doubts about the wisdom of this. He looks at me with those spooky eyes and it's obvious he's scared. So am I. I say, Wa-ai-t a minute, guys, this is crazy."

He took a deep breath as he tilted his head way back; closed his eyes as he sighed it out. He felt the chill in the air as a malevolent tingle. The limpid blue was growing dark over the glistening ripply surface of the lake. He was getting speedy, the tension like a bad taste in his whole body, concentrated in his throat, a pulsating ache in the root of his tongue.

"So why'd you go along?"

"To get along," he said, and looked down between his knees. "It was two for all, and all for two. Because he who is least stoned has to take care of the others, and I'm not like Dan, with his Daddy-looking-after-everybody trip. I wanna be one of the little kids, too.

"Josh said, If these are about average hits, I don't think I'll have any problem. But, of course, he knew, we all did—it's street-drug roulette. You don't know what you've got till you're gone. I suggested we take one cap right then, in the car, and wait till we were in the infield to see if we wanted another one. But no, Kevin wouldn't go for anything sensible. He wasn't the least bit concerned about taking two.

"Actually, he wasn't—. He didn't try to manipulate us. He was saying, You guys do what you want, I'll do what I want. The problem was, Josh and I didn't want to be left out more than we didn't want to, maybe take too much. We talked it over and decided all of us ought to be in the same boat, floating merrily along on the Niagara River."

When her head turned, he added, "If you get my drift." She groaned faux disapproval.

"I should add that it was an incredibly beautiful day. It was the first warm day of spring for us. It was sunny and the sky was Nixonian—perfectly clear. The babes were wearing tight shorts and halter tops. We were up for a Really Big Trip. But we hadn't really thought it through, our choice of venue.

"If Chicago is the Second City, then Louisville is about twenty-second, or -third. Right behind Cleveland. The area around Churchill Downs is an old-fashioned ghetto. The houses are these little wooden boxes, real rural-South type. About like Evanston's ghetto, actually... Well, so, that's our first unpleasant surprise, that we have to go through this slum to get to the Downs. It was a real downer... Okay, okay, that's the last one, I promise. Anyway, we had to stroll through the squalor on the way to help celebrate the dark side of capitalism, which is what I was always taught recreational gambling represents. In short, it was a bummer but we just went with the flow of other small groups of White people. And we started to come up really fast. The sun felt—just incredible, kind of massaging the rushes, right? And we overhear someone say it's going to get up to eighty fuckin' degrees, man. We know it ain't funny, but we laugh. Holy shit, we shoulda brought some Coppertone, man—and gangster shades.

"By the time we got to the racetrack we were feelin' superfine, thinking, Hey, this is gonna be all right. It sure was smart of us to get here early. And then we find out they're not letting people into the infield yet. There's this huge crowd patiently standing body to body waiting to be let in. It takes us a while to sort out what people are telling us and discuss whether to let ourselves get buried in the crowd or hang back on the edge, or maybe even go somewhere else to peak out, a park or—a *regular* zoo, with cages for all the weird animals.

"We didn't see any other long-haired freaks and it was beginning to bother us. We didn't expect to feel so out there, you know, because of our looks. Most of the people in the crowd were college kids, so we weren't getting any mean vibes or anything, but—it was the usual paranoia of being stoned and having to socialize with straights. All these rowdy fratboys and jocks were going to be getting obnoxiously drunk all around us while we're peaking out on a double hit of mesc. I realized it was too late to back out at that point, because we're not near the edge of the crowd anymore, we are 'in the midst of'—as my favorite author would say.

"I was in front of the other guys for some reason, and I just sort of faded out, keeping my attention on the peculiar beings in front of me. Two guy-girl couples. Kind of odd looking, to me: a little nerdy, wearing neat casual clothes, like they were going to a church picnic. Childlike anticipation in the girls' faces.

"I was really coming up fast and trying to ignore it, and, you know how it is, you begin to feel like you're seeing right into other people's eyes. Reading their innermost essential identity right there in plain sight, on their faces and in their eyes. They side-eye you like: It's their little secret, what are *you* lookin' at?

"I was just—. I wasn't looking down on them, really... Okay, I was, but I was actually grooving on them too. You know, I was just letting them be whatever they were. No judgment. Just the facts, ma'am. I felt totally objective, like I was just a movie camera with a microphone, doing an Andy Warhol documentary. *Sexual Banter Among Young Straight Couples on a Double Date to the Kentucky Derby.*

"It was fascinating, believe me. They were entertaining each other with idiotic groaners everyone learns in junior high. And so there I am with my arms crossed, standing behind them, just another hairy face in the crowd, your basic spaced-out hippie trying to look totally inoffensive. They probably thought I was enjoying their repartee, behind my Mona Lisa smile. *Au contraire,* I was concentrating on not thinking about how languid and swoony I was beginning to feel, and how hot and closed in and panicky, et cetera. Did I mention the sun was blazing down on us and we were hundreds of young bodies mashed together with hardly anyone wearing a hat?

"Very gradually I become aware that someone is nudging my shoulder. I turn, my face floating around in slow motion, and there's Kevin's balloony face pressed right up close, kind of distorted, as though I'm looking through a wide-angle lens. He's saying something real casual-like. It takes me a while. I open my mouth, sounds come out, and apparently Kevin gets the message. I don't understand what the fuck he's saying.

"I get it the second time through, while he's working on the third time, and the news is: Hank is not feeling so good and they want to know how I'm feeling. I felt a lot better before he asked. Suddenly I'm not so sure. We look at Hank and right that instant he crumples to his knees and keels over. Just crumples and falls onto his back.

"Kevin gets to him and bends over him. I'm right behind, ordering people to stand back: *Give him air, give him air!* TV reflex, I guess. My first close-up of Hank's face is gruesome. He looks gone, and I mean permanently, not just conked out. Some idiot in the crowd—saved his life for all I know—bends over and tips a can of Coke to his mouth. It doesn't seem to be going in, it's just running back out, the side of his mouth, but then suddenly he's throwing up—while he's still uncon-scious! Vomit comes spurting out. And when it stops, he looks paler—more dead than before.

"I began to think super clearly at this point. I realized we couldn't handle it. I moved away, looking around for profes-sional emergency-handling people, and I spotted one—a state

cop leaning against his car, at the edge of the crowd. He seemed
to be looking right at me, but he was wearing those mirror
sunglasses. I yelled something and waved frantically. He just
casually looked away from me. I decided to go over to him. I
saw it all in the clichéd flash—the Big Trouble we were in, having to confess to the use of illegal agony-and-ecstasy-inducing
substances. But I couldn't see any other choice. I decided to
tell Kevin that I'd get the cop to call an ambulance. I'd do the
martyr bit. He and Josh should just get sober and bail me out.
Josh wasn't around, but I hadn't realized that yet. I had the
whole drama sketched out in no time, but when I go back to
tell Kevin my plan I find Hank doing a Lazarus trip. Thank
you, Jesus. Kevin's helping him sit up.

"We got him to his feet and out to the edge of the crowd,
where people were milling around in some shade by a wall. We
sat him down. He looked really bad but he's saying, I'm all
right, I'm all right. And I'm convinced when he takes out his
Marlboros and lights one up.

"But then the question is: Where the hell is Josh? I ask Kevin
and he says Josh freaked, went running off right after Hank
passed out. I can't believe how unconcerned Kevin looks while
he's telling me this. He's got that serene-beam up as high as it'll
go and he can't quit smiling.

"Well. Kevin doesn't want to go looking for Josh because
he's afraid he'll get lost. I see his point but I think I can handle
it. I can't imagine *not* going to look for Josh. Kevin says Josh
went running off down the street beside the racetrack. I tell
them to stay put. Hank says, Don't worry about that.

"I was getting these constant just incredible rushes. It was heavy but it didn't feel like too much anymore, and I was sure it was mescaline because it was a body trip. I headed off past the crowd, which was starting to move because they'd finally opened the entrance to the infield.

"It was crazy but I felt sure that I could find Josh. Even though I couldn't focus on anything for more than a split second. You know—the old stroboscopic vision. I was on autopilot. I felt like I was thinking so logically and fast that if I'd tried to think what I was thinking I'd have been ga-ga.

"I can't get over it. I've tried to rationalize my decision to head into that Black neighborhood, away from the race track, and away from the direction the car was in, and I just can't put together an explanation that makes sense. I really seemed to be literally following my nose. Or my eyes, rather. I just scanned all around and my eyes kept pulling me down that street.

"I had enough sense to realize I better not get lost. I was getting pretty worried by about the second or third block, but when I tried to think about turning back I couldn't muster the will to turn around. I had to keep going. This weird confidence was leading me. And then at a corner this old Black dude standing on the sidewalk turns around, wobbling some, and looks at me with these bulging bloodshot eyes. Then he looks into the bar on the corner and back at me. I feel like he's telling me something. And when I get right up to him he tilts his head toward the door.

"I understood. I turned into the bar. The door was open, it was come as you are, and there I was—in da wrong place, brutha, lemme tell ya. The lighting is dim and the place feels ugly and the dudes at the bar turn their bored but suspicious eyes on me and just keep 'em there.

"Now, I don't know whether at this point I got another nod from somebody or what—telepathy maybe. But I just look back at them, my eyes saying, Peace and justice, bruthas, I'm just stoned and lost. And I look around. And my eyes go straight to this door in a corner, and the thought hits me that that's the bathroom. And I just know: It's not astounding, it's just there, a matter-of-fact, my subconscious casually saying, Yep, he's gotta be in there.

"And of course he was. As I went through the bathroom door, Josh jumped back. He was just then coming out. It was a Cheech and Chong moment: Whoa. Far-fucking out, man. We babbled in circles for a while, ascertaining that it was freaky as hell that I had found him, and then I told him that Hank was okay and asked him why he ran off. He says when he saw Hank collapse, he just lost it. He had to get away from the crowd, and when he did he began to think that he was headed for the same fate as Hank, because he was beginning to feel very ill. He decided he'd better throw up, to get what might be the last fatal little bit of strychnine or whatever out of his stomach. Does he bend over right there and vomit in the gutter like any drunk in the neighborhood would? No, of course not. He goes looking for a bathroom. He's a nice Jewish kid, his mother taught him not to go barfing, much less dying, right out in public. And that's how he ended up in the bar. Guess who he asked where the nearest bathroom was?

"He said he tried sticking his finger down his throat but he only gagged. Nothing even tried to come up. Gradually, he realized, Hey, I don't feel sick. In fact, I feel like Tony the Tiger. This stuff is grea-a-t.

"I agreed, and we decided we'd better get back to Hank and Kevin before those doofs wandered off. Time for intermission. I need another smoke."

He pulled his head back from his cupped hands, puffing on the cigarette; he took it from his lips and clenched his body to stop shivering. Tamara was hugging herself tight. He laughed. "It's fuckin' cold out here."

Her head urgently bobbed. "I know. Ya so smat why duncha wear a coat when it's cold out, hheh?"

His smile felt forced; her Jewish mommy mimicry was so good it repulsed him a little. He smoked and looked at the dark water, then gazed a moment at the stars. He was hyper-conscious of her silence and again mindful of being right back where he'd been when they first started getting it on: enjoying a cerebrally sexy feeling he'd only experienced once before, with a girlfriend the summer after high school, before she went off to a small women's college somewhere in the South.

Detecting movement, he looked at Tamara. She'd craned her head way back. He lifted a cursory glance. The moon, half-full, was nearly straight overhead. "Come on," he said, grinding out the butt, which, because he was a militant anti-litterbug, he dropped into his shirt pocket. "Let's get going."

"Where?"

He stood up. "Your room, I guess. I could use a cup of that god-awful tea. As long as it's hot."

She awkwardly unfolded herself. He leaned forward, reaching. She grabbed his hand with unexpected alacrity and he braced not a moment too soon.

He put his arms over her shoulders as they walked under the university's observatory, which looked like a looming white metal spacecraft; she unfolded her arm and slid it around his waist. They sauntered down the trail toward the construction mess, rather than get sand in their shoes again crossing the beach. Cal talked shivery fast.

"We decided trying to ride out the trip in the infield would be insane. It was too fuckin' hot. There were too many people, too many of them jocks getting drunk. So we decided to get back to the car and drive to a park or something. Kevin said he could handle the driving.

"We have to go through the slum again, of course, so we are truckin' along pretty good when Hank says he's gotta sit down, he feels weak. Oh, shit. We stop. Look around. Hank says, I gotta get in the shade or I'm gonna pass out again.

"So we look around and shrug about it some and then Hank just goes over to the nearest shack and sits right down on the little concrete stoop in front of the screen door. Talk about weird moments. I guess nobody was home, or if they were they just watched from inside. We tried to make sure by our demeanor, of course, that the shy peekers and frowning gawkers in nearby yards understood that we knew we were intruding and we would move on just as soon as our friend felt better.

"Hank recovered before anyone said anything to us, and we followed Kevin back to the main sidewalk. He said he knew the way back to the car. The three of us had no clue. We were too out of it. We were happy to place our faith in Kevin's confidence. And anyway we felt better just being on the move. After our rest stop, though, it feels like it's taking too long and we start wondering aloud if Kevin is getting us into another adventure here. He just keeps giving us that big goofy smile and says we're going the right way. So we keep on keepin' on and sure enough we come around a corner, finally, and see the busy four-laner and where the car's parked on a big grassy area between the residential street and main road.

"*Whoosh.* What a relief. Not lost anymore. But when we get back to the car, we realize we are completely boxed in. There is no room to move the car anywhere, not until a bunch of other cars get moved. I guess that's when I found out about there being other races before the one called the Kentucky Derby. It wasn't even noon yet and Kevin said the Derby wouldn't be till three or four o'clock."

He turned to get a better look at Tamara's expression. She looked appreciatively incredulous, her smile wincing to a grin.

"Didn't faze Kevin a bit, of course, having to stay put, right there, tripping his brains out. At least it was a shady spot and there was grass to sit on. Hank and Josh quickly accepted the situation. I looked around hoping to think of some alternative. Three or four hours? Wouldn't it be better to keep moving? Find an actual park maybe? Kevin gets out a portable radio from the trunk and a pack of cards. In no time at all he's got

Hank and Josh sitting on the grass between the cars. He sits down and tunes the radio to a rock station. He starts shuffling the cards. Looks up at me, kind of sputters a laugh. You going to play or not?

"I agreed, reluctantly. But as I started to look at the hand Kevin dealt me, I was ready to puke. I mean—after what's just happened, Hank passing out and Josh running off thinking he's about to die. Thinking Hank was already dead. And it happened because we got greedy—for a higher high, an all-time record of revelry and weirdness.

"I just couldn't hack it. I was getting pissed off. It's like everything Kevin and I have been—, have clashed over, and that Josh and I have been arguing about, was all right there, in what had happened to us and how we were not dealing with it—by dealing cards instead, and denying that we'd just had a an experience that maybe we should talk about.

"So I started making my usual snide remarks about the mindlessness of playing cards. Then I quoted Timothy Leary: Show me a tab of acid and I'll show you a religious experience. Kevin says, What's that supposed to mean? With his voice jumping an octave and his goofy-giggly put-down laugh. Kevin's dealing me in for a game of *Hearts,* by the way. Their favorite card game when they're high.

"Hank was being neutral, as usual, looking amused. Josh was looking at me though like he really didn't get what's going on between me and Kevin. He's looking scared, but curious, too, like an earnest little kid. He wanted me to repeat the quote, asks, Timothy Leary said that? Kevin gets mad, says, I'm not listening to any religious discussions. He throws down his cards. I look at Josh and he says, Let's just play cards for now and talk about it later. I look at Hank and he surprises me. He says he thinks we oughta talk about it—but only if Josh wants to. So Kevin chortles and picks up his hand and sorts the cards, figuring that settles that.

"At that point, I reminded Josh about the first time he and Kevin and Injun Joe dropped acid. I came back to the dorm and found them sitting in Josh and Dan's room, talking about their incredible discovery. Wow. Paradise Now and it was right here all along. And trying to figure out what it meant, why so few people know about it, why the human race remains so fucked up when we've got heaven on earth, in our bodies, in our minds, if we really want it. If we can learn how to live with it."

Tamara's shoulder pushed into his ribs and he looked where he was going, veered onto another sidewalk crossing a park-like space between dormitories.

"I wasn't saying anything new. We'd had this discussion before. In fact, it had become a fucking *leitmotiv.* I said, Fine, Kevin can go through life like Mr. Natural, and maybe you think you can, too, Josh, but what happened back there proves you don't really believe 'It don't mean shee-it'—or you wouldn't be feeling so guilty right now."

Cal extended his pause. They were approaching the dorm and other people were around. They uncoupled just before taking the first step of the concrete stairway. Inside the entrance, he had to sign a visitor's log, supervised by a pasty-faced middle-aged male security guard. Tamara's room was on the third floor. They climbed in silence, quickly, Tamara in the lead. She greeted several women descending the stairs, none of whom he knew.

She had a double to herself because her roommate had dropped out a few weeks into the winter quarter. She entered the room talking about how great it was not to have a room-mate. She hoped to luck out in the dorm lottery so she could get a single on north campus in the fall. She asked about his housing plans. He said he was going to wait till after the lottery to decide. He thought he might go for a single, too, if he got the chance to choose. He and the guys had talked about possibly renting an apartment. She was setting up a percolator to boil water.

"Need more water," she said, turning around and holding up a plastic pitcher. "I'd invite you along but…"

He shrugged. "I know—might frighten a prude brushing her teeth."

"In curlers and nightie. Be right back."

She left the door ajar. He bounced from the edge of the bare mattress strewn with books, notebooks, clothes. He recalled the last time he was in this room—the night they'd discussed his Calvinist upbringing and the hang-ups it had left him with. He'd put her to sleep with a rambling monologue in support of his claim that his inhibitions were fundamentally ethical in nature, not sexual.

He walked over to the large built-in desk, identical to the one in his room in the adjacent dorm. One night he and the guys, sitting around stoned, had decided the desk was a plot by some sadistic interior designer. Originally, their dorm, like this one, had been built to house only men. The wall-to-wall desk in each room was shaped exactly like a pair of bikini bottoms: The waistband met the sill of the room's triptych of windows; the concave curves on each side of the crotch was where you sat to read or write or type, or just talk. He tried to remember who'd announced the resemblance. Josh, he thought. Yes. He'd enlightened them about the opposite of phallic symbols: yonic symbols.

It embarrassed him to think how convenient this would appear to the guys. He'd told them he wasn't interested in getting more deeply involved with Tamara. His debilitating case of moral qualms had surfaced unexpectedly after a peculiar month-long courtship, during which they had upset the delicate equilibrium of their distinctly incompatible coteries by establishing themselves as a couple.

He was heartened by how securely content she seemed now. It was her show of romantic vulnerability that had given him cold feet. He'd begun to notice a chronic wincing quiverness in her smile, and how often it accompanied defensive uncertainty in her eyes. He'd felt that she was asking him to be in love, too. And he couldn't pretend.

A poignant wrenching sensation in his gut erased the reverie, and then the apprehension of Tamara's presence slammed a door in his mind an instant before he heard the door behind him shutting.

Designed to maximize the illusion of privacy for two students working within a few feet of each other, the desk was also uniquely suited for intimate conversation. When they looked straight ahead, obliquely toward the windows, each was in the other's peripheral vision. And the window's night-backed mirror allowed a nearly straight-on look at the other's face without risking eye contact.

"You'd compared Kevin to Mr. Natural," she said.

"Oh, right. Kevin considers Mr. Natural a role model, you realize. What he doesn't like, he says, is that I think I'm superior to other people because I insist that some sincerely held convictions about the meaning or absurdity of life are better than others. And he's right, I guess. I am a snob about some things. I prefer Camus to Mr. Natural.

"Kevin hates to talk about the heavy stuff. Period. Mainly because he's not verbal. He's supremely confident but very shy. He flusters easily and the slightest emotional friction rubs him the wrong way. So to speak."

"That was awful," she said.

He slurped at the chamomile tea. "You're right. So is this. You got an ashtray?"

She got up; he took out his cigarettes.

"Sorry, the best I can do," she said, sliding a plastic saucer from the cafeteria onto the desk.

"Anyway, so of course Kevin didn't want to talk about what happened. But it was obvious to Hank and me that Josh needed to talk about it. Whether he needed to talk about it right then, with me, is another question.

"So it's up to Josh and since Hank says he thinks we ought to talk about it, Josh changes his mind, says he wants to talk about it, too. He tries to get Kevin to go along but Kevin picks up the cards and says he can't take it, he's gotta split.

"I don't think he was actually all that upset. It was more like, Okay, fine. You guys do your trip. I'll do mine. I'm going to find a place to buy some beer."

"We're fine with that idea. We'd love to have some beer. Doesn't even have to be cold. It's obvious Kevin's not as spaced out as we are. So we wish him luck. And there we are, the three of us, sitting on the grass in the little bit of shade between the cars, with several hours to kill before they run the fuckin' Derby. Josh and Hank are waiting for me to start this heavy rap I'd insisted on. And all of a sudden I'm not sure it's such a great idea, when I see how vulnerable Josh is. Those big spooky eyes of his really looked scared.

"He says, So—what is it we're talking about? And I get a feeling he's faking it. But he sure looks genuinely out of it. I repeat the Leary quote. Show me a tab of acid and I'll show you a religious experience.

"We're talking about tripping being a religious experience, how it's not like that for us anymore. Religious experience? It's just a crazy mixed-up hilarious adventure. As long as you don't take more than you can handle. As long as you don't try to think about the heavy stuff it's showing you.

"I wanted to get Josh to understand—or just admit—why he panicked and ran off. It was a perfectly normal reaction, so the question was: Why did he feel so guilty about it? I just confronted him with what was in his eyes. I asked one simple question after another. I got him to see that if he hadn't cared about Hank, he wouldn't feel guilty; that, in fact, he loves Hank and he felt guilty because at the moment of crisis he left Hank to die, for all he knew, because he was more concerned about himself.

"I stressed that that's the normal human reaction to an experience like that. When Hank passed out, Kevin and I were worried about ourselves, too, but we didn't feel sick, so we didn't panic. We did things by instinct that Josh would have done, too, if his fear of death hadn't overruled his concern for Hank."

Cal paused to finish up his cigarette, warding off interruption with his eyes. He had been looking at her hands mostly. Her fingers were so long, so graceful and elegant. Even casually curled around a cheap coffee mug, they seemed expressive of the intellectually aristocratic air that had first attracted him to her.

"I don't know what all I said, really, how I connected everything up. I was trying to get Josh to see that maybe J.C. was not so off-the-wall when he put a radical emphasis on the commandment in the Torah to love your neighbor as you do yourself. My point was that Josh's guilt about running off proved that he wished he'd put concern for Hank above concern for himself. I.e., he ought to quit ridiculing me for thinking that the Christian ideal deserves some respect, because he was showing by his reaction that he actually does respect it, whatever he says. He just doesn't want to admit it, because then he'd have to judge himself in light of it.

"One time I quoted W.H. Auden to Josh: We must love one another or die. And Josh said, We'd rather die. So I reminded him of that. I said, You don't include yourself in that *we,* so why pretend that you do? Why not admit that you want to do something with your life to make the world a better place, just like I do? You keep saying that death makes life meaningless, ultimately, from a cosmic perspective. But that's a cop out. It's because we are all going to die, alone and not knowing what if anything comes next, that we worry about not wasting our lives.

"I was saying, Look, I agree with you. We have to base our lives only on what we can really know, not on wishful thinking. So, unless we die and come back, we have to assume that death is it: The End. We have to assume that our consciousness comes from our brains and our bodies, and that when the last brain wave flattens out, the shore is oblivion. No more us. Except, as Josh always says, in the memories of the people who loved us. That's extremely important to him. His family's very close. His parents are wonderful—really warm and open. His dad is devout, Reformed, goes to synagogue early every morning. Josh kids him about it, says his dad just laughs, admits that it's irrational but says it keeps him from going crazy.

"Josh really got into Nietzsche last quarter, Intro. to Philosophy. God, did he get obnoxious. Started suggesting that he was a prototypical *Übermensch* and I was one of the willfully blind, like his dad but not as honest, because I don't admit that I believe what I do because I have to, because I was brainwashed with the whole Jesus schtick as a kid and I'd freak out if I faced up to what the *Übermensch* sees staring supermanfully into the Void: that all of our meanings are stuff we make up as we go along. There is no Truth with a capital T, no God with a capital G. Therefore, there is no essential meaning to life and no ethical imperative dictating how a person should live, if he lives up to what his conscience, based on reason, tells him. The universe is a bizarre accident indifferent to our existence. And we, as a species, are beyond redemption—incorrigibly selfish, greedy, and delusional, we'll destroy the earth in the near future anyway, so what's to worry?

"Josh's favorite hero is Meursault, in *The Stranger*. Only he can't bear to sound intellectual so he calls him *More-salt*. By that great Jewish-American writer Al Kammus.

"Well, he was not feeling so smug about his nihilistic credentials, after two hits of some very strong mescaline. His scared little boy was right there, staring at me.

"Josh is—just incredibly sensitive and empathetic. And so he's had to build up this habitually cynical attitude, for protection. And now his usual defense mechanisms were out of commission. It was right there in his eyes—the knowledge that the God of the Jews said is not far from us, because it's written on our hearts. All I was doing was describing it and showing Josh what it meant: that the fact we all live in fear of, that we're going to die, ought to make us want to live every day feeling as close as possible to the way we did the first time we tripped—marveling at everything in sight, seeing how beautiful everything is, even when it's ugly, really appreciating the miracle of being alive. And wanting to share the trip with others. Because what good is being so alive and aware if you're all alone? Hell, even in heaven.

"I said, Remember the first time you tripped, okay? Now imagine the loneliness of God after he made everything and saw how great it was. And looked around. Tripping his brains out. Fuck. No one to show it to.

"Josh and Hank both were getting into it. We talked about how you can't actually be tripping every day, obviously, so it comes down to staying aware as much as you can, and just trying to fully appreciate things, and people. I don't know, I must've been scanning around about this time and I spotted this kid sitting in a chair on a porch across the busy four-lane road. He looked pathetic. Chubby White kid, sitting on the porch on a gorgeous day, the first real fine day of spring, probably, and all he can think of to do is sit there on his fuckin' porch watching the traffic.

"And then I think—it made me laugh—he could be a goddamn thirteen-year-old perfect master for all I know. And Josh says, What's so funny? So I point out the kid and I paraphrase the verses in Luke where the pious lawyer, trying to get J.C. to limit all this brotherly love he's preaching, to loving the brothers, the kindred, your fellow Jews, but not Romans and

Samaritans and so forth—the lawyer says, Well, okay, we gotta love our neighbor. Who's that? And then you get the parable of the Good Samaritan.

"I always assume too much about what people know about the Bible. Josh said he didn't know the parable of the Good Samaritan, and Hank seemed fuzzy on it, so I had to tell it. And it hits me as I'm telling it that it's pointing a finger at Josh. But he and Hank are listening like little kids, Hank maybe a few years older than Josh, and when I finish, Josh is staring at the dorky fat kid across the road and I see it in his eyes that he's really feeling—*holy*, I guess, is the only word. And he says, I want to go over and talk to him.

"Hank and I look at each other and explain that it's maybe not such a great idea, because of the traffic. And Josh goes, Does he know we love him? And I say, No. How could he? And he says, Well, shouldn't we go over and tell him, then? And I say, You go over and tell him you love him, he'll probably run in and call the cops.

"I said, Look, it's not important whether he knows or whether he wants to love us in return, whether he can. What's important is that we can love him, so we should, but it doesn't mean we're personally responsible for his life. It just means we're ready to be kind, to care, and to do what we can for him if we see that he needs our help.

"Well, we talk about it some more and conclude that if everybody tried for that ideal the world might begin to seem like heaven on earth, compared to the way it is now. So we're grooving on agreement about why we should try for that attitude, without making a big deal about it, you know. We really feel like we've worked something out and we're really feeling together because of it, and right then, of course, is when Kevin comes back.

"Lo and behold, a couple of hours have passed. And he's brought back two cold six packs of Falls City, the local beer. He tells us about getting picked up by a van full of freaks with very short hair—soldiers from Fort Knox. They had some amazingly strong grass straight from Vietnam. It is a really far-out story and he's in a great mood.

"Well, Kevin has noted our good mood, too, and he starts acting curious about what happened, you know, because we're kind of embarrassed about it. He asks if we discovered the secret meaning of life while he was gone. And I say, Well, yeah, we did, but if we tell you, it won't be a secret anymore, will it?

"He laughed and seemed willing to let it go at that. He gets out the cards again, with a look on his face like, Okay, now that we're back to normal here... But then Josh starts telling Kevin what we talked about and how he's decided that I'm right. We ought to really get into loving one another and other people.

"Now, I got uptight about the way Josh was talking, by the desperately sincere way he was coming on, and the really intense energy in his eyes. Kevin thought he was making fun of me, of course, but Hank and I could see that Josh was not joking. And when Josh realized that Kevin didn't think he was serious, he says, really, really grim: Kevin, I love you, man.

"Well, that turns Kevin's face a nice rosy red. And Josh turns to Hank and says he loves him, and he's sorry he ran off instead of trying to help when he passed out. And then he turns to me and says, after a big swallow, that he loves me. Well, I tell him I love him, too.

"It was really a weird scene at this point. It was like he was making it a challenge. He says, But do you love Kevin? And I say, Yeah, he's my brother whether he likes it or not, and Hank is, too. And Josh says I ought to tell them that I love them. So I do. And Hank tells us that he loves us, and Josh looks at Kevin, and goes, Do you love us?

"Kevin freaked. He turns even more red and starts sputtering, says he should have stayed with the GIs in the van because he knew I'd be on a religious trip. He says saying we love each other is stupid because it doesn't change the fact that we still love ourselves more than anyone else and we're always going to put ourselves first, no matter what we say.

"Well. Josh tried to argue with him but I came in kind of on Kevin's side. I was really embarrassed because I agreed with Kevin to a certain extent. I've said almost the same thing to them before, when I talked about why I don't consider myself a Christian. To me, a Christian, as Jesus himself defined following him, practicing what he preached, is someone who lives by the ethics of the Sermon on the Mount, which is just—impossible. Jesus didn't even do it. He didn't turn the other cheek when he threw the moneychangers from the temple.

"It's so crazy. I'm referring to a text, a mythical hero. The only historical Jesus as far as I'm concerned is a figment of words. Meaning, of course, he's subject to individual interpretation.

"Okay, so... The Jesus of the Gospels... What he means to most people is brotherly love, right? Loving others as you love your own self—and right there's the catch. You are a self yourself. And you have to be able to love yourself before you can love others. But what if you don't really love yourself? What if you can't, because of what happened to you as a child, or maybe because you're genuinely just not a good person? And narcissists love themselves plenty but aren't capable of really loving others.

"What gripes me about most born-again Christians is that—. I know them. I grew up with them. I was one of them. And I know that for most of them Christ is like a mirror. Their conception of Christ's love for them, their belief in that, makes them able to love themselves—superficially, without ever *knowing* themselves, at least not as others know them."

He stopped, decidedly. He had gotten lost in conundrums irrelevant to his need to tell her this story. He took a sip of the unpalatable tea, lukewarm now. He sat up straight and pulled his cigarettes from his shirt pocket, glancing at her by way of the window as he lit up. She raised and quickly lowered her eyes. He sucked in another dose of toxic smoke and sighed it out while staring gratefully at the cigarette. He lifted his eyes over to her. She was studying her bulbous-bottomed coffee mug, a rainbow of warm tones—brown, green, orange. She looked confused and wary; and a little intimidated.

"So," she said, "why was Josh acting, tonight, like he thought you were"—her suddenly very poignantly parted lips drew back into that pathetic wincing grin—"a terrible hypocrite?"

He took another drag, and a long moment later, after exhaling, gave her a hapless look. "Not I, but Christ in me."

Her vulnerable grin flashed again, her eyes showing bafflement and dismay. She shook her head, frowning helplessly.

"What I did was totally self-serving," he said. "When we got back to the car and Kevin got all set to play a nice friendly mind-numbing game of *Hearts,* I saw a chance to slip Josh the queen in the mind game we've been playing since we first got to know each other.

"When I saw that 'evangelistic opportunity'—okay? What did I see? I saw that Josh felt horrible about running off. I saw guilt and fear and how blasted away his ego was. He couldn't defend himself. And what the fuck did I do? I attacked his whole way of staying intact. I very kindly showed him the split between what he claims to believe and what he feels, which dictates what he would desperately like to believe—but can't, because he's got too much aptitude for critical thinking and not enough for the kind of sincere but mindless faith he admires in his dad.

"Basically, I was showing him that he's a hypocrite, too, so he ought to stop calling me one, which is what he was doing all the time before, saying in effect: You don't really believe that Jesus shit so don't go wiping it off on us."

She was grimly embarrassed; he was hotly ashamed. At last, he felt that they had gotten somewhere.

"For months," he said, "I've been turning the other cheek, sometimes without even allowing myself the satisfaction of letting Josh know when I've been slapped. When Kevin got out that deck of cards, I saw my chance to even the score. But I didn't let myself see that that was what I was going to do. Oh, no. I convinced myself what I was doing was for Josh's own good.

"He figured it out when he woke up this morning. He's going to be obsessed, for a while, with getting back at me, reminding me, like he did tonight, that there has only been one real honest-to-God Christian so far, and he died on a cross about two thousand years ago. Thus spake Zarathustra. Josh likes to add, Dunt vorry. Iff da fule kumes bach, ve haf vays of making him shut up.

"I don't do the goofy Nazi accent nearly as well. Out of touch with my German heritage."

He sensed an air of equanimity settling over her countenance. He smoked. She dandled the mug in her beautiful delicate hands.

"Was this"—she jerked her face at him—"a rehearsal?"

"Not exactly, no.

"Aren't you going to talk to him, tell him what you've told me?"

"Why? He doesn't want to hear my confession. He knows I know what I did, and that I'm sorry. He knows I know that he knows that I couldn't have kept myself from doing what I did, at the time, any more than he could have stopped himself from running off when Hank passed out."

"But," she insisted, "don't you think it would help to heal your friendship...if you at least go to him and apologize?"

He felt as though he were telling her with his look that she would know now what she was getting into; that whatever happened from here on—she'd been warned. He exhaled a final drag toward the window, catching a glimpse of himself and sardonically accepting one of Josh's more inspired put-downs: "Surfer Jesus."

"I assume," he said, tamping out the cigarette, "that when Josh can handle the further humiliation of having to forgive me, he'll let me know."

CHAPTER FIVE

Diversities of Gifts

SLOUCHED IN THE PINTO'S passenger seat, Cal lifted his eyes from a page of mimeographed typescript. Through a fairly clean arced swath of the slush-glazed windshield, he peered at the sunny blue sky above a plain of shimmering cars. Out the side window he saw a flotilla of puffy cumuli scudding in from the northwest. Beyond the chain-link fence of the parking lot, brown grass tufts sparkled amid melting snow.

He moved his lower back off the armrest and stretched his left leg between the gear shift and the edge of the driver's seat. Easing back against the door, he lowered his eyes to the page. He read quickly to the bottom and flipped it over, pausing to see how much of the stapled sheaf remained. The driver's door opened.

"What a bee-U-tiful day," Josh crowed. He whipped off his parka and tossed it into the back seat. Cal extricated his leg and sat up. Josh climbed in behind the wheel, pulled the door shut, and eagerly rolled down the window.

Cal aped a grumpy expression. Josh teasingly grinned. "Don't tell me you didn't get much sleep last night either?"

"It's not nice to gloat."

"What's ya reading?"

"T(i)lfabra propaganda."

Josh stuck his elbow out the window and took a fat joint from his shirt pocket. "I really think, for a religious group, they need a better acronym." Holding up the joint, he raised his eyebrows, mouth poised between an O and a smile.

"No, thanks. I'm high on life today."

"Yeah, okay. Who needs it on a day like this." Josh dropped the joint into his pocket and straightened himself behind the wheel. "Vamanoose," he said, aping wary expectation as he glanced.

"*Ándele*," Cal said glumly and returned to his reading.

A few minutes after Josh had settled into moderate midday traffic westbound on the Eisenhower, he glanced repeatedly over. Cal ignored him the first few times, then relaxed and left off reading.

"So how's your little sister?"

"She's in love."

Josh tsk-tsked, shaking his head.

"Better be careful," Cal said. "You're showing signs of infection yourself."

"I'm only infatuated so far."

"Who's the lucky woman?"

Josh blushed. "Oh..." He shrugged.

"Good grief. Do I know her?"

"No, and I want to keep it that way for as long as possible."

"Why?"

"I have my reasons."

"The territorial imperative, huh?"

Josh bounced his eyebrows. Cal recalled that a woman he'd never seen lived in the apartment downstairs, an elementary school teacher.

"So," Josh said. "The only relevant question is: Is the guy Rachel's in love with in love with her?"

"Seems to be."

"Is he an okay guy?"

"Yeah, for an intelligent religious fanatic, he's okay. They'll make a good missionary team."

"Well, then—? What's to worry?"

"Do I look worried?"

"You definitely have the look you always get when you become obsessed with some totally irresolvable and useless question, and want me to be concerned about it, too."

Feeling a spiteful tickle, Cal asked: "What do you know about the Holy Spirit?"

"Don't you mean, Holy Spart?" Josh replied. "As in, That little shortstop sho' has spart, don't he Pee Wee?"

"Would you mind being serious for minute?"

"As a matter of fact, I would."

"Do you remember in *Marjoe*," Cal went on, "whether it looked like they were completely out of it when they were speaking in tongues?"

Josh seemed to think about it. Then he rattled off random syllables that sounded like a tobacco auctioneer's rapid-fire chant, ending with "...Sold, American!"

Cal grinned, blushing, and shook his head; he slapped Josh's shoulder with the loosely rolled sheaf of paper and tossed it into the back seat. He crossed his arms and put on an expression of incisively thoughtful frustration.

"You never heard of T(i)LFABRA before, right?"

"I would have remembered that acronym."

"I never heard of them either. But they've been around since the late forties, and now they're in every state and over a dozen countries, quietly spreading their heretical version of Christ inanity, which they claim is what the New Testament actually teaches."

"Good for them," Josh said.

"Jesus is not God the Son, he's the Son of God; the Holy Spirit is just another name for God or it's the bit of Himself that God gives to believers in Christ, i.e., holy spirit—small *h*, small *s*—that gives them the ability to manifest all nine operations of the Holy Spirit, if they just believe hard enough that they can."

"They can do all nine operations of the holy spart?"

"So they claim," Cal said. "You don't even know what they are."

"Sure I do: pitcher, catcher, first base, second base, shortstop..."

"Oh, Jesus."

"He didn't make the team," Josh said. "Had something wrong with his hands. Couldn't catch worth beans."

"I don't believe you said that."

Josh made an uh-oh look.

"Just for that," Cal said, "I'm going to explain to you how the Trinity got misinterpreted into the Bible."

"Okay, I deserve it. But wait." Josh pulled out the joint and stuck it into his mouth. He pulled out the ashtray and jabbed the lighter knob, not quite getting his hand back in time to catch the joint as he started to say—retrieving it from between his thighs as he did say—"I'll make a deal with you." He held the joint out. "I'll pretend to listen if you split this with me."

"Nah. Really, I can't. I'm going to have a hard enough time coping with my mother. She was not pleased when I called to tell her Rachel wouldn't be coming home for Christmas. I expect they're going to think I betrayed their trust, when they hear what I have to say."

Josh dropped the joint into his shirt pocket. "Why doesn't Rachel want to go home for Christmas?"

"Why do you think? Her excuse is that T(i)LFABRA is giving a free feast for poor folks on the South Side tomorrow. But really, she's just not ready to debate the old man yet. She said she might be able to handle meeting with my mom in a month or so. They were really close, you know. Too close, in my opinion, for Rachel's good."

The cigarette lighter popped out; Josh touched it into place. "So Rachel is just as brainwashed as before, she's just changed her brand of soap."

"That's about how I feel about it."

"Is T(i)LFABRA into charity for charity's sake, or is this free feast they're giving mainly to get people to listen to their sermons?"

"I got the impression it's something new for them. I'm sure they will offer the hungry some spiritual grub to go with the turkey and dressing."

"Can they eat and speak in tongues at the same time?"

"Depends... Peanut butter, no."

Cal kept talking. Josh's eyes glazed over with inwardness. Cal was hardly aware of when he stopped talking and continued to himself in thought. He caught Josh presaging speech with an amused and embarrassed glance.

"Look in my coat pocket and you'll find what Santy Claus brought you."

Stretching back between the seats, Cal said, "Which reminds me: I've got a present for you at the house."

"Oh, goody. Something Mexican maybe?"

"Yeah. Getting worried, huh?"

He stuck his hand in one and then the other big pocket of Josh's parka and pulled out a small oblong block wrapped in shiny lime-green paper.

"Ah, you shouldn't have been so...Jewish."

"Good things come in small packages," Josh said. "It's real cute. I even bought one for myself."

Cal peeled the wrapping paper off and held up a miniature coffin of reddish brown wood. It took him a few seconds and two glances at Josh to recognize the thing as a hooded cigarette lighter. He opened it.

"Very good," Josh said. "Now look for the holy spart. Hint: It's the inside that counts."

Cal's first attempt to separate the metal lighter part from the wooden base left him looking doubtful.

"You gotta pull harder than that," Josh said.

"Hey, okay. Sure enough. Ah so, a portable stash."

There were two joints inside the hollowed-out base.

"Merry xmas," Josh said. "Now tell me what my present is. I hate surprises."

"No way. Don't worry, you're gonna love it... I've changed my mind. Let's smoke one of these."

Josh insisted they smoke his; he had most of a lid with him. While passing the joint, Josh filled Cal in on the big news—the Seymour Hersh exposé of the CIA's domestic spying division; the initial story had run Sunday on the front page of *The New York Times*. They talked about the startling revelations, none of which surprised them in the least. Josh turned on the radio and stopped the dial on an FM station playing The Band's version of "The Night They Drove Old Dixie Down."

"I think this is an album station," Josh said.

Cal didn't get the point of that remark until the opening chords of the next song. His grin went whoop-wide. The Band's "When You Awake" was a creedal hymn to them freshman year. They sang along now, making a joyful noise unto each other. At the end of the song, the nasally high hillbilly voice faded so abruptly that the last lines were inaudible. The Nattering Nabobs had listened to the lines over and over on one stoned occasion. Hank, the electrical engineering major, fiddled with the bass, treble, and volume controls until the Nabobs finally reached consensus on the faint final words.

Josh peered teasingly from the corner of his eye as he twanged, "And if I thought it would do any good, I'd stand on the rock where Moses stood." Singing along, Cal substituted *Nietzsche* for *Moses*. Josh made a wryly objecting grimace and then went wide-eyed and intoned "*DundunDUN*"—mimicking the bass guitar and drums opening the next song, "Cripple Creek."

They were counting themselves among the blessed by the time they pulled into the wide sloping driveway of the spacious split-level house owned by the Orthodox Presbyterian Church of Elmore. It sat alone with the church on a large corner lot adjacent to Elmore Estates. Josh had affected awe, as usual, at the sprawling sumptuousness of the lots and the hugeness of the houses. The Cook County suburb his family lived in was not less affluent, but it was at least fifteen minutes closer to the Loop than Elmore Estates. Although the houses, maybe, and the lots, definitely, were a little smaller there, they were also more expensive per square foot, Cal had pointed out—to no avail. Josh liked to pretend that he truly believed this WASP enclave was far and away the wealthier suburb.

After switching off the ignition, Josh pulled hard on the hand brake. "Oh, fuck. I mean, phooey. Fiddlesticks. By gosh and by gum. I just remembered your dad doesn't drink beer."

"How about a nice cold refreshing Tab?" Cal suggested.

"You think you could handle tripping with your mom?"

Cal felt a rush of silliness. "I can't believe it, man. I used to enjoy trying to imagine my parents on acid."

"And I bet you did, too," Josh said. "Maybe we should run to the 7-Eleven—or better yet, drive. And get a nice cold six-pack of Bud."

Cal looked helplessly befuddled. Josh said, "Hmmm... What a time to be shit-faced."

Before unlocking the front door, Cal rang the bell; he was expecting to find the chain lock in place. Despite her faith in the protection of Providence, his mother had become paranoid about robbers and rapists the past couple years.

"Whuddaya know," he said, when the door did not hit the chain as he opened it. He let Josh shut the door, bounded up the short flight of stairs to the living room, calling out: "Hey, Mom! We're here!"

He suspected the house was empty. Thinking of how cottony his mouth felt, he turned around—and almost ran into Josh, who looked instantly whoa-begone, stepping back.

"She's not here?"

"I guess not," Cal said. "All the better, for making ourselves at home." He untied his Mexican sweater.

But then his mother's voice—weak, confused—trembled from the hallway: "Cal? Is that you?" She sounded like she was really afraid it might not be.

"Yeah, Mom, it's just me. And Josh."

In another moment Sarah appeared at the top of the short stairway to the bedrooms, patting at the drab permanent which had been her hairstyle for at least twenty years. Her hair was still without a trace of gray, thanks to coloring that made it a slightly deeper shade of red than Rachel's. But her face shocked him. The resemblance to Rachel was beneath wrinkles and sagginess; she looked haggard about the eyes. Only a few years ago people liked to say that she and Rachel looked like sisters, and only a few years before that Cal could see it coming true—if Sarah remained the same petite, slim, girlish-looking woman she had been for as long as he could remember. She had never liked compliments on how young she looked though. Once Cal had heard her reply: "Well, they say it's how young you feel that counts. And ever since I started having children I have felt older than my years."

"Good afternoon, welcome home, Cal. Hello, Josh."

"Good afternoon, Mrs. Wideman. Sorry to disturb you."

"Yeah, sorry to wake you up, Mom."

"No need to apologize. I only meant to take a short nap. I guess I didn't hear the alarm go off."

She pulled her sweater closed and hugged herself as she came down the stairs. "What would you boys like for lunch? You look like you've put on weight, Cal."

"Do I? Maybe I have."

"I can hardly believe it," Sarah said, embarrassing him with an ingenuously surprised stare. She frowned grumpily and shook her head and turned away. "Your hair hasn't been that blond since you were a little boy," she said, walking toward the kitchen.

Cal looked embarrassedly at Josh; Josh looked dumbly back and did a big shrug. They followed her.

Scanning the top rack of the refrigerator, Cal came across a bottle of wine.

"Hey, how about some—" he began, his voice falling as he lifted the bottle, "André Cold Duck. Sparkling, supposedly, but it looks flat."

"It was just opened the night before last," Sarah said.

"Oh."

"It should still be drinkable."

"It'll do," Cal said, closing the fridge and setting the bottle on the counter. Sarah was slicing tomatoes at the counter beside the stove, her back to him. He felt, or imagined he did, that she tensed up.

"Mind if we finish it off?" he asked.

"Not at all, go right ahead."

He opened the cupboard in the corner, above her shoulder. She glanced up, suppressing annoyance.

"The wine glasses are in the buffet—where we've always kept them."

"No need. These are okay."

He grabbed two breakfast juice glasses. Josh was sitting at the dinette, looking like he'd rather be anywhere else. As he poured the wine, Cal felt an old shame, thinking how much he liked going home with Josh. The Levinsons genuinely enjoyed one another's company, and raillery was their family sport. Mrs. Levinson got teased about being a typical Jewish mother and went right on cheerfully being one.

Cal lifted his glass, filled three fingers high with the barely bubbly red wine.

"Salud," he said.

"Mazel tov," Josh rejoined.

Cal grimaced at the fruity taste and frizzy tingle on his tongue, surprised that it was more acidic than sweet. He pulled the chair out, and sat down across from Josh. He dismissed the urge to light up a cigarette. Josh seemed to read his mind. Sarah was sniffily sensitive to cigarettes, but if Josh were to ask her if she would mind if he smoked, she would say, "Why, of course not. Go right ahead."

"The Calvinist ideal of vino," Cal said, under his breath.

Josh stuck out his jaw and nodded and took another sip. "You'd prefer Manischewitz perhaps?"

Cal pretended to think about it; he shook his head.

"So quitcherbitchin."

Sarah asked Cal to get out plates, soup bowls, and silverware. He had to ask her to move so he could get the soup spoons from the drawer. His elbow nudged her upper arm; she flinched.

Following Cal into a room off the garage, Josh said, "Am I being oversensitive or was she surprised to learn that we Jews go Christmas shopping?"

Cal feebly chortled. "Can't say. She did look confused for a second. Did you notice how quickly she dropped the suggestion of a bacon, lettuce, and tomato?"

"Yeah, I did. It was thoughtful of her. I hate bacon. What is all this junk?"

The musty, dimly lit room—concrete floor, cement-block walls—was cluttered with cardboard boxes filled with pots and pans, small appliances, toys, clothes, shoes, and sundry other items. Cal didn't answer Josh's question; he barely heard it. He picked his way to a dusty ping-pong table shoved against the far wall; on it were the boxes he'd sent from Mexico.

"I can't believe it," Josh said. "Your mother's even worse than mine. Some of this stuff is in semi-perfect condition. Why doesn't she give it to some charity?"

"It doesn't belong to her. It belongs to the church. Families in the congregation have donated all this to the annual white elephant sale."

"Some of this stuff looks practically new. Look at these toys. They could give them to Toys for Tots."

"Yeah, but that wouldn't count as part of what they call Christian stewardship—giving money to support the church and missionaries and other specifically religious organizations. There's a CPA in the church who estimates the fair market value of anything he and his wife donate to the white elephant sale. He puts it down in his ledger as part of his tithe."

"Ah, yes, the tithe that binds," Josh said.

"Even my dad thought of that one," Cal said, opening the flatter and larger of the two boxes on the ping-pong table. "Only he wasn't joking. He used it seriously in a sermon one time."

"Does that accountant figure ten percent of his net or ten percent of his gross?"

"And you call yourself a Jew. Stand back, don't look: I want this to be a surprise, since you hate surprises. Don't you know your Torah, boy? God ordered Abraham to give Melchizedek a tenth of everything right off the top—nothing but the best for the spokesmen of the Almighty."

"My dad's rabbi settles for ten percent of the net. Is that my present? I like blankets."

"You do, huh? Well, you'll love this one. There's a hole in the middle so you can wear it."

Sarah, wiping the dinette when they came up the back stairs from the basement, embarrassed Cal with her usual deadpan simulation of enthusiasm.

"Oh, my. How colorful."

"Josh's present," Cal said.

"It's very nice."

Josh wasn't listening; he stared down at his poncho of many colors, looking goofily awed. It had a diamond pattern composed of jagged-edged bands of yellow and three shades of green on a white background. He put his arms out and spun slowly around, blushing as he raised his face. He reminded Cal of a kid showing off his Halloween costume.

"You didn't have to pay any duty, did you?" Cal asked, to deflect Sarah's attention from Josh's inability to say anything.

Sarah frowned and thought a second; she turned back to the counter. "No, I don't believe so."

"You shouldn't have been charged anything," Cal said. "I followed all the rules, for sending gifts to different people in one box—had to wrap each gift separately. I'll have to rewrap everything in decent paper, though, for tomorrow. Where's the wrapping stuff?"

"I'll get it for you."

"Okay, no hurry."

"Maybe not for you," Josh said.

Sarah turned from the sink, her hands in a towel.

"Well, Josh, it was certainly a pleasure seeing you again. Give our regards to your parents. We wish you, and your family, a very Happy Hanukkah."

Cal almost had to bite his lip. Josh blushed and bashfully smiled. "Thanks. I enjoyed the lunch very much."

Sarah watched them exit from the top of the stairs to the front door's hall-like vestibule. "Give our regards to your parents," she said again.

"I'll do that. Addy-ose," Josh said, stepping down, pushing the storm door open wider.

Cal glanced up at Sarah. "I've gotta get my laundry from the car." Her face went grim. She seemed to swallow; she nodded and turned away.

As he pulled the large and very stuffed blue duffel bag from the Pinto's trunk, Cal said, "I don't know, Josh. I may be going back to the apartment tomorrow, man. Maybe you couldn't tell, but she's acting even more uptight than usual."

"I did notice that," Josh said. "I figured it was because she couldn't bitch at you about Rachel not wanting to come to dinner tomorrow so that she and your dad can bitch at her about the only right way to believe in God. Though I have never said anything to Him about it, I always thought Yahweh made a big mistake by not making the Eleventh Commandment *Bitching is mine, sayeth the Lord. Thou shalt not bitch at anybody about anything*."

Cal slammed the trunk lid shut. It popped open. He slammed it down again. It popped open. He put his hands on it with a look of I'll-show-you.

"Wait a sec, waitwaitwait," Josh said, gently touching his arm and nudging him aside. He raised his face to the sky. "Jesus, how'd it get so cloudy so quick? Obviously, God is trying to tell you something."

Cal snickered and hugged himself, shivering.

"Isn't that right, God?" Josh said, still looking upward.

Cal glanced worriedly toward the house. Josh raised his hands with vatic drama.

"Hey, come on, I'm getting cold," Cal said, and carelessly with one hand flung the trunk lid down. It latched.

"You see!" Josh cried. He lifted his arms again and peered excitedly skyward. "We hear you, God!" To Cal, he said: "You're my witness. God told me to make the Eleventh Commandment *Thou shalt not bitch*. Period."

"Told *you*? You said He was talking to *me*."

"You better watch it, fella. You are dangerously close to breaking the Eleventh Commandment."

Cal took the duffel bag directly down to the laundry room. Most of what he put in the washer hadn't been worn since last pulled from a dryer, but it smelled musty from months of storage. He got the machine going and went back upstairs to the kitchen. He found Sarah—uptightness vibes emanating from her back—standing at the stove, stirring.

On the dinette was an A&P grocery bag, with rolls of wrapping paper jutting from the top. Beside it were scissors and Scotch tape.

"I put a load of wash on," he announced.

She nodded, stiffly. "That's fine. I'd like to talk with you."

"Okay. Now?"

He startled when she banged the wooden spoon against the rim of the cast iron frying pan. She set it carefully on a paper towel and turned down the burner. He pulled out a chair at the dinette and took his cigarettes from his shirt pocket. He sprang to his feet as she turned around.

"Ashtrays in the usual place?" he asked, going through the doorway to the living room instead of past her to the other doorway, which would have taken him directly where he wanted to go—into the dining room. The ashtrays were in the buffet. When he came back, Sarah was seated across from the chair he'd pulled out, her hands clasped on the table.

She gave his cigarette a critical glance as he pulled out the chair kitty-corner from her. He turned sideways sitting down, putting his back against the wall as he lit up. He blew the smoke away from her, toward the stairway to the basement, feeling slightly more justified than guilty.

"Jim and Priscilla and the girls are going to be here tonight," Sarah said. She swallowed with difficulty; she didn't look at him. He didn't look directly at her, but he felt as though he were seeing peripherally an aura of spent emotion—anger and despair that seemed alarmingly intense.

"They're staying here tonight?" he asked.

"Yes." She glanced at him. "Jim wants to present the results of his research on this cult. Your father and I hope you will want to hear what he has to say and give us your opinions, based on what you observed. We didn't realize, of course, that you would be staying overnight at the commune."

"As I told Dad," Cal said, "it is not a commune. They are firm believers in private property and free enterprise. Also, I thought I made it clear that I didn't intend to stay overnight there and would have preferred not to. It didn't seem like a good idea, though, to drive back to Evanston on snow-covered roads, without snow tires, late at night. Also, staying there gave me a chance to talk to Rachel alone. I'm sorry to disappoint you, but I just did not see any evidence that her mind was being controlled, against her will. She has freely chosen to believe—in a different theology."

"And what do you think of it, their theology?"

"Well..." He shrugged reflexively. She looked at him critically. He got serious, eyes on the ashtray as he trimmed the ember of his cigarette, twirling it against the shallow metal bowl. "It's no worse than the theology of most Pentecostals," he said.

She closed her mouth more tightly and lowered her face.

"I don't have the expertise," he said, "to pass judgment on the way they interpret the critical Greek texts of the New Testament. Nor do I have the need to think the various orthodox interpretations are infallible. I'm not on one side or the other. I'm for freedom of belief."

Actually, he thought: freedom *from* belief. He flinched from the cynical hauteur in her look.

"You don't think that boy she's infatuated with, had anything to do with her not wanting to come home?"

"Mark Connor is no longer a boy. He's twenty-six. He was wounded twice in Vietnam and got awarded a Bronze Star for heroism in combat, in addition to the Purple Heart twice. He came back and got a bachelor's in communication from UI Chicago Circle."

"What else did you learn about him?"

"What else? Well, I can vouch that he is bright and articulate and has what they call 'strong leadership qualities.' If it's fruits of the spirit you're concerned about, according to Rachel, Mark's a veritable orchard."

Sarah almost let a sneer show. "We were hoping—in vain, I see—that you would take this matter seriously. Rachel is nineteen. She's had a very sheltered upbringing. She's naïve. She's inexperienced, with men..."

"Well, if Mark's a boy..."

The muscles in her throat tightened. She shoved the chair away from the dinette and stood up. "Your father will have to continue this."

"I apologize," he said, crushing out the butt. Raising his voice, calmly, he declared: "I am taking it seriously. But I am not taking a prejudiced view of it. Jim's been giving you a lot of misinformation."

She was listening, but not looking, having resumed her probably needless stirring of the pot on the stove.

"Rachel said she'd think about talking to just you, without Dad present, the first time, anyway. She doesn't feel confident enough to debate with Dad."

Sarah almost turned her head; but she didn't say anything. Absently, Cal touched the scissors lying on the table. He picked them up, along with the Scotch tape, thinking she wasn't going to say anything more. One of his long-standing complaints about Sarah was that after so many years of taking correction from her, often with scalding emotion, as soon as he was old enough and brazen enough to set her straight on a few things, she had begun to clam up whenever discussion got the least bit heated.

As he was putting the scissors and tape in the bag with the rolls of wrapping paper, she turned partway around.

"Do you think there's a chance she would do that, come here by herself to meet with me? Would they let her?"

"She's not a prisoner, for Pete's sake. They'd let her do whatever she wants. She said she'd consider meeting with you alone—but not right away. In a month maybe. She needs a little time."

He interpreted Sarah's momentary inward gaze as her acknowledging the off chance that the situation with Rachel wasn't as bad as she'd been led to believe. As she turned away, she said, "Jim is sure he can convince you they brainwash their converts. He'll make his case after dinner."

"I'll be happy to compare what he says with what I observed," Cal said. He picked up the grocery bag. "I'll be downstairs, wrapping gifts."

"Fine. Your father will be home shortly. He *says.*"

The presents were already individually wrapped in plain brown paper, each labeled with a name. Cal couldn't recall what each garment looked like, but he had a general idea, from the size and feel of its package, what each gift was. Unlike Josh, he liked surprises. He worried, though, that his delight as the presents were unwrapped might be embarrassingly more genuine than the pleasure expressed by his loved ones—if his mother's reaction to Josh's poncho was any indication of what he could expect.

He remembered how intently he had contemplated each of them, and with what tender affection, while picking out their gifts in a village he had visited on a day trip from Mexico City: *Chico*-something, touted in his guidebook as *the* place to buy handwoven woolens. He'd fallen in love with the stuff and got carried away, deciding on the spot to do all his Christmas shopping in one fell swoop.

He wished now that he'd bought a poncho for himself. He wondered what it would take to set up an import-export business...

"Hello, son. I hope I'm not interrupting."

Though inwardly startled, Cal showed no surprise when he glanced up at his father. "No, it's okay," he said, and marveled at his own composure. He exaggerated concentration as he finished wrapping a bundle in a sheet of red paper decorated with green candles. Martin made his way through the boxes and stepped up to the other side of the ping-pong table.

"I hope you didn't pay anything to Customs for this stuff," Cal said.

"Not that I know of, we didn't."

"I wrapped everything separately and labeled who each thing was for, and the value, so they wouldn't charge duty on the total declared worth. It's exactly the way Postal Service regulations say to do it. Josh got me a copy of them before I left."

Martin looked uncertain. "I don't recall your mother's mentioning having to pay any duty."

"There's a rubber stamp on the box, saying it was opened for Customs inspection and resealed."

"Oh. Well, I wouldn't worry about it. I take it we're in for some unusual gifts. Exceptional ones, I mean."

"Did Mom tell you about the poncho Josh was wearing when he left?"

"No. No, she didn't. She has a lot on her mind."

"Well, that's as good as it's going to get, I guess," Cal said, referring to the package he was wrapping; he'd botched the folding and taping on one side. "Now: another tag..." He stood up straight to scan for the ballpoint pen. "Ah," he said, reaching for it; he bent to write on the tag's snowman, whose happy-face smile made its tiny stick arms look absurdly pathetic.

His thoughts went stereophonic, reminding him that he was still stoned and wowing over the change in Martin's appearance.

"You look like you lost some weight, Dad."

"As a matter of fact, I have. I've started working out on a regular basis. I have a new exerciser, in the room we used to keep this table in. We also had a sauna closet installed. I call it my gym now. You're welcome to make use of it. How long do you think you'll be staying with us?"

"Not long, I'm afraid. I want to go back to Evanston Thursday. I hope you or Mom could drive me to the train station. Or Jim and Pris could drop me off, if they're staying till then."

"It won't be a problem," Martin said. "I guess you're moving in with Josh, for the time being?"

"Yeah. I'll be looking for a job starting next week. Josh's grandfather has a lot of connections in the city, and, he offered to help me find a *chamba,* as they call it Mexico."

"That's kind of him. What sort of employment will you be looking for?"

"Whatever I can get, I guess, that I think I can handle for a while. I still haven't settled on a long-range plan."

"I see. Well, I expect you will need to, build up your bank account again. Were you able to economize sufficiently so that you have enough to get by, until you find a job?"

"I'm all right. I don't have to pay any rent till I get a job—Josh will cover it."

"Oh."

"Yeah, well, the Postal Service pays pretty well, and I'll be sleeping on his sofa. He's got a larger apartment lined up on the Near North Side. I'll start paying half the rent when we move in. I should have a job by then."

"I see."

"His sofa is actually quite comfy as a bed, but then I've slept on a lot worse the past few months."

"Yes, I imagine Josh's place may seem like the lap of luxury compared with many of the homes in Mexico. I can't get over how easily you were able to establish rapport with people, during your travels—to have been a house guest on so many occasions."

"Well, Mexicans, however humble their homes, are incredibly hospitable." Also, he thought, it was easy to establish rapport if you spoke enough Spanish to get by but not enough to follow everything they were saying about you; and if you were reasonably generous with your pesos.

Both men were rapt in thought for a moment. Suddenly aware of that, Cal blurted, "I like your new glasses."

Martin's lips pressed together and he focused quizzically. "Oh, yes," he said, suddenly touching the almost tear-drop shaped silver frames. "Your mother picked them out." He hemmed. "She gave me a full report. Frankly, I'm disappointed that you do not apply the same skepticism to this cult as you do to every variety of orthodox Christian belief."

Cal pulled his hands from the bundle he was working on; he'd messed up the wrapping. Calmly, he ripped the paper off and crumpled it up, muttering, "Too much of the same kind, anyway."

"I'm sorry. There's no use getting into this now," Martin said.

"Why not? You think Rachel's mind is being controlled by Mark and the group. I have news for you: That is not the case. True Life Fellowship is not a crackpot bunch of fanatics as Jim has led you to believe. I can't imagine what distortions he's dreamed up to reach that conclusion, but it doesn't jibe at all with what I heard and saw last night."

With a pinching of his lips, Martin dropped his look, then sighed and raised an expression that was both meek and mistrustful. "We'll discuss it after dinner. Jim believes he can persuade you that you should support us in doing everything we can to get Rachel to see how she's been deceived and manipulated."

"I'm willing to hear him out," Cal said. "But I'm not going to take everything he says as gospel, obviously."

Sadness deflated Martin's countenance. "Obviously," he said, "since you do not even take the Gospel as gospel."

With shrugging nonchalance, Cal recited: "*Therefore hath he mercy on whom he will have mercy, and whom he will he hardeneth.*"

His father tried to lock eyes. Cal averted his.

"I better go help your mother," Martin said.

He moved away, picking a path through the discarded surplus of his congregation's material blessings.

Cal kept his brain geared down to supervising his hands; anger fizzled, giving way to dejection, which became self-pity as he very tenderly labeled the last gift to the favorite of his two nieces, Ruthie.

He took his clothes from the washer and stuffed them into the dryer; he put another load in the washer and started it up again. He used the duffel bag to carry the wrapped gifts upstairs, by way of the garage and the front hall to avoid his parents in the kitchen. He arranged his gifts under the amazingly life-like Scotch pine displayed to street view in the living room's picture window. The plastic boughs were dusted with fake snow and draped with authentic tinsel; the lights were the tiny multicolored variety. Topping the preternaturally perfect Tannenbaum was a many-pointed plastic star, shiny as chrome, its center a blue hollow brightly lit.

When Cal turned around, limp duffel bag in hand, he found his father standing where a wall would have divided the living room from the dining room. His hands were in his trouser pockets, and he was staring somberly at the tree. "The girls had a wonderful time Sunday, when we trimmed the tree," he said.

"You waited till Sunday?"

"Yes, well." Martin pulled his hands from his pockets. "Could you help me with the extra leaf for the table, please?"

Cal tossed the duffel bag onto a chair and walked to the end of the dining room table opposite Martin. They leaned over and grabbed the edges; on Martin's count of three they commenced pulling. Their neck tendons stood out and their faces turned red. Cal felt a rush of camaraderie as they laid the pegged plank into the opening. He wanted to say something banally sociable, but he squelched the question that came to mind: whether his nieces still believed in Santa Claus.

Martin appeared to be fixed on the task at hand; he didn't look up till he was ready to shove the table shut. "Okay," he said, "one, two, three..."

Of course they did, Cal thought. Naomi was only four; Ruthie, two and a half.

When the two seams were tightly closed, Martin said, "All right, that's it. Thank you," and stood up straight, wiping one hand with the other.

Martin went off in the car on an errand for Sarah. Cal availed himself of the opportunity to use his father's home office, which the family referred to as "the study." He left the door open a crack; the plushness of the carpet made him feel as though he were skulking about. He walked around the magisterial mahogany desk. Scanning the bookshelf behind it, he recalled that after God promised to show Philip Lewten the hidden-in-plain-sight meaning of holy spirit, Lewten hauled his library to the town dump, keeping only his Old Testament in Hebrew and his Greek New Testament, along with the corresponding dictionaries and concordances. Lewten said he notified the local pastors that they might wish to salvage some of the expensive books. Cal suspected that he probably sent out a press release as well.

The shelf most easily reached by someone sitting at Martin's desk was solidly packed with Bibles, arranged in descending order of height from left to right. Cal smiled and dragged his index finger over the spines, waiting for the holy spart to say when. He pulled out a large Bible bound in maroon leather and sat down, pushing back the posh executive office chair to a comfy tilt, putting right ankle to left knee. He set the Bible on his thigh, slipped two fingers between the superthin, gilt-edged pages. He resisted the urge to do as he'd done so often as a child—shut his eyes and pick a page, then slide his finger up and down until an impulse picked a spot. His holy spirit had liked to tease a lot. More often than not, even when he passed over the Old Testament entirely, he would end up with his finger on a verse as bereft of possible special meaning as a list of begats.

He stared at the Bible's attractive maroon cover, put his finger on the large gilt-stamped *O* in HOLY, tracing the circle, thinking of one of the first songs he'd learned in Sunday School:

> *The B-I-B-L-E,*
> *Yes, that's the book for me.*

I stand alone on the Word of God,
the B-I-B-L-E.

Unfortunately, he mused, there was no way to erase it, short of severe brain damage or death: Repetition had etched the ditty indelibly into the clean new grooves of his preschooler's brain. If he were in the right mood he could replay the tape from memory's archives and hear it sung sweetly off-key by a chorus of innocents doomed to be taught they were children of the Elect.

Not intending to, he opened to the Bible's title page. The top line identified this Bible as the one his brother-in-law cherished above all others, which Martin routinely disparaged: the New Scofield Reference Bible. Perusing the front matter, Cal discovered that the Scofield's Editorial Committee included the presidents of Dallas Theological Seminary and Moody Bible Institute in Chicago, two bastions of conservative Protestant theology.

The Scofield made minor changes in the text of the Authorized King James Version, updating the translation, principally of names and key words. The space between columns of text on each page, or both side margins if needed, listed cross-indexing notes; the bottom margin varied according to the length and number of footnotes, many of which set forth main points of dispensationalism, a systematic framework for interpreting the Bible that marked a radical departure from the much older covenant theology. Dispensationalism was based on a creative reconfiguration of biblical theology by

John Nelson Darby, an Anglo-Irish evangelist who was among the founders of the Plymouth Brethren, which began in the 1820s as a breakaway movement from the Anglican Church of Ireland.

Jim had a master's degree from Dallas Theological Seminary. Cal had absorbed the notion from Martin that DTS was widely regarded as the U.S. headquarters of dispensational teaching and scholarship. An ordained minister of the Southern Baptist Convention, he worked for an organization that identified itself as "independent evangelical." Headquartered near Schaumberg, where Jim and Priscilla lived, The Institute for Modern Biblical Living was a nonprofit corporation composed of people like Jim who traveled around the country in teams conducting a week-long program of seminars and workshops in churches: several hours every evening and all day Saturday.

The seminars included multimedia presentations and sermonic lectures presenting a mishmash of old-fashioned Protestant principles and lessons from popular psychology found to be supported by the Scriptures. Participants received workbooks mapping out a step-by-step program for reforming oneself, one's family, and one's social relationships. The most harped-upon theme was the need to reestablish "God's chain of command" in the family: the children blindly obedient to their parents; the wife submissive in all things unto her husband; the husband taking orders from and speaking for the Lord Jesus Christ. The Institute had started offering the seminars about the time Gloria Steinem became a household name, and earnings from them were now in the millions of dollars annually.

Cal turned the silken thin pages of the Scofield Bible, sliding bunches at a time, letting his eyes snatch phrases at random. His disgust with biblical literalists had been mainly focused on dispensationalists ever since his older sister brought one home from Wheaton College and announced they were going steady. He thought Martin shared a visceral dislike of Jim Fuller at first handshake, but Martin denied any suggestion that he had ever been anything but happy about the match Priscilla had sprung on them. Cal didn't buy it. It had seemed obvious to him that Martin had merely tolerated Jim until his first grandchild was born, and that Martin still took uncharitable pleasure in drawing Jim into competitive discussions on topics that somehow always involved arcane points about dispensational interpretations of Scripture.

Jim had been shocked by Martin's high-brow hostility. Cal could remember one of their arguments over a best-selling book by the apocalypse-monger Hal Lindsey, another Dallas Seminary man. His first best-seller, *The Late Great Planet Earth,* explicated the hermetic phantasmagoria and vatic declarations found in Ezekiel, Daniel, and The Revelation, laying out a vividly described scenario of modern-day events allegedly fulfilling the apocalyptic prophecies and leading inexorably to the conclusion that The Great Tribulation was nigh: seven years of hell on earth. Christians had nothing to fear, however, and every reason to pray for the horrible destruction and suffering to begin as soon as possible. According to Lindsey's reading of Scripture, Christ would appear in the skies before all hell broke loose and whisk his faithful away to gloryland, bypassing suffering and death. Beam me up, Jesus!

Cal had been amused by Martin's transformation on the topic of The End Times. When Jim first enthused about Hal Lindsey's book, Martin acted as though getting into specifics about biblical eschatology was beneath any right-thinking Christian's dignity. Jesus had stressed that no one would know the exact time of His return. It would happen when no one expected it, so predictions aimed at pinning it down were clearly contrary to God's Word, rightly understood.

As the evangelical world became more and more fixated on the Rapture, Martin began to engage with Jim on the subject. He claimed that only one person before J.N. Darby had ever read the Scriptures to say the Rapture would precede the Second Coming. Martin said that Darby got the idea from a kooky prophetess who'd literally dreamed it up: She'd had a vision in a dream and in trying to make sense of it she concluded that God had revealed to her that the various verses about the Second Coming didn't rule out a preliminary Second *Appearance* in the heavens. In effect, Cal suddenly realized, this prophetess claimed, like Lewten, that God had shown her how to rightly divide the Word of Truth.

The ironies bubbled away in Cal's stream of conscience as he read the Scofield Bible's footnotes on chapters twelve, thirteen, and fourteen of First Corinthians. This morning he'd read Dr. Lewten's exegesis of these three chapters. He couldn't say whether Lewten's novel interpretations of key passages were really defensible, but he could say, and with conviction, that the Scofield was grasping at straws in its attempt to distort the plain literal English sense of Paul's essay on speaking in tongues and other "spiritual things." And he was pretty sure the Scofield was merely representing the orthodox Protestant position on the matter.

Remembering the Nicodemus story that he and Rachel had discussed, he turned to it in the third chapter of the Gospel of John. The King James Version had it that Jesus said, in verse eight, that *the wind bloweth where it listeth*. The Scofield preferred *willeth* to *listeth* but retained the translation of *pneuma* as *wind*. That made no sense at all, Cal saw now, in the context of Jesus' entire speech beginning with verse five, in which Jesus declared to Nicodemus that a man must be born again of water and of the Spirit to enter the kingdom of God. Verse six was one of the examples cited by Mark: *That which is born of the flesh is flesh; and that which is born of the Spirit is spirit.*

No wonder the orthodox literalists got nervous here. Lewten said God gave believers in His Son some of what God is: some *godness*, i.e., spirit. You hear the sound of the spirit, but you can't tell where it's coming from or where it's going—which doesn't necessarily apply in the case of wind, Lewten pointed out, claiming that Jesus was actually alluding to speaking in tongues, *the sound of the spirit.*

Spirit goes where It will. God goes wherever He wants, spirit entering into whomever He pleases? Well, then: Were the True Lifers Calvinistic to some extent? Based on what little he'd read by Lewten and about TLF, Cal guessed that they probably defended some version of the limited free will rationalization, arguing that God, being omnipotent, knew in advance who would accept his offer of salvation and predestinated to the extent of allowing humans to freely choose everlasting damnation, even though He desired that all would be saved.

Calvinists interpreted the same passage in John to mean that Jesus was saying a sinner could not save himself; the Holy Spirit had to do it for him, first by regenerating his soul with the spiritual wherewithal that made true repentance and genuine faith not just possible but one-hundred percent effectual. Calvinists believed that no one could fall from grace. "Once saved, always saved" was their felicitous mantra. But there was a proviso: You had to be *truly* saved.

How did the Holy Spirit choose which sinners to save? By going where He pleased to go, bestowing irresistible grace on some and passing over the rest.

To Cal's delighted disgust, the Scofield's note on the Nicodemus story asserted the first of Calvinism's five main doctrines, though without the traditional shorthand title for it—Total Depravity. The Scofield's note explained that the "natural man" was incapable of entering the kingdom of God; he could not even be made aware of its existence much less feel drawn to it. The note said that being born again was a creative act of the Holy Spirit and not a person's self-reformation—correct, according to Calvinism. But then, obscuring one of the most divisive issues in Protestant theology and church history in a single sentence, the Scofield said the only precondition of the new birth was the sinner's faith in Christ crucified.

The subtle distinction made perfect sense. If the Scofield had translated *pneuma* as *Spirit* in verse eight, the verse would clearly support the second main doctrine of Calvinism, known as Unconditional Election. When Calvinists explicated this passage, they claimed Jesus used the wind-spirit ambiguity metaphorically, comparing the Holy Spirit's entirely unpredictable conversion of some sinners but not others to the apparently arbitrary movements of the wind. Only strict Calvinistic denominations still preached this doctrine, which most of modern Christendom deemed an absurd misinterpretation of Scripture: Faith is not a believer's own doing.

Jesus said that many are called, but few are chosen (Matthew 22:14). Calvinism held that sinners who seem to be saved for a time and then revert to ungodliness or convert to heresy are called by the Word but not by the Spirit; they are those in the parable who receive the seed into stony places: *The same is he that heareth the word, and anon with joy received it: Yet hath he not root in himself, but dureth for a while; for when tribulation or persecution ariseth because of the word, by and by he is offended* (Matthew 13:20-21).

Such was Cal, his parents were obliged to believe. Jim—and Priscilla, once she'd given up her parent's theology to cleave unto her husband's—believed the above but also believed that Cal had been called by the Spirit and initially accepted it on some level but ultimately rejected and even resisted God's will that he be saved and live only to honor Him. They said that predestination amounted merely to this: Before He created the world, God foreknew who would choose salvation and who would not and ordained that it be so.

In *The Bondage of the Will*, Martin Luther raged against the idea that the unregenerated will of sinners could be free to choose salvation, but the church that took Luther's name quickly moved toward the soothing reasonableness of limited free will after his death. John Calvin took up the cause of determinism, writing a systematic theology staunchly affirming the impotence of the human will even to truly desire salvation before experiencing the regeneration of the Holy Spirit, the rebirth about which John's Jesus spoke to Nicodemus.

After Calvin and the Westminster Divines promulgated the Westminster Confession of Faith, the Dutch theologian Jacobus Arminius proclaimed it in error on five main points, all of which stemmed from the free will question. Arminius read the Bible to say that man's will is totally free and not only able to will that which God requires, but also able to achieve the requisite holiness—with a little help from the Holy Spirit. Protestants proceeded to repeat the dispute between Augustine and Pelagius, splitting the hairs ever finer and tightening up the logic of the circular reasoning on both sides of the question.

The Holy Mother Church reinterpreted Augustine's deterministic commentaries and evolved a reasonable middle way between those Scriptures that appear to grant us free will and those that appear to deny free will as a possibility. Protestantism recapitulated the same debate, arguing over God's gift mentioned in Ephesians 2:8-9: *For by grace are ye saved through faith; and that not of yourselves: it is the gift of God: Not of works, lest any man should boast.*

The true Calvinist professes himself to have been totally passive in his salvation because faith cannot happen without grace, which is not of ourselves. The Calvinist if he is truly saved has no choice in the matter; he has faith because God willed it to be so. The limited free will Christian claims to have had one meager, excruciatingly humble, but absolutely crucial part to play in his salvation. He had the final say: to accept the gift of forgiveness and eternal life, or reject it.

Cal's appreciation of Calvinism was born again when he could no longer claim to be a born-again Christian by even the most liberal criteria. During his first year at Northwestern, he took to calling himself a "Calvinist reprobate." When a witness for Christ approached, if Cal had the time, he let himself be imposed upon. He would listen politely and then he would take the Bible from the witness for Christ and read him or her proof texts for Unconditional Election and a related doctrine declaring that Christ died to save only the Elect, not the whole world—Limited Atonement.

At that point, Cal would launch into his "personal testimony," relating how he had been called by the Word as a child but had gradually learned that the Bible contains numerous inconsistencies, contradictions, irresolvable ambiguities, and a lot of stuff that he didn't think was very Christian. Hence, he had found it impossible to base his beliefs on the Bible. If for the sake of dialogue, however, he agreed to assume that it

was the inerrant and infallible Word of God, then he agreed
with Martin Luther and John Calvin that the Bible said there
was not a damn thing he could do about being damned. The
Bible said only God could save him, faith being enabled only
by God's grace, meted out according to God's inscrutable will.
You were among the lucky Elect, or the unlucky damned, and
there wasn't a damned thing you could do about it either way.

In "heavy raps" with a Messiah's dozen Jesus freaks,
Inter-Varsity Fellowship jocks, and Campus Crusaders for
Christ, Cal had defended double-predestination Calvinism as
the most logical and consistent interpretation of the Bible. As
far as he knew, he had not made any converts.

More times than not, he had had to help them with the
answers to their side of the argument, the limited free will position: The reprobate mind can, through the power of the Word,
be shown its bondage to sin and its condemnation before God;
the reprobate heart can then will repentance and faith, but
these are only effectually achieved by the power of the Holy
Spirit when the sinner realizes that his will won't do it and in
abject despair surrenders his will entirely unto Jesus Christ.

When the limited free will scheme of salvation had been
clearly established between him and his latest victim, Cal
would attack the mainstream evangelical line with some dev-
ilishly difficult questions and the most damning of the predestination by God's will passages of Holy Writ. At this point,
most of the followers of Christ got up and shook the dust from
their sneakers. They may still have had plenty to say, but not a
one had known how to knock the wind out of the Calvinist

position. They usually said, when leaving, that they would pray for him.

Cal spun the swivel chair around and settled to staring at the study's floor-to-ceiling bookcase. He scanned the shelf containing a selection of Luther's works, recalling the time a would-be brother in Christ had belittled Calvinism as though it were a perverted distortion of Christianity that everybody knew was totally without foundation in any reasonable interpretation of the Bible. Cal had tried to convince the guy that Luther had preached Calvin's line before him; the guy wouldn't believe it. To prepare for any next time, Cal bought a copy of Henry Cole's 1823 English translation of Luther's Latin treatise written to refute the free will arguments of the Catholic theologian Erasmus. Cal committed key passages of *The Bondage of the Will* to memory. (He was never tempted to read Erasmus.)

According to Luther, if a sinner could do anything at all, even simply choose to believe, in order to qualify himself for salvation, he was receiving a reward, not grace. In *The Bondage of the Will,* Luther argued that it was the highest degree of faith to believe that a God who saves so few and damns so many is merciful; to believe that He is just who will inflict eternal torment upon us for the evil nature we were born with. *If, therefore, I could by any means comprehend how that same God can be merciful and just, who carries the appearance of so much wrath and iniquity, there would be no need of faith. But now, since that cannot be comprehended, there is room for exercising faith.*

When Gutenberg made the Scriptures directly accessible to all who could read, Western Civilization was born again. As a translator, Luther gave Germans the first, and some said still the best, Bible in their language; he earned his place in history by opening up the vocation of Spokesman for the Creator of the Universe to anyone who could out-argue all comers as to what God's Word *really* says.

Rocking slightly in his father's chair, Cal fantasized a World Championship of Christian Evangelists, a televised crusade held in a packed football stadium: the crude and cantankerous Martin Luther reviling Billy Graham as a heretic, in a medieval dialect of German.

The vision vanished when Cal heard his father call from the front vestibule, "They're here."

He shut his eyes and listened to his parents greeting Priscilla and the girls. They actually sounded genuinely warm. As parents they had not even allowed their children to believe in Santa Claus. Every year Martin had explained that Santa Claus was part of the secular conspiracy to cover up the biblical meaning of Christmas—not to be confused with the "true meaning of Christmas," which was part of the cover-up because it made it seem downright ghastly to most people to learn that the Babe of Bethlehem was sent by God to save only a relatively few undeserving souls and to judge unto eternal damnation all the rest.

Cal pulled himself to his feet, put his hands on his hips and arched his back, trying to stretch out the nervousness he felt suddenly, a weak fluttery pathos. He slid the Scofield Bible back into its slot and went to the door, opened it a little more and cocked his ear.

Above his mother's gushy-sweet and his sister's wearily complacent voices chattering to and about the little girls, he heard Jim's cheery, slightly high, slightly raspy voice—"So where's Cal? What did he say?"

A momentary hush, lowered voices, and then Naomi said, "Don't forget the presents, Daddy. They're in the car."

He would give them a couple minutes. He took a deep breath, praying to himself for strength, trying to transform ordinary air into wholly human *pneuma*.

CHAPTER SIX

In the Beginning, Wor(l)ds

MARTIN WAS PERCHED ON a stool in front of the fireplace, making final adjustments to his masterpiece of stacked logs, kindling, and crumpled newspaper. Priscilla was sitting on the sofa, contentedly watching her little girls, who stood primly enthralled before the Christmas tree. Martin unexpectedly threw a look over his shoulder. "Here's Cal," he said.

Priscilla twisted around as he entered the room. "Well, hello, Cal. Welcome home."

"Thanks, Prissy. You're looking well. Hey, Nay, Ruthie. Don't worry, I'm not Santa Claus. You remember me, don't you?"

"Say hello to your Uncle Calvin," Priscilla urged; and they did, Naomi practically shouting and little Ruthie bashfully garbling it.

"Gosh, you're tan," Priscilla said. "I wish I could get a tan like that. You look like a surfer. I like your hair short. Short-*er*, I should say."

Cal had to smile carefully, hiding his innate defensiveness upon greeting her for the first time in a long while. He had come to accept that he might never be able to dispel completely the middle child's resentment. How could he hope to, when she had become a reliable source of pride to their parents, while he was, at best, a decidedly mixed blessing.

The whooshing clap of the front door being shut preceded Jim's voice affecting a jolly bass: "Ho ho ho. Here comes Santa's biggest elf." He stepped into the room hunched over a cardboard box. He acted buffoonishly stunned to see Cal; said, "*Buenas noches, señor,*" and scuttled over to the Christmas tree. "What do you have to say for yourself?" Emblazoned on the box Jim carried was the brand name of a dishwashing detergent.

"Joy," Cal said. "Joy to the world, joy for the dishes with the see yourself shine."

"Is that supposed to be funny?" Priscilla asked.

"No, of course not," Cal said. He sat down at the other end of the sofa, keeping the joke, sorry as it was, to himself. The brand name on the box Jim carried in had reminded Cal of an anecdote that Jim told during one of his first meals with the family. Oblivious to the embarrassment of his audience, Jim had cheerily regaled them a canned anecdote about a saintly old lady's secret recipe for joy: Jesus, others, yourself.

Dressed in identical corduroy overalls and long-sleeve blouses with frilly collars and cuffs, Naomi and Ruth, both with hair as whitish blond as their mother's, reverently approached their daddy. Jim handed a present to Naomi and told her where to put it under the tree. Turning Ruthie around, he said, "You tell Mommy and Uncle Calvin that if they don't be nice to each other, Santa Claus is going to leave lumps of coal in their stockings."

Ruthie gaped at them. "Lumps of coal?" Naomi echoed, scrunching up her face.

Cal and Priscilla chuckled through clenched teeth.

Martin drew the fire screen closed and turned around, wearing a somber, wary look. Holding his hands out, fingers splayed, he said, "I guess I better go wash up. Sarah's about ready to serve the eggnog."

"Oh, yeah, eggnog. Hey, great," Cal said.

"Don't get excited, she's using rum *flavoring*," Priscilla said.

"You're kidding. What a travesty of tradition."

"We're out of rum," Martin said. "There's brandy, though. Help yourself."

"Well, I don't want to be a stumbling block, to a weaker sister or brother-in-law."

"Ha! The devil quoting Scripture," Priscilla said.

"And almost getting it right!" Jim added.

To Cal, Martin said, "She may have already put the flavoring in. If not, do you want her to save some out for you, unflavored?"

"Yes. Please."

Getting to his feet, the empty box hanging from one hand, Jim said, "*All things are lawful for me, but I will not be brought under the power of any.* I could care less if you spike your eggnog, but I've read that smokers have to smoke more when they drink, and, well, we'd really appreciate it if you didn't smoke when the girls are in the same room. They've just gotten over bad colds and they're very sensitive to cigarette smoke anyway."

Cal just looked at him.

"I realize you're careful about it," Jim said. "I don't want to offend, believe me. But we feel it's especially unhealthy for the girls right now, so if it's not too much to ask..."

Trying to make it sound light and look shrugging, Cal said, "*No problema. Suegro mío, tan querido.* I can go outside or up to my room—as I often do, you may have noticed. I don't smoke in this house any more than I have to, you realize."

Priscilla blushingly bowed her head away.

"But, you know," Cal said, "in a large room like this..."

"How about—" Jim started to say. "Maybe you could sit close to the fire and blow the smoke toward it."

Ashamed for letting his irritation show, Cal glanced dumbly toward the fireplace, and felt disappointed to find the animated flames obscured by the black metal mesh screen.

"Oh, don't worry about it," Jim said. "You're right. I'm sorry. I'm just an overprotective father, I guess."

Eggnog was not a choice aperitif, Cal realized, several minutes into the meal. He had put too much brandy in the second helping, trying to keep himself jolly while Jim enthused about holiday missives received from new friends all around the world. Jim and Pris had left the girls with Martin and Sarah for two weeks in July to attend the Conference on World Evangelism in Lausanne, which they followed up with a stay at *L'Abri*, the Alpine retreat run by Edith and Francis Schaeffer, highbrow evangelical authors whom *Time* magazine had dubbed "missionaries to the intellectuals."

"Why don't you use your fork, dear?" Jim asked Naomi. He and Cal were across from Naomi and Priscilla. Jim was next to Martin's end; Cal, next to Sarah's. Ruthie was in a highchair between mother and grandmother.

Priscilla was supervising Ruthie too closely, Cal thought; and he couldn't stomach her mommy voice. Grandma was being aloof and tightlipped. Usually she was right on top of every move the girls made or were about to make. Cal noted that she wasn't letting her eyes light on him even briefly and that he wasn't the only one she wasn't looking at. He wondered what bone she was saving to pick with Martin, who may have been ruminating on the same question: He kept shooting worriedly searching looks at her.

Absorbing himself in delectation of the cheesy chicken-and-asparagus casserole, a dish he'd loathed as a child but developed a taste for as a teenager, Cal thought he might remark to Sarah, but wouldn't dare, that chopped tomatoes and chili peppers would make a zesty variation on the recipe. He smiled to himself after a swallow and the vision of his father staidly taking his first mouthful of the spiced-up casserole and getting a seed-filled slice of jalapeño. Martin looked at him and said, quite coolly: "Cal, why don't you tell us something about how the Mexicans celebrate Christmas?"

Cal grabbed his water and urgently sipped. Sarah affected alarm, and then, when it was clear he wasn't going to choke, chastised him with a frown.

"Sorry," he said. "Almost went down the wrong way. Okay. The Mexicans, uh, are a lot of different peoples, of course. The Yucatec Maya have different traditions than the Zapotecs of Oaxaca, or the Tarascans in Michoacán. Every region has its own pagan heritage embedded in its Catholicism and the traditions vary somewhat... Actually, I didn't get to see all that much of the Christmas celebrations. I saw one thing, in Puebla, a life-size Nativity scene. Not life-size; I mean, real-life. The crèche was done like a scene from a play. They got a young mother and her baby to be Mary and the Christ-child, and a guy, maybe her husband, to be Joseph."

"No... Wait. Oh, that's right. I remembered a mistaken impression. I thought it was a real baby at first, but turned out it was only a doll. I asked a guy if it was a real baby, and he said, *Sí, sí*. Probably didn't even hear what I asked. They had lots of animals standing around—sheep and burros and a cow—all definitely real."

No one at the table had so much as smiled while Cal, in between mouthfuls of casserole, talked. He extended the last pause because Naomi had been grumping and Jim had tried to reprimand her silently; i.e., they had been making faces at each other. Jim apologized and asked Naomi what she wanted. She said she wasn't hungry and didn't want any more. She'd piled the pieces of asparagus aside: little green logs. Jim told her to eat three more bites and then she could start on her carrot salad.

"Puebla?" Martin said. "Isn't that fairly close to Mexico City?"

"That's right," Cal said. "It was my last stop on the way back, from Guatemala. It was—. I was there the night of the sixteenth. That's the night they start the Posadas, which is the most famous tradition, come to think of it, from Mexico. Posadas are reenactments of the story of Mary and Joseph arriving in Bethlehem and looking for a place to stay.

"The Posadas are movable fiestas. Friends and relatives get together and go from house to house, celebrating. I didn't get invited to any. If I'd stayed in the countryside, in some village, I would have gotten invited to some, for sure."

Jim asked, "So is that like their Twelve Days of Christmas?"

"No, no," Martin said, blushing. "Well—."

Priscilla said: "Jim, the Twelve Days of Christmas!"

Jim looked puzzled, then sheepishly smiled, shaking his head. "I guess I never really thought about it."

(Cal flashed on Spencer Tracy as Clarence Darrow asking William Jennings Bryan, "Do you ever think about things that you *do* think about?")

"Well," Martin said, "the Twelve Days of Christmas begin on Christmas Day and end on what used to be quite an important religious holiday in its own *rites*—Twelfth-day, the day of The Epiphany, January sixth."

"Oh, yeah," Cal said, "in Mexico that's the day kids get Christmas gifts, from the Magi. They act out that story, too, with guys dressing up as the Three Wise Men. They even have a name for each of them."

"Well, most of that's folklore, of course," Martin said. "The Gospel of Matthew simply states that wise men came from the East. It doesn't say how many—or identify them by name."

Cal stifled the urge to comment by stuffing his mouth with a last forkful of casserole. *Do you think maybe Joseph used the wise men's gold to pay for the flight into Egypt?* He recalled a cryptic couplet, probably by that prolific poet Anonymous. *How can compassion, which has no defense, / Flee the slaughter and still claim innocence?*

And it came to pass that Jim, the brother-in-law of Cal, was seated in the living room in a chair, holding open upon his lap a binder, of the type with three metal rings; in the binder were sheets of paper on which were typed many words. And Jim, the brother-in-law of Cal, had put upon his nose spectacles like unto a lawyer's whose eyes have been sorely troubled by years of fine print.

And Cal entered from the kitchen, and seeing his brother-in-law's intent, he made bold to walk past him, saying, "With your *permiso*, counselor, why don't we conduct this inquest over by the fireplace?"

And Cal did not wait for his brother-in-law to answer, for he had already decided the thing in his heart; he set the vessels he bore before the hearth, and himself sat down upon the floor, where it was carpeted and like unto his hind parts as a bed of new moss. And looking up, Cal found his brother-in-law peering at him over his spectacles, whose lenses were in the shape of half-moons. And his brother-in-law saith unto him: "I was here first. Why don't you take the other chair?"

"Oh, come on," Cal said. "We have a nice fire going. Just turn the chair around and push it over."

With an affected grimace of acquiescence under protest, Jim stood up, placed the open binder in the chair, swung the chair around, and shoved it over between the recliner and rocker, which were angled toward each other to either side of the fireplace.

Cal sipped at his coffee. Settling himself in the chair, Jim reached under his rust-colored V-neck sweater and pulled out a ballpoint pen. He clicked it repeatedly as he silently scanned a page, turned it, and continued reading.

"That looks a little long to be a brief," Cal said.

Jim indulgently smiled and raised his pleasant, chubby face. It surprised Cal to realize Jim was nervous.

"Martin told you, didn't he? I was put in charge of our Cult Truth Squad. It was my idea that we move into this ministry. There's a pressing need for it."

Cal passed, taking a sip, translating "ministry" to "market" and "pressing need" to "big demand."

Jim said, "I think I've worked harder the past four months than I did whenever I had to cram for an exam in seminary. I've had to dig up and process a small library of information with only one administrative aid and a secretary."

So what's your new title—General Verity? Cal wanted to ask. "So—?" he said. "You're giving seminars on this?"

"Not yet. I expect to start training a seminar team next month. First I have to do a rush job on getting some materials published, that boil everything down." He looked down at the binder. "I've got reports on the Big Five about ready to edit for a book."

"TLF is one of the Big Five?"

"Yes, indeed. Of the new cults, which make an antiestablishment appeal to alienated young people, convert them with hyperemotionality and coercive peer pressure, and then keep them docile with various mind-control methods—borderline brainwashing."

Jim looked as though he would welcome an objection. Trying to appear as blasé as possible, Cal took a sip of coffee. "So how big is TLF?"

Jim lowered a disappointed look. "I can't give you any reliable numbers. They claim they don't have members, as such, so they don't keep track of how many attend their fellowship meetings regularly. Without a doubt, though, the size of their following puts them in the top five cults. The consensus—we're not the first ones getting into this area, just the first ones east of California to see the need for it—the consensus is that Mr. Moon's—I refuse to call him "the Reverend"—his Unification Church is definitely number one in membership. And that means in money, too, of course. After them, the order is probably the Hare Krishnas, TLF, Scientology, and the Divine Light Mission."

"Divine Light Mission?"

"That chubby teenage guru's outfit."

"Oh, him," Cal said.

Jim inclined his head over the notebook and frowned, reading rapidly. Cal lit a cigarette. He blew the smoke toward the fireplace. The light in the dining room went out. They both looked. Martin stepped from the dimness.

"We decided it'd be cozier over here," Jim said.

Martin came up and stood beside the recliner, *his* chair; he looked both peeved and chastened as he assessed the fire. Cal assumed that Sarah had picked the bone clean, whatever it was. Martin stepped over to the rack of hearth implements and pulled out the poker. Cal scooted over, looking toward the nearest kitchen doorway as his mother stepped into it.

"Do you have enough light in here?" she asked.

"It's adequate," Jim said. "Well, maybe I should have this other lamp on."

She turned it on and sat down in the rocking chair, whose green upholstery matched the recliner's. She pushed it back to give Cal more room. Cal put out his cigarette. His eyes were drawn to the periphery when Sarah's feet, in her favorite house shoes—maroon penny loafers—began softly to push and fall.

Martin gave the wood a final poke, studied the flames a moment, and stood up. He put the poker back, glanced at the handkerchief in his hand, wiped the other hand with it and sat down in the recliner, setting it back one click. He left the mesh screen open.

"You're not going to be too warm, are you, Cal?" Sarah asked.

"I don't think so. Feels good." He noticed Jim's hesitating glance and said, "Go ahead and open with a prayer if you want."

Martin's jaw clamped, producing his anger's early warning signals: dour dimples—a tiny pit in each cheek.

"Well," Jim said, "the Lord has heard our prayers the past week. He knows the burden on our hearts... I want to begin with some general observations, to put the problem in the context of what's happening all over the country. Currently, there are more than fifty recently founded cults with sizable followings scattered around the United States. About two-thirds of these cults grew directly out of the so-called Jesus Movement. What they have in common is that they are all heretical deviations, though in various ways, from the orthodoxy articulated in the Apostle's Creed. True Life Fellowship and Biblical Research Association is the largest of these, although less well known than some others.

"True Life Fellowship—TLF for short—has been operating for about twenty-five years, though not in its present form. Its founder, a man named Philip Lewten, had the foresight a decade ago..."

Cal was an expert at listening to lectures; he had developed at a tender age the knack of keeping track of main points while intermittently attending to his own thoughts. He mulled the situation as it appeared to be shaping up: Jim intending to prove that TLF's way of speaking in tongues was borderline brainwashing and Sarah already convinced; Martin, then, was the only possibly still undecided arbiter of probable truth in this case; and he himself, the only impartial one.

"You have to understand," Jim read, "that the slavish proselytes for Lewten's lunacy don't come right out and say that they're preaching a different Jesus, a different Spirit, a different Gospel. They employ the tried and true orthodox Christian vocabulary, but they use a dictionary edited by Philip Lewten in collaboration with modern liberal theologians and ancient heretics. It's only when the targets of the cult's 'love-bombing' are lured into taking a course that they learn that TLF's Holy Spirit is not the indwelling Third Person of the Godhead and that Jesus Christ the Son of God is not—according to Lewten—God the Son."

"May I interrupt, please?" Cal said. "I'm sorry, but I can't let that go by, because it's not true. Not in the case we're discussing, anyway. Rachel told me that her first contact with TLF was on the campus of Covenant Christian when she stopped to listen to Mark debating a seminary student about the Trinity. And the seminarian, in fact, denounced Mark quite vehemently for defending the Arian heresy."

Jim looked skeptical. "Rachel told you that? Or Mark?"

"Rachel. Mark was not with us at the time. She was bragging on him. It was real, believe me. As long as I'm being rude I might as well add that if you don't have to affirm the Trinity and you know how the doctrine gradually got hammered out over the first three centuries of the Church, you might want to give Lewten's ideas, at the very least, an honest looking-into.

But to do that, you'd have to get out your Greek New Testament—and that's just for starters."

No one said anything for a moment. Cal listened to his pounding heart.

Martin bowed his head till his chin doubled and checked on the cleanliness of his fingernails.

Jim said, "Lewten's Church history and Greek scholarship are as bogus as the *Doctor* he puts in front of his name; he got it from a correspondence school, a degree mill."

"But he has a master's in theology from Princeton," Cal said, "and his about-the-author note on the one book I looked over says he completed all the coursework for a doctorate there. Maybe he couldn't get his dissertation proposal past his committee, or maybe he said something he shouldn't have during the orals, like that friend of yours from Dallas."

(In the oral exam to present and defend his dissertation proposal, the friend of Jim's admitted he favored the mid-Trib Rapture position, arguing that the best reading of the relevant Scriptures suggested that Christ would appear in the skies and rescue his faithful exactly halfway through the seven years of the Great Tribulation.)

Cal noticed that Sarah had stopped rocking and that they weren't looking at him; they seemed to be simmering in uncharitable vibes. Martin sighed and shifted in his chair so as to have a better view of the fire; or maybe his hemorrhoids were bothering him.

Jim looked at Sarah. "Please continue," she said.

"All right. Let me explain Lewten's Doctrine of Christ. That Covenant student Rachel mentioned hit the nail on the head about this being the Arian heresy all over again."

That ended Jim's attempt at speaking extemporaneously. He bowed and read to himself, flipped a page and then another, saying, as he continued to skim, "Anybody with a grounding in Church history would be able to identify Lewten's new interpretation for what it really is—history repeating itself. Like Arius and a host of other heretics—among them Paul of Samosata, Marcion, and Saturninus—Lewten preaches a different Jesus, a different Spirit, a different Gospel, such as Paul warned against in Second Corinthians 11:4.

"Lewten's Christ is a created being: He had no existence before his birth in Bethlehem." Jim looked up. "Bear with me, this is essential. You see: Lewten developed his Christology after his reinterpretation of the Holy Spirit, and made the former fit the latter... Okay."

Cal managed not to look embarrassed and his was the only eye-contact that Jim received when he glanced around. Cal felt sorry for him. Jim continued reading:

"Lewten's dogma on the nature of man mixes orthodox truth with subtle error. He correctly reads Genesis to say that God created man as body, soul, and spirit. But he errs in teaching that Adam's spirit was the part created in God's image and likeness; not, as orthodoxy proclaims, man's soul. Lewten further builds upon solid ground by teaching that the spirits of Adam and Eve enabled them to have direct personal fellowship with the Spirit of God while they were in Eden. In Lewten's interpretation, as in orthodoxy's, Satan took the form of a serpent and tempted Eve to seek the power of the knowledge of good and evil through the body's five senses, in flagrant disobedience to God.

"Here is where Lewten begins to go astray on this doctrine. With no scriptural basis whatsoever, Lewten claims that God took the spirits of Adam and Eve completely out of them, so that, from then on man's nature was twofold: body and soul—no spirit at all, rather than, as orthodoxy affirms, threefold, with a dead spirit needing the gracious power of the Holy Spirit to be resurrected unto direct personal relationship with God."

Cal had listened intently, hoping to hear a divergence from Calvinist doctrine. He hadn't caught anything, but Martin had, evidently; Cal had glimpsed the dour dimples momentarily on his cheeks. When Jim looked up, checking for feedback, Martin cleared his throat.

"I just want to point out," he said, "before Cal pounces on it, that there are far fewer similarities between what Lewten teaches and what Reformed doctrine teaches. Lewten is building his house on the same sand as Hal Lindsey, who also teaches that Adam and Eve were created body, soul, and spirit. Of course, Lindsey posits the image and likeness of the Creator in their souls, which possess the limited attributes that God possesses infinitely—intellect, emotion, will, morality, and eternal being." Martin paused; faced with their silence and Jim's earnestly blank look, he continued.

"Naturally, a trichotomous Doctrine of Man has a strong attraction because of the Trinity. I realize it's widely accepted in evangelical churches—mainly from lay ignorance and pastoral inattention. I had planned to lend you a book by Charles Hodge in which he argues the Scriptures against all forms of trichotomy."

Cal had to keep his head bowed and his breath bated.

"But, Marty," Jim said, forcing a chuckle, "the Bible clearly distinguishes between soul and spirit."

"No, I firmly believe it does not," Martin said. "Even the Scofield is careful not to draw too fine a line, much less to construct a complete edifice of doctrine on the subtle distinction it does make. In its note on First Thessalonians 5:23, the Scofield points out that the several terms for soul and spirit in both Hebrew and the Greek are often used interchangeably. The editors approve a distinction that seems valid in some passages: that spirit is that which knows and is capable of consciousness of God and communion with Him, whereas soul is the seat of the emotions and the will."

Martin paused again—with an air of replenished confidence. "I don't agree that the Scriptures cited by the Scofield support that or any other distinction. One of the verses, First Corinthians 2:11, clearly supports the Reformed position on the prevenience of regeneration. The verse implies that unregenerate man has a spirit knowing the things of man, as opposed to the things of God, which no man knoweth but the Spirit of God, and in verse twelve: *Now we have received, not the spirit of the world, but the Spirit which is of God; that we might know the things that are freely given to us of God.*"

Cal glanced from Martin's countenance of grave humility to Jim's look of nervous chafing under bluff condescension. With a shifting of his eyes Jim intimated why he didn't wish to pursue the digression: Sarah was staring forlornly at the fire.

"But the Greek verb translated as *received* in that verse," Cal said: "Which one was it?"

Martin flinched. "What difference does it make?"

"Plenty to Philip Lewten. He says that there are two Greek verbs translated as *receive* but meaning entirely different types of receiving—one type is passive and subjective and the other is *receiving into manifestation.*"

"By which he means speaking in tongues," Jim said. "Marty, I'll look into the soul-spirit distinction and we can take it up at some other time."

"Please do," Sarah said.

"I'm sorry I brought it up," Martin said.

"Ah, come on: You are not," Cal said.

Sarah nudged him with her foot; it was close to a kick and he looked at her with mock alarm. Her eyes blazed back.

Jim scanned a page. "The point I wanted to make was that Lewten's Doctrine of Man dovetails with his Arian Christology. Okay, here it is. Man's soul, according to Lewten, is merely the animal vigor of the body, the life-force, which resides, according to Leviticus 17:11, in the blood: *For the life of the flesh is in the blood.* After the Fall, man no longer possessed his original likeness to God, which was his spirit. When God took Adam's and Eve's spirits out of them, man was reduced to the level of the animals, which have the same 'life of the flesh' in their blood, according to Lewten. When man or animal dies, the soul simply ceases to exist. Of course, Lewten has to reinterpret many Scriptures on the fate of unbelievers to get away with that."

Jim looked up at them; he seemed more relaxed and began to ad-lib, with a weightier, more intimate tone.

"Now, Lewten's insistence that the blood literally contains the human soul comes in when he discusses the Virgin Birth, in his Christology. A human fetus makes its own blood in the course of its development. The mother's blood and the fetus's blood do mix to some extent, sometimes with unfortunate or tragic results, when the Rh factors are not the same, for instance. But Lewten ignores the biological facts and teaches that the soul, which is in the blood, is passed on in human reproduction entirely by the sperm.

"Don't ask—I don't know where he got such an outlandish idea. It was probably suggested by what he was trying to prove, which is that Jesus had sinless blood. The blood contains the soul-life and the soul-life has the sin-nature, so Lewten concludes that Jesus' flesh was in the line of Adam and David, through Mary, but his blood, being directly from God the Father when He impregnated Mary, gave Jesus a perfect, unblemished, sinless soul."

"Absolute rubbish!" Sarah interjected. Exasperation left her breathless for a moment. "That's the stupidest vain imagining

I've ever heard attributed to God's Word." She glared grumpily at Jim; he flinched a half shrug, haplessly smirking.

Squinting thoughtfully, Cal said, "So, taking what you said before, then Jesus didn't have a spirit until God gave him *the* Spirit at his baptism by John."

"That's the line Lewten takes. His conception of the human soul is so limited, you see, he has to conclude that Jesus was little more than an ordinary man except for being born without a sin nature. He was—"

"Exactly like Adam," Cal interjected, excited to find the last piece of a puzzle in his grasp. "Lewten's Christ wasn't God so he could have sinned, he was capable of sin, but he fulfilled God's Law perfectly under his own power. And as a reward, his Father, God, gave him some of His essence, His *pneuma*, when he was baptized by John."

"That's it," Jim said. "In a nut's hell, as a professor of mine used to say."

"Dynamic Monarchianism," Martin muttered.

Sarah was agitated. "But how does he get around the first chapter of John, or of Colossians? And Titus! Does he just ignore—. You couldn't. There's too much."

"He has a variety of means for subverting the Word, some of them quite ingenious," Jim said.

"Well, he insists he's just rightly dividing the Word of Truth," Cal said.

"Thanks for reminding me," Jim said. "Lewten has a convenient idea of rightly dividing, for one thing. He claims that the Gospels should be considered part of the Old Testament and together with it are secondary Scriptures for Christians. How does he figure that? Romans 15:4: *For whatsoever things were written aforetime were written for our learning.* In other words, they're nonbinding. Lewten says that *aforetime* means everything before Pentecost. With that premise, of course, he eliminates a lot of thorny questions by giving more weight to the Scriptures he favors.

"He also claims that the New Testament was originally written in Aramaic and that the occidental Greek-speaking Church paganized the teachings of Christ and the Apostles. When he can't get rid of an offending Scripture by 'correcting' the traditional translation of it, he throws it out, saying it must have been added to the original inspired text by a copyist. With that kind of exegetical leeway, he can have the Bible say whatever he wants it to say."

Jim looked at Cal. "As you pointed out, of course, he insists that it's never his interpretation he's expounding. The sales pitch for TLF's Bible research is that it will enable the students to learn how the Bible interprets itself. The keys to unlocking the hidden truths are provided by the textbooks used in the courses. They're all written by Philip Lewten. Consulting any other biblical commentaries is strictly forbidden.

Cal was sitting with his ankles crossed, his arms around his knees, his right hand clasping his left wrist: a position that matched the tense equilibrium in his mind. He noticed Jim's extended pause had turned strangely silent.

Sarah's sudden sobbing behind him withered Cal's inner composure. Turning his head, he saw that her face was all mashed up: like an astronaut's during liftoff. She daubed at her cheeks and eyes with a crumpled tissue. Her mouth twisted open and a sob bounced from her throat.

Martin and Jim peeked from averted looks. Cal fixed a calmly open stare, tender sympathy poised in his eyes, tightening his throat. He couldn't get any words out. He was too ashamed, accused by her face all squeezed up, red and wet. He released his arm and shifted into a different position, his back more to the fire, his head bowed over his crossed legs. He was mortified to find his old devil of anger and resentment holding at bay guilt and empathy.

"Sarah," Martin said, "is there anything we can get you?"

She shook her head, pulling another tissue from the pocket of her corduroy skirt. "I'm sorry," she said, her voice weakly high and sodden with mucus. "I'm so sorry. I just—. It's just so...awful and crazy. I just can't imagine her believing those STUpidSTUpidSTUpid LIES."

She blew her nose and wiped her cheeks. Sounding drier, surer, she declared: "Obviously, Rachel's not in possession of her faculties. They've brainwashed her. Tell him, Jim. Tell him how they do it, with that gibberish chanting they train them to do."

Cal couldn't meet her eyes. He felt as though an enervating toxin had been released into his blood...into his soul.

"Last night, did you witness a manifestation of tongues?"

Looking at Jim from behind a mask of somber impassivity, Cal flashed on Edward Munch's *The Scream*. He took a deep breath. "Yes, I did, as a matter of fact. During the worship service last night, three people, one of them Mark, spoke in tongues and interpreted what they'd said in the language of the spirit, as they call it."

"Didn't you think it was phony as all get out?"

"Well... I admit that I was more or less expecting Mark to go into a trance and have a spaz attack centered in his organs of speech. What he manifested wasn't like that; so, yeah, it struck me as kind of phony at first.

"Mark appeared to become intensely into his...most passionate feelings, I'd say. But, from the way he went into it and came out of it, I don't think it could be called a trance. He was consciously there the whole time, it seemed to me, letting his breath go where it would, apparently, in making speech-like sounds. The sounds were gibberish; babble. But they had a pronounced rhythm that reminded me, oddly enough, of Old English poetry. I'd call it voice music. Like an Indian chant, or Hare Krishna chant, but without the monotony of constantly repeating the same sounds. Jazz voice music with meaningless random syllables."

"Don't take me too humorously," he went on quickly. "I am serious about this. I felt that the glossolalia I heard last night was a harmless ritual. It communicates intense emotions, makes them present, and communal, in a way that— You know, ritualistic words and phrases in church-service prayers kind of do the same thing.

"The important consideration for me is that True Life Fellowship doesn't let its ritual get out of hand, the way I've seen Pentecostals do it, in a documentary I saw once. Rachel told me they have no more than three people do the speaking in tongues at any one service and each one has to translate what he said in the language of the spirit, afterwards. The translated prayers were pretty ordinary stuff.

"I've read Lewten's apologia on this practice, and he makes it clear that they don't go into a trance when they do this: They don't control the stream of sounds they make—just when it starts and when it stops."

Jim glanced urgently from Martin—whose keen interest had kept Cal talking—to Sarah, who looked only grudgingly curious. "That's right," Jim said. "It's like an on-off switch; they hit the switch, but once it's on, the gibberish works like self-hypnosis. It keeps them passive and easily controlled by the authority figures in the cult."

Cal caught Martin's eye. "You used to say basically the same thing about Catholics saying their rosary."

"He never said any such thing," Sarah retorted.

Yes, he certainly did, Cal thought, only glancing at her.

Jim set the binder aside. He took his glasses off and leaned forward, propping his elbows on his legs. His tired myopic eyes triggered a twinge of sympathy in Cal.

"In the very first spirit power course," Jim said, "they teach everybody how to speak in tongues, *their* way. It's a step-by-step self-hypnotic procedure. There's nothing spontaneous or the least bit mystical about it. The students are coached until they get it right and then they're told to do it constantly—even when they can't do it out loud, to do it silently, in their heads. That's how the organization keeps them docile while they squelch their personalities, in order to re-make them around identities entirely dependent on the cult.

"It's all very subtle and soft-sell, compared to other cults. But once they get them into a household of faith, the authoritarian peer pressure; a complete lack of privacy; and constant speaking in tongues to drown out the voices of doubt and conscience; also the effects of a starchy diet and a regimen that allows for too little sleep—it all adds up to the creation of total psychological dependence. The new converts soon have no effective will of their own. To prove it, all you have to do is remove them from the cult—and watch what happens."

Cal couldn't meet Jim's eyes, though he tried. "I didn't see any evidence of that last night," he said. "The people I talked with and observed seemed to me to be"—he pushed his lips out and looked around for the word; shrugged—"ordinary religious people happy with their lives, happy to be where they are, doing what they're doing to serve the Lord. I got a definite sense of individual personalities who have freely chosen to live in this household of faith." He stifled a further thought: The TLF household struck him as similar to the family religious retreat he'd attended with his parents and Rachel when he was fourteen. It was held at a rustic lodge in Michigan's Upper Peninsula.

Sensing that he hadn't spoken forcefully enough, he became more adamant. "I did not see or sense any evidence that this group was destroying personalities and fabricating new ones. Rachel's personality hasn't undergone any change in its essential spirit—if I may use the word in a secular sense. In my opinion, the only thing different about her now is that she's happier with her beliefs—for the time being. I fully realize it's possible, maybe even likely, that she'll become disillusioned with them, eventually… That's life—live and learn."

Shamefaced, he looked away and saw that the fire was low. He stood up and grabbed a chunk of wood. Stepping back to watch it taking flame, he turned partially toward his mother. "Give Rachel time and I think she'll agree to meet with you eventually, for all the good it will do. You won't talk her out of her new beliefs, but at least maybe you'll be able to see, as I did last night, that she's very much in control of her will to believe them."

Sarah bowed her head and wrung her tissue. She took a deep breath and lifted her eyes to Cal. "You think she might be willing to meet with me, alone?"

"Yes. Not right away. But—just to talk, the two of you. If you'd like, I'll call her and try to get her to set a date. And maybe a place, besides here. Maybe in a coffee shop or a restaurant."

The idea seemed palpably to enter Sarah through her eyes and to be slowly absorbed. She looked down at her tissue. "I'll have to think it over," she said. "If you'll excuse me now, I, want to…"—she took a big breath—"be with my grandchildren, for whose sake, I hope we will all put our differences aside. The carolers will be upon us at any moment. Let us know as soon as they arrive, if you are going to continue with this."

She stood, with magisterial weariness.

"We won't be long," Martin said. She nodded, swallowing a response.

"I have a question," Cal said, when she was out of the room. He took a few steps to the side of the hearth and turned, feeling like Perry Mason about to taunt the truth out of a hostile witness. Martin propped an elbow on the armrest and leaned his head against his hand, middle finger pointing to his temple. Cal squelched his titillation.

"If Rachel had joined a Pentecostal church," he began, "one whose way of speaking in tongues was exactly like TLF's but whose doctrine was otherwise orthodox, you would be upset about it, but you wouldn't be claiming that this hypothetical church's way of speaking in tongues was a mind-control technique. Is that a fair assumption?"

Jim indulgently smiled. "What TLF calls speaking in tongues is not the spontaneous ecstatic utterance practiced by charismatic churches."

"Oh," Cal said. "But you don't think Christians ought to be *practicing* spontaneous ecstatic utterance anyway, do you? Isn't that still taboo in your Bible?"

Martin's hand fell from his face and he sat up, looking smugly bored. "It might interest you both," he said, "that last January in Washington, D.C., at an ecumenical conference of charismatics—to use the term now becoming popular—a clinical psychologist from New York Theological Seminary reported research proving that speaking in tongues is learned behavior. All the variations of glossolalia which he and his students had recorded and analyzed exhibited a very limited range of linguistic phenomena, a mere half dozen types of sounds. The conclusion this brave man proclaimed to that assemblage of charismatic Christian leaders was that no one can speak in tongues without first hearing how it's done."

Becalmed by admiration, Cal got out a cigarette and grabbed it with his lips, picked up the ashtray and sat down in the rocker, whose seat cushion was still warm. As he lit up, he said, "Some guy had the gall to tell that to a convention of ecstatic utterers?"

"They did not accept his findings," Martin said.

"Well," Cal said, "Philip Lewten does. He says it's something you have to learn how to do. He teaches that the person has to turn on the switch, like Jim said; the believer has to turn it on, and then the holy spirit in the believer—little *h*, little *s*—takes over and communes with the capital-letters Holy Spirit—God."

"As far as I can see," Cal concluded, "Lewten goes strictly by the B-I-B-L-E on speaking in tongues. I guess I never looked that closely at the fourteenth chapter of First Corinthians until this morning. Man, was I ever surprised."

"Perhaps you should look at it closer still," Martin said, "in the context of the two chapters which precede it."

"I did. And Lewten does. However, he changes the orthodox translation in spots, based on what he says are better interpretations of the Greek."

"He changes the entire meaning of chapter twelve," Jim said, "with a translation no scholar of New Testament Greek would accept as being remotely possible."

Martin looked over at Jim, and Jim explained: "He claims that the Greek says that a believer can exercise any and all of the operations of the Spirit."

"Well," Cal said, "I can see why you wouldn't want to translate it that way if you could avoid it. True Life says that any believer has the potential to do faith healing."

"It's not a valid translation," Jim said.

"Maybe not," Cal said. "I'm not qualified to say, but it seems unlikely to me that TLF would be much of a threat to you if Lewten's translations are totally off the wall. If they are, why don't you just get some renowned classics professors—preferably non-Christians—to go on record saying that Lewten's Greek is bogus, that he's bullshitting."

Martin turned to Jim. "Cal has the unbeatable advantage, you realize, that he isn't compelled to say only what he truly believes. I think we ought to table the discussion. The carolers will be here any minute."

"Hey, you can't back out now," Cal said. "I hear the prompting of the spirit of truth-seeking." He daubed out the cigarette and stood up. "Let me get a Bible. I truly believe you're wrong about Paul's position on speaking in tongues, and I don't have to know any Greek to prove it."

At the top of the stairs, he glanced over his shoulder and caught Jim looking back over his shoulder while leaning toward Martin. He chuckled and shook his head as he strode down the hall. He stopped in at the bathroom.

In the study he noticed that one of the buttons on the phone was lit, the one indicating that another extension was being used. The unlit button was for Martin's private unlisted number, which he used for counseling.

Martin, alone in the living room, seemed irritated by Cal's reappearance.

"Is Jim calling somebody?" Cal asked, sitting down in the rocker, bridging his thighs with the large, somewhat floppy Bible.

"Not that I know. He went downstairs."

"You sure he's coming back? He really likes Charlie Brown. You know, I remember when you talked about TV as though it were a mind-control device."

His father's eyes bowed away. "You're not making a very fine discrimination. Or you don't mean what you say. In either case, you're being dishonest."

Jim came in—rather excitedly, Cal thought, and he noted that Jim seemed to hide something in his initial look.

"They're happy," Jim said. "Charlie Brown's doing his thing." He took his seat, looking at the Bible in Cal's lap. "That's not your father's favorite Bible, you know."

Cal looked up. "I know. Look, right here in First Corinthians fourteen..." As Cal bowed his head to read, Martin recited:

"*I had rather speak five words with my understanding, that by my voice I might teach others also, than ten thousand words in an unknown tongue.*"

"Which verse is that?" Cal asked, looking for it.

"Nineteen," Jim said.

"Ah," Cal said, "but you left off the initial clause: *Yet in the church I had rather speak*...et cetera. And verse eighteen says what?"

Silence. Cal aped astonishment. "Surely, you're just being modest." Martin grimly blushed. Cal read: "*I thank my God, I speak with tongues more than ye all*...but—to paraphrase—in the church I think it's better to preach. And verse five: *I would that ye all spake with tongues.*"

"Read the rest of that verse," Jim said.

Martin recited: "*I would that ye all spake with tongues, but rather that ye prophesied: for greater is he that prophesieth than he that speaketh with tongues.*"

Cal looked up, laughed, and read the rest of verse five: "*except he interpret, that the church may receive edifying.*"

Cal glanced incredulously at his father: Did he really memorize selectively like that? Martin's eyes said: Of course not. I know what you're getting at.

"I read Lewten's exegesis of this," Cal said, "and he is absolutely right. Paul does indeed put prophesying—which Lewten also says, as do ye all because of verse three, I take it, means preaching—above speaking in tongues in group worship, but he says that praying in tongues—speaking in tongues silently to yourself—nourishes the spirit in you, even though it does nothing for your understanding."

Martin looked blandly away, dimples showing.

"Come on, how can you deny it?" Cal asked, his voice nearly cracking. "It's right here in black and white. Verses fourteen and fifteen: *For if I pray in an unknown tongue*—and the word *unknown,* remember, was added by the translators—*my spirit prayeth, but my understanding is unfruitful. What is it then? I will pray with the spirit, and I will pray with the understanding also: I will sing with the spirit, and I will sing with the understanding also.* One more to clinch it. Verse two: *For he that speaketh in an unknown tongue speaketh not unto men, but unto God: for no man understandeth him; howbeit in the spirit he speaketh mysteries.*"

Cal paused and raised his eyes to them, although without letting any of their eyes really connect with his. He continued in his smoothly insouciant classroom voice: "The central message of this chapter is that speaking in tongues is a mystical form of communication between the holy spirit in the believer and Holy Spirit God; it builds up the believer's spirit, but not his understanding; therefore, in group worship, a person shouldn't speak in tongues unless he or she can provide an interpretation so that everyone listening will understand."

"That's not what it says," Jim said. "Read—"

"Yes," Cal said, "I know, I know. Verse twenty-seven says that someone other than the one speaking in tongues has to interpret, which would discourage the practice, I would think. Lewten says the translation is wrong here, the Greek word translated as simply *one—and let one interpret*—means *the same one,* which seems possible because verses five and thirteen exhort the one speaking in tongues in public worship to do his own interpreting for the group.

"Verse twenty-eight is also mistranslated, according to Lewten. *If there be no interpreter* really says, in the Greek, *If there be one who can't interpret*, et cetera, let him pray in the spirit, i.e., speak in tongues to himself for his own benefit, but not out loud if he can't follow up with an interpretation for everyone's benefit.

"You recall that I said three people spoke in tongues last night at the worship service. Verse twenty-seven says only two or three at the most should speak in tongues during any one service, and verse twenty-two says that speaking in tongues publicly is a sign for unbelievers, but doesn't do the believers present any good without the interpretation, because, presumably, all believers present should be able to speak in tongues."

Martin was staring at the carpet between the three chairs as though at a chessboard. Jim shrugged and flashed a condescending little grin. He said, "I forget which verse it is, Paul says if a nonbeliever were to attend a service where everyone's speaking in tongues, he'd think they were all crazy; but if he hears them preaching, there's a chance he'll see that God is with them, and repent."

Cal looked to the text. "Actually," he said, "I was bothered by that verse, twenty-two, but then I realized that it's simply reinforcing the argument that speaking in tongues in public worship ought to be done in moderation and only when followed up by the speaker's interpretation. It's okay as a sign to unbelievers, but it can get out of hand if more than three speak at any given service, with each one providing his own interpretation. Those are the rules for speaking in tongues in public worship that Paul establishes, right here. True Life Fellowship follows them to the letter. Do orthodox charismatic churches?"

Jim shook his bowed head, simpering. Martin lifted a look presaging readiness. Cal hurried on.

"I was also shocked by verses twenty-four and -five, which describe what I would call authoritarian peer pressure—if I didn't mind being redundant. I sure wouldn't want to wander into this church: *But if all prophesy, and there come in one that believeth not, or one unlearned, he is convinced of all, he is judged of all: And thus are the secrets of his heart made manifest; and so falling down on his face he will worship God, and report that God is in you of a truth.*"

Cal looked up, wide-eyed. "Good thing no one takes that verse literally." He turned to Jim. "Sounds almost as bad as group therapy with a bunch of liberal ministers."

Jim hotly blushed. Martin barked an aborted laugh. Cal was awestruck to see his father put his fist to his mouth as he turned his face away; alas, he got the tickle under control. Taking off his glasses and pulling out his handkerchief, Martin said, "I'm sorry, Jim." His sad-looking eyes blinked rapidly as he wiped under them.

A while back Jim had joined a Transactional Analysis therapy group composed of more liberal clergymen. He'd enthused over a book titled *I'm OK — You're Okay* until the group unanimously told him he wasn't and he quit. It appeared to Cal that Jim's Parent was telling his hurt Child to be a good sport and laugh at himself.

Jim said, "That was hitting below the belt. But I can take it. You know, actually, I think transactional analysis offers a good way of seeing what Paul is trying to get across to the Church at Corinth in these three chapters. Paul was stuck with this parent-to-child relationship much of the time when dealing with his congregations, and here is a good example. Thanks for suggesting it, Cal. The whole thrust of Paul's message on speaking in tongues is that it's immature. It's one of the childish things to be put away by the Church."

Cal gave the devil his due, sincerely relieved he'd bounced back. Martin, still a bit flushed, stared at the embers glowing among the ashes in the fireplace. He looked chastened.

"What does the Scofield say?" Cal asked, feeling humbly triumphant. "Let's see. There's a long footnote here that says: Chapter fourteen 'regulates the ministry of gifts in the primitive, apostolic assembly of believers in Christ.' Hmmm. Here's their conclusion: 'Tongues and the sign gifts are to cease; meantime they must be used with restraint, and only if an interpreter is present.'

"Now. Where do they read that tongues and sign gifts are supposed to cease? They cite verses one through nineteen and twenty-seven and twenty-eight. Nowhere in those verses does Paul say that tongues and sign gifts are to cease."

"Chapter thirteen, verse eight," Jim said.

"You think so? Let's see. They've changed the King James a little here, love instead of charity, a change I know the Reverend Wideman doesn't approve. *Love never faileth; but whether there be prophecies, they shall be done away*. Ugh. The editors have done away with the parallelism. And that changed the meaning a little, didn't it?"

Cal glanced at Martin. "Let's translate back to the King James Version: *Charity never faileth; but whether there be prophecies, they shall fail; whether there be tongues, they shall cease; whether there be knowledge, it shall vanish away.* Now. You want me to lift the *whether there be tongues, they shall cease* out of context and take it as an imperative from the Lord that his worshipers stop yammering at him in the language of the spirit?

"You're not serious, are you, Jim? I mean, to be consistent, if that verse is to be taken that way, then Paul is also saying that prophecies are going to fail—so much for Hal Lindsey's best sellers. Or are these prophecies merely the preachifying kind. I'd have to know the Greek to say whether Paul means predictions when he says prophecies, I guess."

Martin looked impatiently at Jim; Jim looked sheepishly back. Martin heavily sighed and looked bemusedly at Cal. Cal looked at the text. "I'm just trying to find the scriptural basis for the orthodox position against speaking in tongues. I honestly do not see it."

"Well, of course not, because it pleases you not to," Martin said. "It doesn't matter to you one way or the other. I'll tell you where to look, anyway: at chapters twelve, thirteen, and fourteen as a single coherent text. As you no doubt realize, it was not Paul who divided the text into chapters and verses."

"In the verse you just read I would not take *whether there be tongues, they shall cease* to be a divine injunction against speaking in tongues, any more than one should take an isolated verse from chapter fourteen to mean that Paul is totally in favor of speaking in tongues. Look at the verse you just read in the total context and you might begin to perceive the beautiful subtlety of the argument."

Cal bowed his head to read and after a moment looked up, glanced at Jim, and huffingly chuckled. "I give up. Why don't you just show it to me."

"Well," Martin said, haughtily glancing away. "Paul is urging the Church at Corinth to abandon practices taken over from pagan and gnostic cults, practices that were an impediment to spiritual maturity. Jim is correct: Paul was speaking as to children here—adolescent children, perhaps. Paul does not issue an outright injunction against speaking in tongues. That's evident, as you've shown. Wisely, he did not alienate his flock over the issue.

"But you have to blind yourself to the implicit meaning of the three chapters as a whole not to see that Paul considers speaking in tongues and sign gifts to be childish things, things to be done away with in favor of cultivating faith, hope, and charity. And in explicit direct contrast to speaking in tongues, Paul exalts prophesying, which he defines in verse three of chapter fourteen as speaking for the purpose of bringing edification, exhortation, and comfort to men...and women."

And children, Cal thought, diverting the impulse to object that the verse Martin just cited didn't define prophesying, it merely listed advantages over speaking in tongues for public worship. What Greek word did Paul use that King James's scholars translated *prophesieth*? What was the etymology and usage history of that word? How much of orthodox Christian doctrine relied on readings of texts whose ambiguities had been erased by biased and insufficiently knowledgeable translators and made unthinkable by ecclesiastical traditions?

Surprised by Cal's appearance of respectful attentiveness, Martin continued, after almost shrugging.

"And we haven't mentioned chapter twelve. I can't imagine how Lewten manages to translate the Greek to have it say that every believer can exercise each of the spiritual gifts. The central metaphor contradicts such a notion. You ought to be impressed by that, honors literature student that you are. *For as the body is one and hath many members, and all the members of that one body...* And look at the ending of that verse: *Are all apostles? are all prophets? are all workers of miracles?*"

Cal bowed his head to read verse twenty-nine. "You forgot teachers," he said.

"Read the next verse," Martin replied.

Cal pushed up his lips. He read: "*Have all the gifts of healing? do all speak with tongues? do all interpret?*"

"There you are," Martin said, "the separation of the one who speaks in tongues and the one who's supposed to interpret, just as, earlier, the division of gifts, the very last two in the list being: *to another divers kinds of tongues; to another the interpretation of tongues.* What could be clearer than that?"

"Well," Cal said, "I should have brought Lewten's book. He goes through the key terms in Greek and shows how this translation is all wrong."

Martin's dimples punctuated a look of exasperated resigna-
tion. His eyes focused suddenly past Cal. "I believe the carolers
have arrived."

Jim jumped up and looked. "That's them all right. I'll let
them know downstairs." He scurried away, tugging at his
sweater as he straightened his back.

To one side of the Christmas tree, through the ersatz snow
on the picture window, Cal saw candles and parts of faces.
The church's carolers always began their roving a cappella
concert at their pastor's house, referred to as "the manse," an
old-fashioned term that had always amused Cal because to him
it suggested a Scottish lord's country estate.

Looking at the Bible on Cal's lap, Martin said, "Would you
mind putting that back where you got it, please?"

"Okay," Cal said, pricked by the tone meant to put him in
his place. "It sure is a nice book," he said, standing up. "I wish
Jim had given me one."

"Well, if you don't like the book he did get you, I'd be happy
to trade. But don't tell him I said so."

Sitting at Martin's desk, Cal read the verses from the end of
First Corinthians fourteen, which he had saved as his trump
card and hadn't used: "If any man think himself to be a
prophet, or spiritual, let him acknowledge that the things
that I write unto you are the commandments of the Lord.
But if any man be ignorant, let him be ignorant. Wherefore,

brethren, covet to prophesy, and forbid not to speak with tongues." What could be clearer than that?

A line from "The Boxer" came to mind, one of his favorite lyrics by Paul Simon, sadly shrugging off the ineluctable fact that everyone only hears what they want to hear. Philip Lewten did it, too; most glaringly in explaining away the male chauvinism in First Corinthians 14:34—*Let your women keep silence in the churches; for it is not permitted unto them to speak, but they are commanded to be under obedience, as also saith the law.*

What chutzpah! Paul citing the Jewish law to back up a misogynist commandment to those he said were not under the law anymore. Lewten claimed the *your women* meant the wives of the prophets and the Greek word for *speak* there was closer to *gab*; so the best translation would be something like *Prophets, don't let your wives gab during the worship service. It takes attention away from what the Spirit is saying through you.*

Cal looked over his shoulder at the shelf of Bibles but resisted the urge to check the verse in The New English Bible—whose translation he had previously considered the most likely to be the best of all possible words. Now he felt that he'd never be satisfied with any translation but his own. Fleetingly, he envied Rachel's linguistic ambitions.

He could hear the carolers singing now: *O, come all ye faithful, joyful and triumphant...*

He propped his elbows on the desk and put his hands over his ears; shutting his eyes, he peered deep into his mute pre-thought zone and out popped a question that had flashed to mind during his father's impromptu lecture. Why didn't TLF call it *agapé* like everyone else? No wonder he hadn't recognized it last night, when Mark said *agapao* shouldn't be translated *charity* or plain old *love*. Of course not: It was a special divine love that only believers who spoke in tongues could experience. Talk about childish things.

He opened his eyes and saw the door opening. Priscilla, looking demurely mischievous, stuck her face in.

"Go away, I'm praying," he said, without uncovering his ears. He dropped his hands and sat up.

"I've been sent to tell you that you can come down off your high horse now," she said.

He snorted.

"Mom called Rachel," she said, stepping timidly into the room.

He glanced at the phone. "What? Just now?"

"While you machos were having your little ego contest. Jim came down while she was talking, but I shooed him away. You men are terrible about handling situations like this."

"I couldn't agree more," Cal said. "I think we'd have a much more reasonable Bible if God had inspired women to write it."

She flashed a smirk. "Mom set it up that she's going to meet Rachel and talk to her by herself. Somebody has to pick Rachel up Thursday morning, real early—like around six o'clock?"

"Somebody. Meaning me."

"Yeah, well, that's what Rachel wanted."

"Pick her up at the mansion in Lake Forest?"

"Yes. When they come out of the gate, Rachel will get out of the van."

"Do they know that, the group?"

"Oh, yeah. It's just that, they don't want to have to give her a ride anywhere."

"Well. I'll do it. Which car do I get to take?"

"Mom will give you all the details. She called a friend in Kenilworth. You're supposed to take Rachel to her house. Mom's got it all worked out. She'll explain... So why don't you come downstairs now? We want to open a few presents as soon as the carolers leave."

"All right. I thought you guys opened presents in the morning."

"We decided to let the girls open one each, so they'll go to bed. Also, since, that's the way we always did it."

"Remember how we bragged about getting to open all our presents on Christmas eve?" Cal asked. "So we could wake up Christmas morning with the world's Christmas out of our system, and be all set to act like we couldn't care less about the presents displayed under the tree for all the visitors to admire."

Priscilla put on a pitying look. "They're only human, Cal. Being a parent is no picnic, believe me. You really find out about yourself when you have children. Mom and Dad made mistakes, but a lot of them were just because of how they were brought up, and what most people thought about raising kids, back then. They've grown a lot the past few years. They wouldn't do some things the same way today."

He'd leaned into a corner of the chair, his elbow on the armrest. "Apparently," he said, and put his hand to his beard, pulling at it. "They sure seem a lot nicer as grandparents."

Priscilla moved a few steps closer, looking at the Bible open on the desk.

"How come you read that so much, if you hate it?"

"I don't hate it," he said. "I love it."

"You really are a sophist. If I'd said you must really love it, you'd have said you hate it."

"That's right," he said, flashing a small smile as he looked away. "You can read me like a B-I-B-L-E."

He glimpsed the instant in her eyes when she assented to the Holy Spirit's prompting. She bowed her head. "I'm no psychologist, but I took enough courses in it to know that you really want to be a Christian, Cal—or you wouldn't be so obsessed with the Bible the way you are."

He gulped. She continued in that special soft voice of intimate pleading.

"I know, you've got a lot of anger in you, because of the way Mom and Dad were so strict, and cold and everything, but...we were loved, Cal. And we knew it.

"You need to forgive them for teaching you that the truth of the Bible is contrary to human reason and only for a select few people to really understand. I think that's what's keeping you from rededicating your life to Christ, that you haven't been able to forgive them. And me, too, I guess."

He could not speak. He swiveled the chair away, blinking furiously. It seemed absurd to hide it; but it was too pathetic to face. He turned the chair all the way around.

"Cal, I want you to know that I love you. No matter what happens, you're my brother, and I love you. I'm sorry that I didn't act very loving when we were growing up. I'm carrying a load of guilt over that. I need your forgiveness, Cal. Do you think that you can forgive me?"

He felt a burning stab of heartburn rise from his solar plexus and swallowed hard to provoke a muffled burp.

"Please, Cal. I'm not asking for some ha-ha happy impossible change, or anything. I just want us to be more loving with each other. I forgive you, Cal, for all the times you hurt me, or wanted to hurt me, even—just out of sheer habit really, without being conscious of it. I truly do forgive you, but that's not enough for us to improve our relationship. I need you to forgive me."

"Why?"

"Why?"

"Yes. Why do you need me to forgive you?"

"Because we can't begin to be really loving until we forgive each other for all the hurts we gave each other, that we're still carrying with us, deep inside, in our unconscious minds. And we need to be able to forgive ourselves, which we can't do, completely, until the ones we feel guilty about having wronged have forgiven us."

"You treated me about normal, for an older sister," he said, feeling steadier, having intuitively found a handle. She was following instructions; it must be more pop psychology from The Institute for Modern Biblical Living. He swiveled around. His glance recoiled from her look of pitying beggary.

"I should have been more loving," she said. "You should have too."

He found himself looking at the Bible. "Agreed," he said. "Kiss me."

"What?"

"Kiss me. Greet your brother with a holy kiss for once in your life."

"All right. If you'll say you forgive me...and really try to."

"Priscilla, I hereby forgive you."

He didn't change his pose of relaxed hauteur; she almost asked him to confirm that he was serious. But her lips relaxed. She lifted her chin and moved swiftly around the desk. She pecked his reflexively lifted cheek with such precise alacrity the unprecedented moment was condensed for him to an infusion of perfume and the sudden pounding of his heart.

"Well," Sarah effusively sighed, vigorously rubbing her hands as she came up from the front hallway. Her lightly freckled face was red from the cold and attractively wrinkled by happiness. She bowed to Ruthie, who looked up gape-mouthed. Sarah took her chubby cheeks between her hands and gave her a loud smacking kiss on the forehead.

"Grandma's hands are co-ol-OLD, aren't they, sweetie?"

"Where's Daddy and Grampa?" grumpy Naomi asked. She was kneeling beside the largest of her presents.

"They'll be right here," Grandma fairly sang. She sat down on the sofa at the end near the girls.

"So, Cal," she said. "Priscilla talked with you? Would you do that for us, be our chauffeur for a day?"

"Sure. I pick her up when they come out in the van Thursday morning. Mark and the group definitely know that Rachel's going to be getting out and going with me, right?"

Sarah looked hesitant, as though checking with herself. "Yes, there's no problem. You were right to that extent—she's not a prisoner. I suggested that we have our talk at the house of some friends, former parishioners who moved to Kenilworth several years ago, Edith and Harry Schultz? Do you remember them?"

He didn't, until she'd fleshed them out with description. Several minutes later, Jim and Martin made a commotion coming in the back door to the kitchen. They'd gone to the church to fetch a gift. The sight of it put Sarah near to ecstatic utterance.

"Oh, my goodness, Marty! Wait, put it right here on the counter."

It was a microwave oven. The children acted very grown up about the postponement of their delight, while the adults became child-like over the miraculous appliance. Cal poured himself some brandy and repeated a story, probably apocryphal, about a woman who had tried to dry off her poodle by putting it in her new microwave oven for a few minutes. The pooch exploded.

So did Cal's audience, chiding him from their midst. He retreated to the rocking chair; smoked and sipped brandy and gazed at the fire. Verily he did become teary-eyed with sardonic awe when he heard his mother cheerfully reading aloud from the owner's manual.

CHAPTER SEVEN

Bring Hither the Fatted Calf

LATER THAT EVENING, AFTER performing at a hospital, three nursing homes, and a reformatory, the carolers of the Orthodox Presbyterian Church of Elmore returned to the manse for refreshments and a gabfest. Cal, fleeing the spirit of Christmas present, ducked out the front door and slunk around the garage. As he came to the back corner, the general memory of a multitude of like moments flashed, lit by a solitary streetlamp at the edge of the church parking lot. It looked forlorn, as though missing all the moths of summer nights.

Strolling over ground he had trod innumerable times behind a lawn mower, he experienced an absurd gush of nostalgic affection for the grass. His eyes went from the porch at the back door of the church's low office-and-classroom wing to the ground-level spotlights along the sanctuary. He focused on the nearest basement window; in the dim fringe of a spotlight's aura, he made out the top of a cement wall. Each basement window had a sunken niche; they made perfect foxholes.

What year was it that the TV show *Combat* premiered? He was in—what? Going into fifth grade, he thought. He remembered his devotion to Vic Morrow, whose part he had always claimed when his buddies from Sunday School came around with their Army surplus stuff and plastic guns. His prized weapon had been a Tommy gun.

Before entering the shadow of the sanctuary, he lifted his eyes to the watchtower-like steeple, which was surmounted by a tall, illuminated, sword-like cross. The congregation's favorite hymn was Martin Luther's "A Mighty Fortress Is Our God."

He sat down on the concrete stoop, his special late-night roost. The porch was not visible from the three roads that made an island of the odd lot the church and manse occupied. He assured himself that anyone who might notice him from a window on the backside of the house would assume he was smoking a cigarette.

He sucked in the sweetly acrid smoke that Rastafarians swear is the very air of heaven. He coughed as he exhaled and watched through a teary blur the smoke hurried away by the breeze, whose chill he only then noticed. Shivering, he took another toke. Barely able to hold it in against the scratchy stinging of his throat, he peered skyward again. He spotted a moving point of light, which disappeared while he was exhaling, swallowed up by the overcast. Dreamily nudged by the wisenheimer within, he gave the incorrigible imp a voice, softly singing to the tune of a favorite Christmas carol:

> O, great big world of Bed-ed-lam,
> How paranoid you are.
> Above thy deep, nightmarish sleep,
> Spy satellites drift by.

Noting how floaty he felt, he questioned whether he ought to smoke the whole joint. He got a rush of mirth. Providence had bestowed upon him an absurd stroke of luck. To show appreciation, His servant Cal should get really ripped.

He lapsed into stuporous reverie; tardily, he remembered to toke. He thought a *Gracias* to the Holy Spirit for having approved, ex post facto, the foolishly extravagant escapism that had depleted his savings.

Once the microwave oven had been tested, boiling a cup of water in record time, the family sat down in the living room. Naomi and Ruth had selected a gift for each of the adults to open. Sarah cheerfully urged that Cal save the one that Naomi started to lift for him—obviously a large book. Martin had bounded down the stairs waving an envelope and gave it to Naomi, for Cal. "This is a present?" she asked, crinkling her nose like Shirley Temple.

A stab of heartburn countered the warm tickle of the next toke's afterglow. Cal licked the thumb and forefinger of his left hand then used them to tamp the joint's glowing tip till the ember came loose. Feeling swoony above a soft drunken smile, he twisted the singed end and slipped the half-smoked joint back into his lighter's secret compartment.

A veritable Christmas miracle: The Holy Spirit had induced Martin Wideman to write three digits to the left of a decimal point on a gift check not going to some missionary.

He imagined Martin mulling over the distinction between spirit and soul asserted as biblical fact by Hal Lindsey. Suddenly the Holy Spirit says, "By the way, you ought to give Cal some money. It is Christmas after all." The Rev jots a note in the margin of the legal pad on which he's keeping track of the subtle errors in Lindsey's book. And any good points, of course. The note he jots says, "Cal—$?". What he thinks when he sits back is: "Ask Sarah." The next time he's with her, he says, "Cal's going to be needing money more than anything else when he gets back. What do you think would be a suitable amount for a gift?"

"Martin, I asked you to think about that *last week*."

The signature on the check was Martin's, but the amount was clearly Sarah's largesse. Martin often came off as stingy from simple inexperience as a spender; by contrast, Sarah seemed generous to a fault when it came to her children—and now her grandchildren. When Cal was on their dole, he had always asked for less than Sarah had expected he would need. And when they last gave him a big check, at graduation, he'd politely protested that it must be the last gift of money he took from them.

This time he was mortified to be so instantly greedy and couldn't look them in the eyes. "Wow. What's all this for? I mean, it's way too much, for a gift."

"Oh, don't give us that song and dance again, please," Sarah said. "If it'll make you happy, we'll promise never to give you another penny. But you will need more than you imagine just to buy yourself a decent wardrobe for interviews. You've been living on a student's budget for so long, you don't realize how much things cost nowadays."

He let the *non sequitur* pass.

"There's an addendum to the gift, on the stationery," Martin said.

Dumbly, he lifted the sheet of fancy typing paper which had been folded around the check; beneath his father's letterhead were typed the names and business titles, business addresses, and phone numbers of three members of his father's congregation: the vice-president of an advertising agency; the general manager of a commercial real estate company; and a senior partner in a four-name law firm.

"I want you to know," Martin said, "that I did not solicit those for you. I know you would have mixed feelings about using family connections to land a job, but no one's guaranteeing they'll offer you one. They are willing to talk with you, to ascertain, mutually, if some opening they have would be a position you might really be interested in and could apply yourself to."

Hearing Martin's defensive embarrassment, Cal was able to raise a somberly respectful look.

"It was Clyde Milner's idea," Martin added. "He spoke with the other two. They didn't need persuading. They all think very highly of you. They are certainly not trying to do me a favor. Don't feel obligated if you're not really interested in at least hearing what opportunities they might have to offer. They'd be happy for you to use them as references, in any case."

Cal had professed humble gratitude, his mind undivided, his feelings sincere, until he went so far as to suggest that he might be interested in the law firm job. Jim eagerly encouraged that choice: They'd always said he'd make a great lawyer. He could get an introduction to the world of lawyering and earn a decent wage while deciding whether to apply to law school or...graduate school, or whatever.

He gulped air and let out a raucous belch, which brought up a throat-stinging perfusion tasting strongly of nutmeg and brandy. He blamed himself for the heartburn momentarily; the self-directed animus somehow diverted his thoughts toward his mother. He'd overheard Sarah chatting with a woman who'd asked about Rachel: "Oh, she's busy with some group that's putting on a charity banquet tomorrow, on the South Side somewhere."

"How brave. A group from Covenant Christian?"

"They're a Bible study group, mostly young people... How is your father getting along? I meant to ask you last Sunday."

His Mother Hidden in Mystery: Besides Martin, Rachel was the only person in the world, he supposed, who had a loving feel for Sarah McAdam's most intimate self. In truth, he thought Rachel had a better feel for it than Martin.

He burped and stood up on the top step. He peered through the dark at the backside of the manse. The empty view through the brightly illuminated kitchen window made him think of a painting by Edward Hopper. He sighed and descended to the sidewalk. He felt strangely conscious of walking as a process going on between his legs and the dimly lit cement path.

She'll just have to get used to the idea. What's one more bit of cognitive dissonance in the scheme of a Calvinist's psyche? She's losing her baby girl to some heretic who must have cast a spell on her. What else could explain it? Drugs?

Why the rush to judgment? Why not resort to their usual "pray and wait on the Lord"? Rachel will get disillusioned eventually, with Mark or the group...the usual personality politics. She'll realize soon enough that the ego tripping just becomes more passive-aggressive. And woe be unto her if she takes issue with something Mark feels strongly about.

Cult Truth Squad. Jesus. If speaking in tongues is learned behavior, by God, it's just as much a mind-control technique for the World Assemblies of God as it is for TLF.

Ah, but WAGs believe in the Trinity. Their minds are controlled in the Truth, or close enough so it's okay, at least on that doctrine.

The rituals of faith, you hypocrites. Mindlessly reading the Bible is a mind-control technique.

I love my Bible, Pris. I hate YOURS. And you hate Lewten's. My Bible says—. Fuck. This is what doesn't make sense. If Rachel's professing heresy and refuses correction it means she was never really called by the Spirit, so of course her mind is controlled, according to Calvinism. Just like mine, or any sinner's. So what gives, Dad?

"What if God, willing to show his wrath, and to make his power known, endured with much long-suffering the vessels of wrath fitted to destruction... That he might make known the riches of his glory on the vessels of mercy, which he had afore prepared unto glory... Even us, whom he hath called, not of the Jews only, but also of the Gentiles."

Right THERE, Jim. He's talking about the Elect, Jews AND Gentiles, not one versus the other.

"Therefore hath he mercy on whom he will have mercy, and whom he will he hardeneth."

And I bet the Scofield doesn't cross-reference that verse to Ephesians 2:8. The FAITH that saves you is the GIFT of God, by GRACE— not of your will in any way, including really and truly surrendering your will, as you say.

And let us not forget the Gospel of John chapter one, verses twelve and thirteen. "But as many as received him, to them gave he power to become the sons of God," but keep reading: "Who were born NOT of blood nor of THE WILL OF THE FLESH nor OF THE WILL OF MAN...but of God."

Christ, that clinches it right there. How do they worm their way out of that one?

Hmmm... Yeah. Same way: You realize your will is impotent to save you so you surrender and then by the will of God you are born again. But then your WILL is involved: The giving up is something you did to get the grace.

Billy Graham ain't telling it like it is, say Luther and Calvin. It's absurd, and in more ways than that God would love a worthless sinful little shit like you.

What say you, Saint Paul? "Thou wilt say then unto me, Why doth he yet find fault? For who hath resisted his will? Nay but, O man, who art thou that repliest against God? Shall the thing formed say to him that formed it, Why hast thou made me thus? Hath not the potter power over the clay, of the same lump, to make one vessel unto honor, and another unto dishonor?"

There it is, all you self-righteous Bible-quoters. You believe the Bible is the literal inerrant TRUTH, do you? Fine, then don't forget to quote that bit of it—

GOD MADE SOME VESSELS UNTO HONOR AND SOME HE MADE SHITPOTS.

So fall down and kiss Jehovah's ass. And when you're feeling sorry for all of us in hell, just remember: There you would be also but for the grace of God—and not because of anything you did or didn't do.

You can cry your eyes out, Mom. God hath promised to wipe away every tear.

Cal stood before the 7-Eleven on Joliet Road, looking at the hand-scrawled sign in the door:

Closing 7pm 24th
Regular Hours 26th
MERRY CHRISTMAS!

"Thank you, Jesus," he muttered. Looking around, he fixed on the tall transparent closet lit up at the corner of the little parking lot. He considered phoning Josh—to tell him he'd be coming by tomorrow, and why.

The mere thought was consolation enough; he started to walk back the way he'd come—to the house that hadn't felt like it was truly his home for quite some time.

Ephesians 3 something: "I bow my knees unto God...that he might give you, grant you, something...to be strengthened by his Spirit in the inner man..." Close, but no cigar. Okay, yeah: "That

Christ may dwell in your hearts by faith; that ye, being rooted and grounded in love..."Hmmm. Maybe not in the original but the translation's definitely redundant. How about just "rooted," Paul? "...and to know the love of Christ, which passeth knowledge, that ye might be filled with all the fullness of God."

Holy shit, Batman, it must be gnosis. *Right: putting down the Gnostics. The love of Christ beats their* gnosis.

But is the word for "love" there agapao? *Be nifty to know the Greek, all right. Also could be a different word for "to know" to distinguish knowledge of the love of God from* gnosis. *Or: What if it's "gnosis of the love of God?" Might support Lewten on* agapao.

Details, details. Anal retentive bookworms looking for the fullness of God in semantic distinctions. Even if Lewten's right, he's wrong. Meaning Paul's wrong. HE'S the one who started all this. The letter killeth, huh. Right. Then why'd you write so much? Why didn't you do like John: "Keep the faith, brothers and sisters. I'll be coming to see you soon. In the meantime, love one another." John could've sent his epistles by pigeon...or dove.

Love makes a pisspoor theologian. Love doesn't make all these diddling distinctions. Love just loves. And if it says it does and doesn't, any fool can see. You don't need gnosis *to know the love of Christ. Just a little imagination and an open heart, to see the children we all used to be. The innocence that experience always crucifies.*

As he drew near the Joliet Road intersection with Spencer Boulevard, the main entrance to Elmore Estates, he heard voices call out, "Merry Christmas!" and "Good night!" over the racing idle of a car's cold engine. Spencer bordered the church's property on the parking lot side. The manse faced Elmhurst Drive, formerly a two-lane blacktop meandering through woods and cornfields; now it crossed Spencer at one of the three corners of the church's almost fan-shaped lot and snaked through the countrified suburb. Cal went around to the front door to avoid passing people cutting across the back-yard to their cars.

Three men, none of whom he recognized, stood in front of the fireplace listening to Jim. Cal gave a nod and smiled when one of the men, and then Jim, glanced. Jim didn't pause; Cal caught: "The televised crusades are fine, they'll always be needed, but with cable TV—just think of it..."

He hurried up the stairs and went straight to the hall bath-room, sighing relief to find it unoccupied. The medicine cab-inet was chock-full of stuff but the only remedy for heartburn was an ancient-looking bottle of milk of magnesia.

He went to his parents' bedroom. The door was slightly ajar. He knocked softly, waited a second, and breezed in. The beds were piled with coats, the men's on his father's bed, the women's on his mother's. He snorted, wondering how such a tradition had come about and whether it might be traced to some primitive Teutonic ritual.

In the medicine cabinet of their bathroom he found another icky-blue bottle of the same stuff. It was *New! Mint Flavored!* He braced himself and took a swig. The mint was a distraction from the awful chalkiness. He wiped the residue from his lips, hating the stuff as much as ever—but also grateful to have it.

Slurping water from his hand, he smelled marijuana on his fingers. He washed his hands vigorously with the bar of highly perfumed soap.

While still in the hallway, he heard Priscilla make a joking remark; the group laughed. He hardly glanced at them as he came down the stairs. He swung left and breezed into the kitchen. His mother was standing with another woman in front of the microwave oven. The woman asked, "Are you going to cook your turkey in it?" Sarah said, "Oh, no, I wouldn't dare experiment on that." From the corner of his eye he saw her glance his way.

He emptied the dryer and started folding clothes, thinking about the project described by a Peace Corps volunteer he'd met in Oaxaca, a guy named Alan with a BS in agricultural engineering from Virginia Tech. Alan had worked in Guatemala in a small village two hours by jeep or a day by burro from the nearest paved road. He spent two years supervising the installation of a perpetual protein contraption: rabbits in cages set over fishponds; the rabbits ate choice leaves gathered from the surrounding jungle and the fish ate choice rabbit shit; both multiplied and replenished the village's stewpots.

That was the theory anyway. Alan had run into one problem after another, from mysterious rabbit diseases to excess organic matter in the pond. He was confident, though, that the system could be fine-tuned and implemented all over Latin America. He was going to work on it for his master's degree—at an ag school in Puerto Rico near some great surfing beaches.

What could a technically ignorant BA in English do in the Peace Corps, Cal had inquired.

Oh, lots of things, Alan assured him. Teach English as a Second Language, translate stuff. No, really, lots of things. You could just try your luck and submit an application, see what happens, or you could research Peace Corps projects in particular countries, contact the embassy about a project that interests you. If you're already fluent in the local language, that in itself could be your primary qualification.

Ever since talking to Alan, Cal had been drawn to the idea of joining the Peace Corps. The hesitation that weighed most heavily in his mind was the idea that to be accepted he'd have to express more altruistic idealism than he could sincerely muster. Mainly he just wanted to live a more primitive life without having to join a group of rugged collectivists with embarrassingly weird beliefs, one of the "new age" groups growing organic vegetables on some ramshackle farm, part of what Cal thought of as a back-to-the-land hippie diaspora.

Communes had intrigued him at one time—in the abstract. Cal had often told Josh that if he'd been born Jewish American, he'd have gone off to Israel and joined a kibbutz—despite his sympathy for the Palestinians. And now he could see himself living in an indigenous village in Central America, the resident outsider, a missionary from the First World carrying out his assignment to instruct and guide the natives in some simple practical community project.

"Cal, are you down here?" Martin called.

Cal startled, then hurriedly folded another T-shirt as he answered: "Folding clothes, Dad."

Martin stepped into the laundry room.

"Are you about done? We could use some help upstairs. They bought tricycles for the girls, and Jim's afraid it'll take him all night to put them together. And you know how good I am at that sort of thing."

"I'm, kind of worn out, actually..."

"Jim is going to open a bottle of French champagne that he brought back from Switzerland."

"Champagne?"

"His visit to *L'Abri* liberalized his views apparently. He still considers hard liquor inexpedient, but beer and wine are all right in moderation—so long as his denomination doesn't find out. He had some wine the other night at dinner."

"Oh, yeah, the Cold Duck. Jim actually drank some?"

"A very little bit."

"For the sake of his stomach, huh?"

Martin smiled. "Please don't tease him, Cal."

The women were posed on the sofa in attitudes of prim expectation. Jim was standing on the other side of the coffee table, untwisting the cage on the cork. Grimacing, he glanced up when Cal and Martin came down the stairs. "Here goes," he said, turning toward the fireplace.

It didn't go.

"Push it with your thumbs," Martin advised.

Jim made a wryly fearful face at the loaded bottle. "You're such an expert, you do it."

"Cal, why don't do the honors," Martin said.

Modestly, Cal took over. The cork was stuck good, and when it finally popped, it made him jump. Expecting the bubbly to gush out the way it always did in movies, he needlessly jerked the bottle so it would be over the coffee table, and in so doing, spilled some.

"I'll get something," Priscilla said, and hurried off to the kitchen. Cal began to fill the tulip glasses. "Hey, where are the champagne flutes?" he asked.

"These are now *de rigueur*," Martin said, glancing at Jim. "It's the new standard for connoisseurs—so I've been told."

"That's plenty for me," Jim said.

Martin offered an old Scottish toast: "To sum up all, be merry, I advise. And as we're merry, may we still be wise."

As he quaffed, Cal marveled at the subdued cheerfulness of the group's mood. He was alone in refilling his glass, though, and only filled it half way.

"How would you like to join Santa's workshop?" Jim asked. "Martin can read the instructions while you and I ignore him and figure it out for ourselves."

The written instructions were comically illiterate and didn't seem helpful, so Martin joined Jim and Cal in assembling the plastic tricycles with low seats and large front wheels. As necessary, they referred to colorful photographic depictions on the boxes and crude black-and-white schematics in the instructions. Sarah and Priscilla looked on, chatting about good old-fashioned metal tricycles, the plastic awfulness of toys today, and the shameful ploys of TV advertisements aimed at little children.

When the task was done, the men stood to admire their handiwork: two spiffy modern versions of kids' trikes. The boys next door had them, Priscilla said. All the kids wanted them. Ruthie's was smaller than Naomi's; there was discussion over how long it would take her to get the hang of pedaling. Cal wandered over to the tree, preparing to say good night. His eyes fell to the large gift-wrapped book from Jim and Priscilla.

"Jesus," he muttered, lifting it, laughing at how heavy it was; seeing Jim's blush, he lied and said, "I'm sorry; it slipped out."

Sarah was in the kitchen and didn't hear; Martin, as usual, played deaf. Pris thought it was funny; too much champagne, Cal thought. Jim mimed a shushing reprimand at her.

"What's so funny?" Cal asked.

Priscilla went into a giggling fit. Cal started to laugh, saying, "Come on, what's the joke."

"You'll find out tomorrow," Jim said.

"Oh," Cal said, disappointedly. "I get it: another book about the man from Nazareth."

Jim made a disgruntled face at Pris, then turned with mock humility to Cal. "Can you forgive us?"

"That depends," Cal said. He tore the wrapping off. "Wow. What a gorgeous book. And I don't even have a coffee table to put it on. Thanks, guys."

It was excellent champagne. It did not mix well, however, with mint-flavored milk of magnesia. He lay awake, burping and wallowing in bitter ironic disgust.

Finally, he propped himself on an elbow and turned on the lamp. The beautiful book was on the night table: *Jesus Rediscovered* by Malcolm Muggeridge. The cover of the jacket showed a gorgeous Byzantine mosaic Christ—a graven image with real class. It made Cal's heart ache to look upon the nobly compassionate but stoically aloof countenance.

Muggeridge was a conservative British pundit specializing in trenchant satirical commentary on popular culture and the arts. Cal had always hated to read his columns—and rarely passed one by. *Jesus Rediscovered* was not his latest book; Cal could remember having read reviews of it when he was a senior in high school. This new edition was deluxe: large, with many graphic embellishments—photographs, illustrations, and maps of the Holy Land. The text was the ubiquitous evangelical genre—personal testimony.

Muggeridge went to Israel to make a documentary on the New Testament for the BBC. He observed Christian pilgrims from all over the world often paying homage at shrines whose relics were fraudulent and whose locations were a matter of pious tradition discounted if not disproved by archeologists. The former Labor Party utopian, now Tory curmudgeon, wrote that he was awed by the faith whose power he saw in the faces of the pilgrims and whose beauty he heard in their conjoined voices singing hymns. He came to realize that the historicity of the shrines did not matter; faith made the shrines authentic to the believers.

Cal put his head back on the pillow and squeezed his eyes shut. He wanted to put the book down and go to sleep, but he was enthralled by this wickedly intelligent sophisticate's building up to a confession of faith with a tone of transcendental naiveté. He blinked to clear the blear and again read the passage in which Muggeridge said that he became mystically aware of the historicity of Jesus Christ, a man who was also God. He did not "become convinced"; he became aware, from one moment to the next, apparently. He felt Christ's presence; a certainty seized him; it was "almost magical."

Cal stared unfocused at the page, waiting for the shadowy welter within to throw up a response. Nothing: a dry heave of spiritless disdain. He sighed and closed the book, put it on the night table, turned out the lamp, and lay down, putting his hands under his head. It amazed and disgusted him: Jim and Pris really thought Muggeridge's book might do the trick. Why? What did they think he had in common with Muggeridge? Word smarts? Intellectual arrogance?

You believe God is love, but you want me to worry about everlasting damnation? It says right here in your excellent book, "Take no thought for the morrow." Also, by the way, please may I have some money? "Give to him that asketh of thee, and of him that would borrow of thee turn not away." And at the biblical rate of interest, how's that grab ya? Zero, baby.

One has to read the Sermon on the Mount in the context of the entire Bible... It's almost magical. Now you see it, now you don't.

I wish you all would take it half as literally as you say you do. You say that the Spirit of Christ in you gives you the love of Christ. And the best definition of that love is found, you say, in First Corinthians thirteen...

Hmmm... Paul doesn't say anything about love forgiving all things. Just "beareth all things" and "endureth..." Until the judgment day, by God. And then you sinners are gonna get your eternal comeuppance... I mean "everlasting," of course. How could I forget that distinction?

But Jesus said to forgive as many times as you are wronged, essentially. To love your enemies. That's the love of Christ, right? The Jesus of the Sermon on the Mount preaches unconditional love, but elsewhere says that God's mercy is conditional—you have to accept it, or be damned.

Calvinism makes more sense than that. God's mercy is totally unconditional. It's just a big fucking mystery why He decided to save only a few.

You're the one who's absurd, Jim. You say Jesus himself at the Final Judgment is going to condemn me to eternal torment in the Lake of Fire. Wouldn't that make him a hypocrite? He preaches infinite forgiveness but doesn't practice it himself?

Wait: He says that all things are given unto him by the Father, right? So what's to keep Him from forgiving everybody in the end? Maybe after a spell in purgatory, reliving their crimes from their victims' minds...

Ah, of course: He and the Father are one. The Trinity to the rescue again.

Jesus, Jim. Why do you want to be yourself forever and ever anyway? You really think heaven is like a parallel universe but without dying? And you're going to be you, eternally ecstatic, glorifying God, God in you, you in God. I see what you're after. Thank you, Jesus!

But which one? What a convention that would be: All the Jesuses that have ever been written or preached about...gathered in McCormick Place. A Jesus Christ convention. Featured debate: Jesus the original communist utopian versus Jesus the senior sales VP for enlightened capitalist enterprise. Do unto your customer as you would that...and rapid promotions will be yours, sayeth the Lord.

At intermission, a book fair: the 70,000 or so biographies of Jesus. And at the closing dinner, a keynote not to be missed, by Satan: "Does God Have a Sense of Humor?"

Do the Son and the Father ever get drunk with the Spirit and get to laughing so hard...?

No, no, not the God of the Bible. That's why His chosen people produce so many great comedians. Nowhere does the Lord God Jehovah laugh. And if J.C. did, it was left out, like his hard-ons. We can assume... Oh, sure, you can assume any fucking thing you want...except fucking and laughing.

I oughta freak 'em all out. Get my Zen Jesus down pat, memorize those verses from the Gospel of Thomas. It's the earliest of the Gospels, man! "When the inside is like the outside and the above is like the below..."

Too serious though. Too synoptic. Have to write my own Gospel. That hippie Jesus with the big mellow grin. Talks like George Carlin.

Hey, diggit, this is heaven, man.

If you can see it, you know, keep it to yourself.

Don't worry, man, you'll run into other freaks who know the secret. Right?

They might not know they know, is all. And don't you fuckin' tell 'em, whatever you do.

Jesus, man, don't go trying to pretend you love everybody. There are real shits out there.

Just mind your own mind. You dig? See what's in back of your eyes and you might find what you're looking for. Your face before you were born.

If you do, guard it and go your own way.

Frequent nude beaches.

And be kind to others, as unto your own secret child.

In Jesus' name, or Buddha's, or—what's yours?

"Ahhhhhh-ahhhh...mennnnn," he kind of sang aloud, and then let loose a long two-tone belch.

Chapter Eight

The Fool Shall Be Servant

SPORTING A SANTA CLAUS cap with a fluffy white ball on its flopping tip, Josh pulled down a rebound. Dribbling toward the street, he stopped and pulled the ball to his chest, scrunched down and squinted at the yellow Volkswagen Beetle that had pulled to the curb. Cal beeped the horn.

Josh's brother Elliot came up behind him and poked at the ball. Josh danced away, making the time-out sign. Elliot darted after him. Josh spun around, hurling the basketball toward the basket. It fell well short and rolled past the movable pole and backboard into the open garage.

Josh clambered into the passenger seat chattering about how cold it was. He unzipped a dark blue windbreaker to reveal a purple Northwestern sweatshirt. He took off his knit gloves and blew vigorously into his fists.

"I always thought you needed a fool's cap," Cal said.

"Like it? It's from my dad's rented Santy Claus suit. His synagogue did a charity thing, and it was his turn to be jolly Old Saint Nick."

"It's too fuckin' cold to play basketball," Cal said. "It's too fuckin' cold to be outside, period."

"That's *almost* what my mother said."

"Aren't you going to remark on my vehicle?"

"Nice vehicle you got here. Where'd you steal it?"

"Santy Claus gave it to me."

"You shittin' me, boy?"

"I shit you not."

"No shit?"

Cal pressed his lips together and watched Elliot striding back with the ball, glancing gloomily toward them, deep exhalations violently whipped away. "Must be ten degrees with wind chill."

"Your parents actually gave this to you? How many miles it got?" Josh leaned toward the steering wheel to read the odometer. "Eighty-four, almost eighty-five. Doesn't look that old."

"It's a '67. Seems to be in great shape. The guy who owned it was a fuddy-duddy engineer in my dad's church."

Elliot shouted for Josh to finish the game or forfeit.

"I'm ahead by a basket," Josh said. "Five more and I win. You can watch from the garage."

"Finish the game and then let's drive around for a little bit. I need to talk."

"Sounds serious," Josh said, looking out the window. Elliot disappeared into the garage.

"No, it's a big fucking joke. I'm seriously thinking about joining the Peace Corps."

Josh peered at him. "Uh-oh. Another attack of Schweitzer's Syndrome. Okay, don't panic. Sit tight, I'll get this over quick."

He lunged out the door and yelled, "Ell-eee-AAHHT. Get your skinny ass back here!"

As Josh hustled toward the garage, the ball came shooting out. He jumped aside, slapping it down; retrieved it and loped in for a layup. Elliot came diving out just in time to foul him on the arm.

Cal rolled down the window a crack. After lighting a cigarette, he pulled open the ashtray and merged a scoffing sigh with the first smoky exhalation in his new car. The ashtray looked virginal. Again, he felt unworthy of the gift and guilty for wanting to gloat about it.

He watched the game, concentrating on Elliot, who was Rachel's age, he thought. Elliot was about the same height as Josh but he was slender. His face was enough like Josh's that you might suppose them to be brothers if you saw them together, but you'd look closely and still not be sure. Elliot's head was a different shape—longer and thinner—and he didn't have Josh's bulging eyes.

Elliot played with morose caginess, dribbling back and forth across the driveway just in front of Josh, feinting toward the basket then abruptly backing away, sometimes whirling to take a quick jump shot just as Josh lunged at him. Josh invariably bullied his way to right underneath and took some kind of shot. More often than not he would be fouled, but he never complained and didn't retaliate—meaning only that he didn't need to, Cal knew.

Josh won on a hook shot from the edge of the driveway, a twenty-footer from a tough angle that swished the red, white, and blue net. He leaped and bounced on his toes, hurling his fist and otherwise hamming up the victory mania. He trotted over and hung his arm over Elliot's neck, reaching his other hand around to poke his ribs. He lifted Elliot's blue watch cap and spoke into his ear, then slapped him on the back and whirled away. He took a little skip-step and broke into a jog. Halfway to the street, he turned around and yelled as he backstepped, "Tell Mom I'll be back in an hour."

He looked embarrassed to be so happy when he settled into the seat.

"He hates to lose," he said.

Cal pushed the stick shift into first and looked over his shoulder. "Why not let him win then?"

"I do, most of the time. But I gotta win once in a while or he'll catch on."

"This clutch is tight," Cal said, launching them with only a slight jerk. "You think he hasn't figured it out by now?" he asked, covering pride and silly slight reflexive excitement. Shifting into second was easy.

"Probably," Josh said. "But he still prefers the thrill of victory to the smell of defeat." He looked askance suspiciously.

"That really stunk," Cal said. "Will you take off that hat so you will look a little less goofy."

"I don't look goofy. I look jolly."

"Pretty please?"

Josh pulled off the Santa cap and stuffed it into the big center pocket of his sweatshirt. With both hands he brushed at his hair and swept the curling recalcitrant strands back behind his ears.

"This isn't all that my generous parents bestowed upon me," Cal said. "I also got a cashier's check for five hundred bucks, which they suggested I'd need to get by while hunting down a decent job. And they supplied me with some easy targets. Three members of my dad's church have issued a standing invitation to talk to them about job opportunities. One's a senior partner in a law firm and another's an advertising VP. The third guy's a big shot in a company that develops shopping malls."

Josh glumly considered for a moment. "Take the advertising job. They'll probably let you keep your beard. And with my help you'll be Junior VP for Vapid and/or Idiotic Slogans in no time. Then you can give me a hefty annual retainer to be your idea man."

"Great plan, but—. I don't know, maybe I got addicted to escapism. That's what you're going to think, and I can't deny that's part of it. But there's more. As I said in my letters, I really dug the peasant way of life. It's not 'getting back to nature.' They never left. I loved their simplicity and their earthiness, their sense of humor. They really are a lot like hippies in the way they think, and do things. In their priorities."

Josh's O was upon his mouth. "Keep your eyes on the road," he complained.

"I don't have any altruistic illusions," Cal went on. "I wanna do it for very selfish reasons. I want to try living on the simplest most basic level, day to day, just getting by. Work directly connected to eating. I like that. Food directly connected to community; the center of it, the reason for it... They have a saying down there: After God, the stewpot."

Josh jutted his chin out as he nodded. "That's almost what I always say."

"That's why I said it."

Cal gave his full attention to watching the green light and the oncoming cars at an intersection with a divided four-lane road. He had to hurry to make the left turn on yellow and almost blew it, letting the clutch out too fast. When they were tooling along in the slow lane, headed for the interstate, he looked over.

Josh said, "*Yo no sé nada.*"

"But I know what you think."

Josh did a big disgruntled shrug.

"I'm sick of this country," Cal said. "I'm going to check out the Peace Corps, find out what it takes to join at least and what kind of assignment I might be able to get. If it doesn't seem like such a good idea after that... I don't know. On the way over today I was thinking about driving my freedom machine here down to the Yucatán. I could get a job down there easy, maybe in one of the new resort hotels. There are half a dozen cities in Mexico I wouldn't mind living in for a while."

"Can you do that?" Josh asked. "Just drive your car across the border?"

"With a permit. You get it with your tourist card, when you get to the border."

"Can a tourist legally get a job?"

"No. But I can look for one. You find a company that'll hire you and they take care of the legal stuff, one way or another. You're supposed to get working papers, just like here. If you run into hassles getting them, though, you just pay a bribe or two. The bribes are usually a bargain, all things considered. And I could probably get along without working papers. In the touristy cities for sure: There's all kinds of marginal stuff you can do. Pay the bribes if you get caught. I'd save my money, and move on when I got tired of a place. Eventually, I'd like to take a big trip down through Central America, and bum around in South America for a while."

"Just don't go swimming in the Amazon," Josh said.

"Right. Piranhas."

"Nothing those piranhas like better than fresh gringo."

"Yeah, yeah."

They were silent for a while. Cal said: "I'm gonna turn around. I guess I've said what I needed to say."

"Well, I haven't," Josh said. "Obviously, I can't be impartial about this, because I would prefer that you stick around. In fact, I was counting on it. You're the only friend I have who tries to steal my puns."

After a tight few seconds, Cal said, "But think of all the good letters you'd get."

"I can steal all the good letters I want at work."

Cal wanted like hell to casually state what Josh already knew; he couldn't bring himself to. He was stuck on the thought that while he was Josh's closest friend, he wasn't his only good friend; whereas Cal had no others. "I don't really know what

I'm gonna do," he said. "Maybe it's just the culture shock. Also: I can't take being around my family anymore. Shit, I haven't even told you about the thing with my sister."

"That's what I thought this was going to be about."

"Nah, that worked out okay. The two sides have agreed to hold talks."

"Blessed are the peacemakers," Josh said.

"For they shall get it from both sides," Cal rejoined.

"I was referring to the Colt revolver known by that name in the Old West."

Cal withheld so much as a smile, though affection welled up as his concern eased that Josh's feelings were hurt. He gave him a brief account of the previous night's anticlimactic adventure, culminating with a description of Sarah's peace initiative. Josh expressed relief and said he hoped it would all work out. Cal agreed and found he had nothing more to say. They rode along in silence. The streetscape of service sector monotony—gas stations and fast-food joints, small shops and crammed car lots—seemed poignantly bleak. It was almost dark enough for headlights; there wasn't much traffic.

They said nothing more until they were stopped at the curb in front of the Levinson house. Josh glanced at the ignition and back to Cal. "Aren't you coming in?"

"I don't think I can handle the warmth and good cheer," Cal said.

"Don't forget the delicious leftovers, big new color TV, and sayre-VAY-za."

"Really: I'm just not up to it."

"Why don't we go to a gen-u-wine Mexican restaurant in Mextown sometime?" Josh asked.

"Okay by me," Cal said.

"You sure you don't want to come in? What's your hurry?"

"I need to be alone."

"We have three bathrooms."

"Very funny."

"How you been in that department, by the way?"

"If you must know, I'm back to normal."

Using his Maxwell Smart voice, Josh said: "AhHA. So the secret meaning to life is found by a simple process of elimination. In fact, it *is* the process of elimination."

Cal sighed and looked up and away. "When you going back to work?" he asked.

"Not till Monday. Feel free to use the bed until Sunday night. Just in case, you know, your streak of luck continues."

"Yeah, right. I'm used to the sofa now anyway. Make excuses for me to your mother. I'm sorry, about...being so antisocial."

"No, you're not. If you want, you should come over Sunday. We can watch football, the conference championships, and shoot some hoops if the weather's good."

"Okay. I'll think about it. Make up a good excuse for me to your mom. For me not coming inside, at least to say hello."

"I'll tell her the battery in your new used car is weak, and you're afraid the car won't start again if you turn off the ignition."

Conscience pricked, Cal said, "You know, if it weren't for you, I wouldn't even think twice about going back to Mexico... I'd just go."

Josh's mouth made an embarrassed O; his eyes took on a teasing glint. "We could both become lawyers and start our own firm." He opened the car door and stepped out but held it open as he leaned back in. "I'll let you do all the research and courtroom appearances. I'll handle the clients after the verdict. I'm very good at gallows humor."

"I'll keep it in mind. Why don't you say good night and shut the goddamn door?"

"But...parting is such sweet sorrow."

"IT'S TOO FUCKING COLD FOR THIS!"

"You're right," Josh said, looking very merry as he put on his Santa Claus cap. "Good night and shut the goddamn door." And he did just that.

Cal's automatic inner copilot drove cautiously, following by barely conscious memory the sequence of suburban streets, four-lane roads, and interstate highways that would take him past O'Hare—not the most direct expressway route to the North Shore suburbs from the Levinson's house, but the route of choice for contemplative drivers.

He was just getting settled into the lonesome dark lateral views on I-294 when the thought struck that the very same road was connected by two thousand miles or so of other modern highways to Mexico City. There were so many American, British, and Canadian companies there that he was sure he could land a job; it didn't matter to him doing what. It would be short term; maybe as long as a year, depending.

He lit a cigarette and pondered the bureaucratic hassles he would encounter. They were trivial and quickly dissolved in the heady glow of wanderlust. He definitely had to leave Chicago. And soon. He could pack his trusty yellow Bug with a selection of clothes and books, record the best of Josh's albums onto cassette tapes, and then hit the open road. Wouldn't have to be to Mexico. Why not try out California first? By way of the south, to avoid the cold and snow... *Route 66*!

He flashed on that television show first and, only then pondered the actual route. He thought it must go west from Dallas. He guessed Phoenix was probably along its path, and Albuquerque. He pictured the classic landscape of Westerns—scrub desert, mesas, rocky snowcapped mountains on the horizon.

He only knew the route the Nabobs took on the Great California Van Odyssey of freshman year: I-80 from Chicago to Salt Lake City, from there to Vegas and L.A., and then up the coast to San Francisco, whose mere name held a magical glow. He was passing O'Hare when he saw, in mnemonic imagination, that great American icon, omega to the Brooklyn Bridge's alpha: the Golden Gate.

He'd had this wistful daydream numerous times and as always it faded into practical considerations. What sort of job could he hope to find there? Too many others about his age had the same laid-back ambition—to live in the most beautiful and hip city in North America. He had the notion from magazine and newspaper articles that cab drivers with PhD's were not uncommon in San Francisco. What could a measly BA with no connections hope to find? A gig bussing tables in a rustic vegetarian restaurant?

He considered the only types of jobs he thought he could count on: clerking in department stores and grilling burgers at McFranchise. He figured he could endure such humiliation while he kept looking for a better job, one for which he needed his degree to qualify at least, and that paid enough for him to rent a place by himself. He saw his worldly aspirations compacted into a one-room apartment walled by brick-and-board book shelves.

He pulled another familiar fantasy from his files. He could use his aptitude for math to get a job that would allow him to rent a *nice* apartment, one with a bay window. He had scored in the upper two percent on the math portion of the SAT, and after four years of a college curriculum that had allowed him to avoid even a single math course or math-using science course, he'd somehow managed to score in the top five percent on the math portion of the GRE. He'd been told his aptitude for math, logic, and language made him a natural for computer programming. In the Mexico City airport, waiting for his flight, he'd seen the January issue of *Popular Electronics* on a store rack. He'd skimmed the cover story, about a miniature computer that some company in New Mexico was selling by mail order, calling it a microcomputer. It sounded pretty cool, and only cost about four hundred dollars.

He reviewed the outlines of a plan: He'd find a minimum wage job to start, get something he could stand to stay with for a while, and after establishing himself as a bona fide Californian by living there a year, he'd start computer courses at a community college or San Francisco State. Hell, he bet his parents would co-sign for a student loan if his next degree practically guaranteed a decent-paying job.

The scheme of becoming an itinerant geek beguiled him. He'd be able to spend as much money as he wanted and still have enough left each month to save a tidy sum. When he got a bundle saved up, he'd quit his job and travel. When he ran out of money, he'd come back and get another job. He saw himself slouched in an overstuffed armchair in the bay window of a one-bedroom San Francisco apartment reading *The New Yorker*. Chamber music was playing on an expensive stereo. His bare feet were splayed in an oblong of sunlight stretched across the gleaming wood floor.

He pictured himself entering a funky little theater showing a foreign film. The ticket taker looked like Karl Marx. He revised the theater to a coffeehouse and sat down at a table near the door. There was an open poetry reading going on. He sipped at his cappuccino and nervously smoked a cigarette hand rolled from Drum tobacco. A painfully uptight young woman, who bore a faint resemblance to Tamara, was reading feminist laments.

Modestly but with obvious confidence, he made his way to the lectern; upon it he opened a stiff black binder. He was not nervous, but his voice was a little shaky as he announced that he didn't write poems; he translated poetry. The first poem he would read, first in Spanish and then in his English translation, was by Pablo Neruda. He read the Spanish with exquisitely deft enunciation and flawless emphasis. Looking up near the end of one thrillingly ardent poem from *The Captain's Verses,* he fell headlong into the rapt stare of a Chicana whose face was all bones and passion.

He remembered the woman who'd swiped her tits energetically across his back as she squeezed past him on a bus in Mexico City. She had flung a slyly amused, heavy-lidded glance at him, her naughty smile opening to mutter something before she pushed hurriedly toward the front. He saw himself sidle forward in the aisle, squeezing into the compacted throng, giving chase.

Cal missed the Dempster Street exit off the Tri-State Tollway and ended up going well out of his way to get back to Josh's apartment, which he also had a hard time locating. He wasn't familiar with the neighborhood and, in the dark, he wound up driving around for ten minutes before he found the street. And then he wasn't sure which house it was, so he pulled over and consulted the address written on a scrap of paper in his wallet.

In the kitchen, he got out a beer and fixed himself a ham and cheese sandwich. The food and alcohol renewed his spirits and he returned to considering his options. He realized he envied Tamara for having launched a career in journalism, however loosely defined. He'd abandoned his major in journalism after coming under her influence. Now she'd become a journalist, and he'd become a literary aesthete, which is how he had regarded her central intellectual focus when they became a couple.

Journalism was a career that he genuinely respected, and it still held gut-appeal. Having abandoned his place in the prestigious Medill School of Journalism after the required introductory course, the notion of applying to a master's program there or anywhere else evaporated as soon as it came to mind. Why not just join the Peace Corps, get assigned to some country in Latin America, and start writing about his experiences? Or he could keep the Peace Corps as an option, try winging it in Mexico City first. Maybe get into travel writing!

The first step was to move to Mexico City then. Step two: Find work, probably off the books, to cover room and board and pocket money. Step three would be to look for a journalism job while researching and writing tourism and travel articles he could submit to newspapers and magazines in the states. Or maybe he could find English-language publications in Mexico City to write for.

If he hadn't found himself a sustainable niche after a year or so, he could join the Peace Corps, request assignment to Guatemala. While living in a gorgeous mountain village, he could work on magazine articles or maybe even a book, a memoir.

He heard the tea kettle's whistling, finally. While the tea steeped, he lit another cigarette. It occurred to him that the ex-Jesuit priest in whose small Chicago bookshop he'd worked over the summer might have connections in Mexico. He guessed at what sort: some U.S. Catholic lay organization doing social work.

As he sipped the Earl Grey, he began to envision the possibility of employment with such an organization in exchange for a subsistence wage. He'd gain firsthand insights into social and political problems, which he could write about, for the organization but also as a freelancer. He'd investigate and make connections on a whole range of issues. He'd work his way into the cabal of Mexican investigative reporters; they'd give him leads on material they couldn't touch without risking their lives. He savored the sweetness of entirely uncommitted conjecture and swallowed the honey-thickened last sip of tepid tea.

About an hour later, as he was leafing through a *Penthouse,* dumbfounded by how far the photos were going now, the doorbell buzzed. He stalled, pacing around while mentally castrating himself. On the way downstairs, he decided the person most probably on the porch was Josh's mystery girlfriend, and he opened the door with a look of ingenuous expectation.

Two men were on the porch. He did a double take and frowned, recognizing Mark on the other side of the storm door's filmy plexiglass. His buddy Larry was beside him, and they looked only a little less surprised to see him as he was to see them.

"Hey, Mark," he said, pushing open the door. "What's up? Is this about tomorrow?"

"It's about tonight," Mark said angrily.

"What about tonight? Why the look, man. What's going on?"

"Your parents have kidnapped Rachel."

"What? But— How? I was just there, this afternoon, with them. What happened?"

The fatigue-jacketed Vietnam vets glanced at each other, confirming their skepticism. "You mind if we come in?" Mark asked.

"No, no, of course not. Come on in. Upstairs."

As they climbed, Cal leading, he said, "How did they get her away from you? They didn't know where that, that charity feast was being held. I told them about it, but I didn't know where it was coming off."

"They took her from your house," Larry said.

"My house? My parents' house? I just left there, around three. What were you doing there?"

He pushed open the door and stood aside; they entered brusquely.

"Mind if I use the bathroom?" Larry said.

Cal said, "It's through the kitchen, at the end of the hall."

Mark followed Larry into the kitchen and turned around. "So you didn't know anything about this?"

"No, of course not."

Mark turned toward the kitchen and Cal, stepping closer, caught Larry indicating a negative answer—he'd looked into the bedroom and bathroom.

"Come on, you guys. Would I be here if I'd known about it? I didn't have any idea this was going to happen. My mother said she called Rachel last night and Rachel agreed to meet with her tomorrow. She told me I was supposed to go to your place early tomorrow morning and pick up Rachel when you guys came out in the van."

Larry looked tentatively accepting of this but also disappointed; Mark shifted nervously, not ready to let go of his suspicions.

"Why did you take Rachel to the house?" Cal asked. "You left her there alone?"

Mark turned away. Larry said, "Your mother wanted her to come and get her Christmas presents."

Mark perched on the edge of a chair, looking ready to spring to his feet. "You knew your mother called Rachel last night?" he asked, staring hard at Cal.

"Yes. We had a discussion after dinner. I stood up for you guys against my brother-in-law. I thought that my mother had called Rachel on an impulse and, talking with her, on Christmas Eve and everything... All she told me was that Rachel had agreed to meet her, alone, at the home of some family friends in Kenilworth. I was supposed to be her chauffeur, early tomorrow morning."

Larry looked at Mark looking at him and half shrugged. "Sounds straight to me."

"Your mother's one hell-of-an actress," Mark said. "She was crying. Got Rachel crying. She said your dad wouldn't be there, that she only wanted five minutes alone with her. And we were stupid enough to believe her."

"You're on our side, right?" Larry said.

"Well, yeah," Cal said.

"So you'll help us figure out where they've taken her, right?"

"Sure. If I can. I don't have any idea though—really."

"You have the address of that house in Kenilworth," Mark said. "We'll have to check that out."

Larry stood up. "We've got three more with us in the van. You mind if they come in? It's cold out there."

"No, I don't mind. Of course, bring them in."

"We didn't expect to find you here," Larry said.

They moved into the living room. Cal went to the kitchen and came back with a dinette chair. He retrieved his cigarettes and an ashtray and sat down. Mark was slouched in the arm-chair, eyes serenely closed, his hands limply on his legs. Cal waited half a minute before deciding he didn't mind possibly interrupting a private prayer.

"How'd you know to come here anyway?"

A minute or so later, Mark opened his eyes and sat up. "You said something."

"Yeah: How'd you know Josh's address?"

"Rachel was going to write you to tell you what happened so you'd have her side of it. I knew it was Evanston, and I remembered Josh's last name."

Cal nodded, relieved by the mundane logic. He heard footsteps on the front porch; the foursome climbing the stairs sent reverberations throughout the house. Just as Larry walked in, the phone rang.

Mark snapped to his feet. Catching his look at Larry, Cal said, "It's probably for Josh. It might be Josh, in fact."

"Yeah, but it could be them," Mark said.

"There's only one phone. You can listen over my shoulder if you want."

"Listen," Mark said, "if it's them try to fake them out. Pretend you want to help them. Maybe that way they'll tell you where they're keeping her."

"Now wait," Cal said. "After defending you guys last night the way I did, there's no way they're going to believe that I'd go along with them on this. I mean, I'm... What do you think they're planning to do?"

"Just answer it," Larry said.

Whirling from the chair, Cal glimpsed Bob's daughter, Annie, hesitantly stepping through the doorway.

Mark followed him into the bedroom and stood on the other side of the bed from where the phone sat on a nightstand beside an alarm clock.

"Hello?"

"Cal, it's me," Priscilla said.

"Oh. What's up? Just a sec, let me tell Josh. He thinks it's his new girlfriend." He muffled the mic with his hand. "It's my older sister, Priscilla, Jim's wife."

"Fake her out," Mark whispered urgently.

Cal grimaced; he uncovered the mic. "Okay, so what's up? Is this about tomorrow?"

"Indirectly," Priscilla said. "Before I tell you, I want you to know that I didn't know it was going to happen like this when I talked to you last night, about picking up Rachel tomorrow. You don't have to now."

"Why not?"

"Mom and Dad took Rachel back into their custody."

"What do you mean by that?"

"I mean Rachel is now with Mom and Dad, so you don't have to pick her up tomorrow."

"Rachel is with them of her own free will?"

Priscilla said nothing.

"God, I can't believe this," Cal said. "They kidnapped her?"

"No, that's not what it is. Dad has full authority over Rachel."

"They kidnapped her," Cal repeated, looking at Mark. Mark threw up his hands and disgustedly whirled away.

"Where are they now?" Cal asked.

"I'm not going to tell you that, of course."

"I can't believe they did this. What—? How did they con her into leaving the group?"

"I can only tell you that she came to the house with people from the cult and left with Mom and Dad."

"Right. I know she didn't go willingly."

"The cult controlled her will; that's why Mom and Dad had to get her away from them."

Mark had turned away, hands on his hips, inspiring Cal's next question. "And Mark and the others just let her go?"

"They didn't have anything to say about it."

"Why not?"

"Mom and Dad took her out the back door."

"Oh, I see: to a car waiting in the church parking lot... So you don't consider this kidnapping? Well, okay, maybe technically it's just unlawful imprisonment. Were you there?"

"No, I was not. Before you say anything else, I have a few things to say. The first is that I don't think you want to admit that Rachel's mind is being controlled. For obvious reasons."

"Such as?"

"If you're half as smart as you think you are, you can figure it out for yourself. You have your own selfish reasons for defending the crazy beliefs of this cult."

"Why don't you figure it out for me, Miss Not-a-Psychologist-But-Took-Enough-Courses-to-Know-it-all."

"You know damn well, Calvin Wideman, Rachel would never believe all that crap if she were in her right mind."

"I do *not* know that. What she believes now is no more unreasonable than—"

"Blahblahblah... You talk a blue streak but you don't believe any of it. You know damn well that TLF perverts the Scriptures. But it's all a word game to you. You're glad that now it's not just you making Dad and Mom suffer... It's blinded you to what's really going on. Haven't you ever fallen in love?"

"As a matter of fact, I have. So what?"

"This is the very first time Rachel's ever fallen in love, Cal."

"Oh, come on." He glanced at Mark.

"You wouldn't know. But I know. I had a long talk with Rachel last summer, about love and sex and married life, so I happen to know that Rachel had never fallen in love and in fact she'd decided never to get married."

"Why? Wha—?"

"She decided that Paul...that she didn't need to get married, for the reasons Paul gives, and so she ought to stay single, to dedicate herself entirely to Christian service."

"So she changed her mind about staying single. That means she's been brainwashed? For that you're going to force her to 'listen to reason'?"

"Just shut up and hear me out," Priscilla said. "Jim has a handbook for TLF leaders that was probably written by Lewten himself, and it tells the leaders to target individuals of the opposite sex, to love-bomb them. Didn't Jim tell you about that?"

"Not specifically. Look, it doesn't matter. I've got news for you: I'm going to do everything I can to see to it that the lawbreakers in this case are brought to justice. And you're an accomplice in this crime, Priscilla. I'm calling the police."

"Good. You do that. The police are on our side, Cal. Dad's lawyer informed the Elmore police in advance that Dad was going to exercise his parental rights over Rachel."

"Oh, fuckit," Cal said, giving Mark a look that bore a trace of regret and apology.

"The main reason I called," Priscilla said, "is to warn you that the people in the cult may think that you were involved in this."

"Why would they think that, I wonder?"

"Not because of anything we did. Didn't you invite Rachel to have dinner with us today?"

"You mean this was already planned? You fuckers. You used me."

"We did not. It wasn't until after you called Sunday that Jim presented the option, of forcing Rachel to listen to reason. Dad and Mom were against it. First they wanted a chance to discuss things with her. But then last night Mom realized from what Jim said that there was no chance Rachel was going to listen to reason on her own, voluntarily."

"Oh, I get it. So she called Rachel last night and told her what, Pris? What lie did Mom tell to get Rachel to come by the house?"

"She asked her to come by and get the gifts we had for her. I swear I didn't know when I talked to you, Cal. Mom lied to me, too; not that I blame her. She kept it to herself until this morning."

"Oh, don't worry, I believe you," he said. "I've known for a long time that Mom's a gifted liar."

"That's exactly what you are. You lie to yourself so much you never know what the truth is."

"I sure as hell know what it *isn't*. Why don't you guys try to deprogram me? Man, I'd love that."

"It's not the same thing, Cal, and you know it."

"You fucking hypocrite. You know what—?"

A sharp clack made him pull the handset away from his ear, and then he heard only the loud dial tone.

"You fucked it up, man," Mark said grimly. "You didn't even try to fake her out."

When they returned to the living room, Larry asked, "What did you find out?"

"How could he find out anything? He went and told her right off that he was on our side."

"She already knew that," Cal said. "I couldn't have faked her out...just like that. She's my older sister!"

Cal's apoplectic glare drove home the point, and Mark disgustedly looked away. He said, "You could have acted...like maybe it wasn't such a bad thing, their kidnapping her. You didn't have to—"

"Didn't I? You guys were acting like you thought I was in on the whole thing. If I'd tried to fake her out...how would you know I wasn't faking *you* out?"

"How do we know you aren't now?" Mark retorted.

"All right, come on, let's cool it," Larry said. "What's done is done."

Annie appeared from the kitchen, where the other two guys were hanging out. "I think we should call Bob."

Mark gave Cal a grudgingly apologetic glance. "I think we ought to pray it out first," he said. "And then...talk it over with Cal and try to get some ideas before we call Bob."

"Let's do a prayer circle," Annie said.

Turning to Cal, Larry said, "You two met, the other night, right?"

"Yes," Cal said.

Annie's shy smile tried to bloom but wilted to an abashed, sympathetic grimace. "How are you feeling, Cal? I know this must be really difficult for you."

He kind of shrugged. The two other guys edged into the room—one pudgy and short, the other tall and skinny.

"That's Stuart and that's Rob," Larry said.

"So what about that prayer circle?" Annie said, looking around at the guys.

"Let's do it," Larry said glumly. He took off his jacket. Mark stuck his hands in his hip pockets and, with a sulky glance at Cal, stepped into place in the circle being formed, hands finding hands without awkwardness. Annie smiled a glum plea with a hint of irony, and Cal felt attraction stirring, despite her being at least a decade older.

"We'd like to share the comfort and power of the prayer circle with you," she said. "Why don't you join us? Just be part of our circle. You can pray or meditate however you want. Or just be here with us, feeling it."

"I think I'll sit this one out. Thanks anyway."

She took off her parka. "Can I put this here?"

"Sure," he said, appreciating her physique as she draped the parka over the back of the sofa. She had the black leotard on tonight without the lumberjack shirt; her beltless bellbottom jeans were low on her hips.

Annie stood back and held out her hand as she smiled at Cal. "Come on, it won't hurt. It's silent. We just pray together in the spirit and feel it magnified in us."

"One body in the Lord," Larry said, his look inviting Cal to take the space between him and Annie.

"All right," Cal said, stepping toward them. "But if a circle of faith is only as strong as its weakest link, you'd be better off doing this without me."

"You don't need faith to start," Annie said. The warm soft sureness of her hand embarrassed him so much he didn't give much thought to also taking Larry's large calloused hand on his other side.

They all closed their eyes; the believers tilted their heads back. Cal did likewise: It made it easier to peek. He didn't see any lips moving and no fibrillation under chins. It seemed to him they were all raptly absorbed in adoration of the pleasure centers in their brains—as good a way of praying as any, he mused. But he couldn't get his pleasure center switched on—until he felt the strong warm flow of energy coming into his palm from Annie's.

CHAPTER NINE

But Woe unto You, Scribes and Pharisees

THE NAME OF HIS parents' lawyer was on the tip of his tongue. It was an easy name, but apparently too common to stick in memory. He could picture him with disgusting clarity: a pipe-smoking, hail-fellow-well-met; Republican Party hack and elder of the Plainfield United Presbyterian Church; looked like John Mitchell's even more porculent brother. But what the hell was his name?

Gritting his teeth, Cal pushed the pedal to the floor and swung into the passing lane. He barely made it by the eighteen-wheeler, in whose wake, he realized, he'd been shielded from the headwind. After a few minutes of getting buffeted, he let the semi pass and pulled up close behind it again.

He could just see Rachel heeding the Holy Spirit's reminder not to resist evil, letting herself be taken away, quietly as Christ in Gethsemane. But she could have grabbed the bronze praying hands from the fireplace mantle and hurled them through the picture window, screaming. Mark and Larry would've come running, fueled by the holy juice of adrenalin and the holy spirit of righteous outrage.

Even if she refused to talk to them, how long would it take for them to wear her down? Jim would tear apart

Lewten's theology with sneering sophistry. Mommy would "love-bomb" her. Daddy would come on as Mr. Reasonable: the sympathetic mediator of classic interrogation techniques. Their talk torture would be unrelenting, and she would begin to feel crazy whether she tried to argue back or not.

The clincher would be if Martin broke down and, weeping along with Sarah, begged Rachel to forgive him for being such a cold and remote almighty father.

Cal summarily declared his father guilty of violating some basic precepts of doctrines he held dear. Martin had caved in to Jim and Sarah, he was sure of it. Only, of course, after his lawyer assured him that the law on such matters was not cut and dried, that a worst case outcome was really unlikely. Fine. Probably true. But where was the scriptural justification Martin's conscience surely would have required? Jesus said to admonish a transgressor before the congregation, and if he wouldn't repent to treat him as a heathen or tax collector.

Cal eased off his anger, snickering at the irony of Matthew putting tax collectors on a par with heathens, given that he was a tax collector himself, supposedly.

What could they be thinking? Imagine Jesus trying to de-program a Pharisee. And Paul didn't approve of what they were doing either. In his memo to Titus, Paul said to reject heretics after two admonitions—which was the basis for the Amish punishment of shunning.

John Calvin and company established a one-two-three SOP for handling miscreants in the church: admonition, suspension from the Lord's Supper, and excommunication. Martin had admonished Cal privately for questioning sound doctrine and suspended him from taking Communion when he was a high school senior; he had quietly dropped him from the church membership roll during his junior year at Northwestern.

So why hadn't Martin stuck to his scriptural principles in Rachel's case? Cal scoffed at himself for asking. Even Calvin had approved the Pope's proof text to justify *autos-da-fé*: I Corinthians 5:5. "Deliver such an one unto Satan for the destruction of the flesh, that the spirit may be saved in the day of the Lord Jesus."

Calvin tried to deprogram the heretic Miguel Serveto, who wasn't a Catholic but, like Rachel now, preached a different Christ than Calvin. Calvin first tried to convince Serveto to recant his belief that Jesus was not coequal with the Father, and when he wouldn't, Calvin let the civil authorities in Geneva pass sentence. Praying and reading from the Word, Calvin watched from his window the several hours it took the Spaniard to die, smoldering at the stake.

The way Jim figures it, what's to keep him from trying to deprogram me? Or any other sinner? If the reason I don't accept the Truth is just because I'm perversely stubborn, and if the eternal fate of my soul is at stake... Why don't they kidnap me and torture me with talk until I surrender my will to the Lord?

"Because it's against the law," he answered out loud, and found comfort in the sound of his voice even though he was not at all sure that what he had said was correct. He thought the famous deprogrammer Jack Bristow must have mounted a

legal defense that was at least partially successful, from the little
he remembered reading about it. But his defense couldn't have
been based on parental rights: He'd been hired by the parents.
Parental rights weren't relevant in Rachel's case anyway. The
age of majority in Illinois was eighteen; she was nineteen.

Cal then recalled talking with Josh about the "lesser of two
evils" defense used by anti-war protesters. The moral imperative to fight an unnecessary and corrupt war machine justified
their unlawful actions to break minor laws, like burning draft
records.

"So they think this is legal because she's brainwashed," Cal
said aloud. "They have to violate her rights. To save her...from
what? From trying to follow her heart, her spirit, in Jesus'
name, amen. Even though they brainwashed her as a child to
accept beliefs that most Christians think are absurd. They're
all crazy. Nonono, just *religious*."

*If it's your religion, you can be as crazy as you want. So long
as you're sincere. And don't try to overthrow the powers that be.
Religious liberty, the All-American oxymoron.*

The Christmas tree lights were shining brightly in the picture
window, and there were other lights on in the house. The
shock to Cal's expectations triggered the impulse to drive on.
He circled the block. He reasoned that it must have been dark,
the lights already on, when they snatched her. So why were the

lights still on? Maybe someone from the church was holding down the fort?

He drove around the block again, screwing up his courage to carry off the attitude Mark had scoffed into him: He had a key to the house, he had right of entry, so he could damn well go in and make himself at home—and look for clues to where the kidnappers were holed up.

He parked around back of the house in the church parking lot, choosing the darkest corner. He hurried around to the front door, mindful of the stark edge the cold added to his excitement. He unlocked the deadbolt and then turned the key in the doorknob keyhole with his right hand while turning the knob and pushing in with his left. He mashed his nose when the opening door abruptly stopped, caught by the chain lock.

Bowing away, he hissed and muttered profanities into his gloves. The porch light made him feel like he was on stage. He pushed the door to the limit and shouted into the crack: "Anybody here?"

After a moment, he yelled again, less loudly: "I'm Calvin Wideman. I'm here to help. Please let me in."

He looked casually up and down the street, then rammed the door with his shoulder. The chain felt more solidly attached than his upper arm. He pulled the door shut and whirled about, scanning the dark windows of the only neighboring house, an old brick farmhouse on the corner of Spencer and Elmhurst. Mrs. Hanson was hard of hearing and half blind—assuming she was still alive.

He jumped off the porch and slipped behind the bushes under the picture window. Standing on one foot on the jointed gas main, he looked in over the border of fake snow to one side of the Christmas tree: A lamp in the living room was on, and the kitchen light. What he could see of the living room appeared neat and orderly as usual.

He went around to the back of the house and tried the door to the garage, which was locked. He crouched down directly underneath the breakfast nook's bay window. While folding clothes last night, he'd noticed the basement window that the dryer's vent pipe passed through had changed: The glass had been replaced by plywood.

He could feel that the bolts holding the plywood were the kind with mushroom-cap heads; the wood had been thickly caulked all around. Undoubtedly, this was the work of the church's volunteer handyman, a retired contractor. Carl Knudsen had done another fine job: He was a real stickler for details.

Cal considered kicking in one of the other basement windows. He would have to make sure he got every last sliver out of the frame though: It would be a tight squeeze.

He sat down and pushed the cold rubber soles of his tennis shoes against the plywood. He wished he'd thought to wear his boots. He glanced toward the garage, freezing up, thinking he had heard something. He realized he was in the same pose as a Mayan chacmool sculpture. He grit his teeth and stomped; the plywood's solidity perplexed him. There had to be an easier way to get inside.

He was just getting to his feet when he saw a flashlight beam moving on the ground past the corner of the garage. He froze; sprang to his feet just as a person stepped around the corner.

The man lurched a step back, swinging the powerful light. A second before Cal shut his eyes to it he saw the cop draw his gun. They shouted simultaneously:

"Don't move!" "I live here!"

"Keep your hands up where I can see them!"

"This is my house. I'm Cal Wideman."

The policeman walked carefully up to him.

"That your car over there in the church lot?"

"Yes, sir." The beam dropped; the gun was already back in its holster when Cal looked for it. The cop was young and vaguely familiar looking.

"You still living with your folks, Cal?" The guy smirked. "I'm nobody you'd remember. You're not doing anything I could arrest you for, are you?"

"No, no, I was just, looking for a way to get in. I left my key back in Evanston and my parents aren't home."

"You know what's happening with your little sister?"

"Yeah. In fact, that's why I'm here. My older sister, Priscilla, called me—"

"Save it, man. I left the car running, and I gotta call this in before they send someone else out here."

A fuzzy-sounding female voice came back over the patrol car's radio: "Does he want to come in and make a statement?"

Safety Officer Ron Cushing lowered the mike and looked over—and possibly down his nose—at his high school class's valedictorian.

"Yeah, I guess so," Cal said. "But since nothing's happening till the D.A. gives the word, how about if I do it in the morning?"

Ron raised the mike. "He'll come in tomorrow."

"And he wants to support the complaint against his parents?"

"Affirmative," Ron said.

"Will he be staying at his parents' house tonight?"

"If I can get in," Cal said.

"Affirmative," Ron answered her.

As Ron hung up, Cal said, "You got any suggestions as to how I can get in?"

"Yeah: the kitchen door. One of the crazies knocked out some glass to break in. I guess he was your sister's boyfriend."

"Mark?"

"He had a ba-a-ad go-tea."

"So did you arrest him?"

"Yep. But your dad's lawyer posted bail, said your parents may want to drop the charges." Ron smiled. "I like your old man's style." He cocked his head. "He didn't fool around. Made his move, but then let us know through his lawyer what was happening. If this outfit is legit, like you say, a judge could order your parents to let Rachel go—or order she be brought in so's he could question her." Ron waited till Cal looked at him squarely, then said: "It'll be interesting to see what happens—now that you're going to go up against your old man."

"You don't think the D.A. will do anything?"

"That's where the old timers are putting their money. Your dad's lawyer and the D.A. are like this." Ron twisted two fingers together and jerked the hand up as though flipping the bird.

"Bob Miller here. What did you find, Cal?"

"Hello, Bob. Not much, I'm afraid. The family car is gone, the one my mother usually drives, a Buick Century, four-door, light brown."

"You know what year it is?"

"I think it's a '70."

"Okay. What about Jim's car?"

"He and Priscilla and their kids came in a Country Squire station wagon, with wood panels on the side? Whatever make that is. Priscilla probably has that car. Jim has a red Camaro the last I knew."

"It's not important. So Priscilla called you and told you what happened?"

"Right."

"Was she involved in the abduction?"

"Well, she said she wasn't. Said they didn't tell her what they were planning. Not sure I believe her, of course."

"I see."

"I think she probably knows where they are, and I wouldn't be surprised if she's staying in touch with them by phone."

"I see."

"But if her husband's involved, you couldn't make her testify against him, could you?"

"That's for the lawyers to worry about. Where can we find Priscilla, do you know?"

"I assume she's at home. She has two little girls to look after, which is the only reason she's on the sidelines, I'm sure—if she really is. They live in Schaumberg. James Fuller. The number's in the book. If she's not there, I have no idea where she is."

"All right. And the only place you can think of that seems—logical, where they might have taken Rachel, is that lodge in Wisconsin?"

"Right. Owned by the institute that Jim works for."

"Right, right. We've got that. You can't remember exactly where the lodge is?"

"I've tried. I ran across a Wisconsin map, when I was looking for clues. I've only been there once. I know we passed Wausau, that was the last big town, on the interstate."

"Do you remember how far you drove after Wausau?"

"I'd say it was about...maybe a half hour before we got off the interstate. And it was at least another half hour of slower driving after that, on backroads."

"It's quite isolated then."

"Very much so. I think it's definitely the perfect place, except—it seems too obvious. They know I'd think of it and tell you guys about it."

"That might not matter to them. It's private property. Probably has protected access...right? And it's what? About a five to six hour drive from the house."

"Yeah, I guess so. It's definitely in the boonies."

"I've called our Wisconsin headquarters in Madison. They're going to notify the state police and do some checking, try to pinpoint the location of this place. Do you think the Institute would give Jim permission to use the facility up there?"

"I don't know. I—, I have no idea, really."

"Probably not, officially," Bob said. "Well, all right. Cal, we're grateful for your cooperation. We have lawyers going into action tomorrow. The lead attorney is Kyle Fustenberg. He said he'll want you to testify on Rachel's behalf—as soon as we can get a hearing. Tomorrow, if things go better than I guess we can expect. You think the D.A.'s office in Will County will stonewall us?"

"Definitely."

"Fustenberg has handled this type of case before. He knows the ropes. Are you staying there at your parents' house tonight?"

"Yes. I told the police I'd come in to give a statement in the morning."

"That's good. We'll include you in our prayers, Cal. We know that God will restore Rachel to us. Paul said, *For the kingdom of God is not in word, but in power.* Rachel possesses that power, which is the mind and spirit of Christ. It can't be taken from her. Before too long your parents will have to realize that they have erred in their judgment of us. We will pray without ceasing until they do, as I'm sure Rachel is doing at this very moment, even as they shamefully mistreat her."

Cal let the silence hang awkwardly a moment too long before he said, "All right then. Well. Good night, Bob."

Sitting at the dinette sipping coffee, he pondered the awfulness of what was happening to Rachel; his emotions were thoroughly muddled with irony. He felt a little ashamed that he couldn't achieve a more empathetic angst.

He failed to identify the three chiming notes strangely stroking the silence. The doorbell sounded again.

Jerry Edwards, looking dapper despite funereal grimness, peered guiltily through the glass of the storm door. Jerry was the assistant pastor and director of youth activities at the church. His wife Sally had a master's degree in musical ministry and was the choir director. Cal didn't know them well; they had been hired the fall he left for college.

Cal pushed the storm door open a crack.

"How's it going, Cal?"

"You tell me. Have they gotten Rachel to recant, or are they talking *auto-da-fé* now?"

"May I come in?"

"Of course. Why not?"

Cal thought Jerry exceptionally well suited to be Martin's assistant. He was a few inches shorter than Martin, not as handsome, not as richly voiced or blessed with as keen a mind for rhetorical finesse; but he was plenty bright and a much warmer, more approachable person.

Cal sat down at the dinette, lit a cigarette, and sarcastically gestured for Jerry to take a seat.

Getting out of his coat, Jerry said: "I guess, uh, you're, probably looking for someone to...vent your anger on."

He draped the wool coat over the chair next to the one he pulled out and sat down directly across from Cal. Cal eyed his blatantly matched dress shirt, sweater vest, and tie, surmising that they were a packaged Christmas present. A deep crease across the vest verified his deduction.

Jerry scooted the chair forward, set his hands on the table, and interlaced his fingers. Cal watched without looking, apparently absorbing himself in his cigarette. He was stuck in a pose of contemptuous relaxation, well back from the table.

Jerry put his fist to his mouth briefly and cleared his throat. "Priscilla asked me to come over. She thought you might be here, since she didn't get an answer when she called your friend's apartment."

Cal glanced, then turned his head away, exhaling.

"There's a group of us, gathered at our house, from the church," Jerry said. "We're going to be there all night, praying for Rachel's speedy deliverance. You are not seeing the situation as it is, Cal. It's a real shame, that you can't at least give your parents the benefit of the doubt."

Cal took a sip of coffee. Jerry finally drew his look with a hurt and baffled stare. "This cult has made a virtual slave of your sister. I just don't know how to relate, to your not being able to see that."

Cal stifled the impulse to mock and gingerly felt his way toward a sincere attempt at dialogue.

"I believe that some cults make their converts virtual slaves," he said. "If Rachel was in one of those cults, I'd want to help get her out. If I thought it was doing to her what you think TLF is doing. But TLF is not one of those cults. I went to the TLF house; I observed them, talked to them; I also talked to Rachel alone. I concluded that she is there of her own free will and the Christianity she practices now has just as valid a claim to Constitutional protection as your church does, Jerry."

Cal took his time taking another drag. "I'm going to give a statement to the police backing up the complaint against Jim and my parents, and if the D.A. or a judge doesn't do something tomorrow to put a stop to this *re*-programming, I'm going to take the story to the press. I bet Royko would have a field day with it."

Jerry shook his head slightly, staring at his hands.

"You don't think Rachel has the right to choose her religious beliefs?" Cal asked. "Why? Because she's not twenty-one? She's old enough to vote but she's not old enough to decide which religious beliefs make more sense to her? I've talked to her recently. Have you? Her mind is not being controlled by others; it's being controlled just as it was before, by her own intelligence, judgment, and will to believe.

"We're talking about freedom of religion, a basic Constitutional right, remember? Your religious beliefs include an admission of how absurd they seem to reprobates, like me. Why don't you try to deprogram me? Huh? What does the Westminster Confession say about how to handle heretics, Jerry?"

Jerry lowered his eyes as he began to speak, choosing his words carefully. "Rachel is not a confirmed and willful heretic. She is an impressionable young woman who has lived a very sheltered life, as you know. She has been seduced, brainwashed, and led astray by a group of seemingly happy and spiritual young people who are deeply indoctrinated in this cult's false gospel. Although she is not a minor, she had accepted remaining under her father's authority and care after reaching the age of majority. If she truly was in control of her own mind, wouldn't she have told her parents when she became involved with Mark and TLF? You know how close she and Sarah have always been. Surely, you can see that the way she went about making this radical change in her life, doing it in secret, pretending to her family that everything was going along as normal, when actually she had dropped out of Covenant."

"She dropped out?" Cal asked, clearly taken aback. "She says she took a leave of absence."

"Yes, well, that's part of the ruse, isn't it?" Jerry said. "If she'd been honest about it, she would not have requested a leave of absence, which guarantees her readmission within a certain time frame."

"She told me she didn't want to burn any bridges with the college," Cal said. "At some point she'll want to transfer her credits to another school."

"And you think that's the real reason?" Jerry asked. "Isn't it more likely that she just wanted to give her parents false hope? To keep them mollified, for as long as possible."

Cal said nothing for a long moment. "Maybe so," he said at last. "Moot point as far as I'm concerned. I'm going to cooperate with TLF. We're going to try to convince a judge that my parents have misjudged True Life Fellowship. In any case, they had no right to kidnap Rachel and subject her to torture by endless biblical bickering. They have clearly broken the law and should at least be stopped, if not punished."

Jerry sullenly studied his hands as he twirled his class ring. He put his hands flat on the table and stood up.

"I'll let myself out... Are you going to be staying here tonight?"

Cal answered with silence, contemptuously. Jerry put on a long-suffering look along with his overcoat. He hung onto the fur-lined lapels a moment; sighed and stared pleadingly. "Jim says that with your help, they could make the initial break-through by morning."

Intuitively alerted, Cal averted a glance to his mug of coffee.

"If you don't help them now, your parents are going to be extremely disappointed."

"They've found out it's not going to be as easy as they thought, huh?"

"Nobody thought it would be easy."

Cal picked up the butt he'd just ground out and swept it around in the ashes. "I'll be staying here tonight. Suppose I do change my mind, how do I get in touch with them?"

"Through Priscilla. Don't get the idea we'd take you directly to Rachel. And—it has to be tonight. Tomorrow the situation will change. Please, Cal: Think about it again. I'll tell Priscilla to call you in an hour or so."

"How about if I agree to be a neutral observer?"

Jerry turned in the doorway to the living room, pulling gloves from his coat pocket. He stepped back into the kitchen, frowning slightly as he put on the gloves.

"I promise not to interfere," Cal said. "Rachel doesn't have to know I'm there. I could stay in another room, just listening. If I could just be there to monitor what they're saying and how she's reacting, maybe I'd decide it's best to come in on their side. I don't know, I can't promise that, but I'd promise not to try to stop them—beyond arguing with them, out of Rachel's hearing, if I felt that, that—. Do you trust Jim to admit that he's made a mistake? Or my parents, upset as they are? If Rachel is steadfast in her faith, how far are they planning to go with this? If she doesn't give in, how long do they intend to keep torturing her?"

"If a deprogramming isn't interrupted," Jerry said, "it's only a matter of days before the cult victim's initial catharsis. The only deprogrammings that have ever failed never really got started or were interrupted before the process could be completed."

"That's gotta be bullshit," Cal said.

"I'm sorry: It is well documented fact."

"Documented by whom? Jack Bristow?"

Jerry looked surprised, which disarmed Cal. "Oh, come on," he said, "Don't tell me they hired Bristow? Isn't he in jail yet?"

"No," Jerry said, "Jack Bristow is not involved. But yes, his experiences substantiate what I said. Of course, if a deprogramming isn't properly conducted, the process can take much longer. And that increases the chances that the cult victim will escape, or be found by members of the cult and forcibly removed from the deprogramming. If the process is allowed to run its proper course, however, it doesn't fail. No one who has been fully deprogrammed has ever chosen to return to the cult from which they were rescued. Doesn't that tell you something?"

Jerry leaned forward. "Look, Cal: I really don't get it. You say you're aware that some cults make virtual slaves of their converts. It doesn't make sense that you deny this cult does the same thing, with its mechanical, hypnotic method of speaking in tongues. Is it because their slaves seem happy?

"TLF systematically breaks down their converts' identities and builds cult personalities which are so instilled with paranoia that they cannot function apart from the cult. Rachel is demonstrating that right now. Her personality is buried alive in the cult personality.

"The first step in a deprogramming is to make contact with the person's true self. Given enough time, deprogrammings always succeed. How do you explain that?"

Cal sighed and looked away. He couldn't find the will to go on talking. He wanted to listen and wished he could be convinced.

"Deprogramming can be a long process," Jerry said. "The paranoia programmed into a cult victim's mind may cause them to experience terrible dread and trauma for months after the initial catharsis. Deprogramming breaks the hold the cult has on the victim's will, but it can't erase the paranoia just like that. Ex-cult members suffer anxiety attacks, nightmares, ulcers, hallucinations—a whole gamut of psychological problems after they've been deprogrammed. Complete recuperation can take years.

"Rachel will need to be protected from contact with the cult until she fully recovers. She'll need all the loving care you and your family and her friends and the church can provide. She'll need special counseling."

Cal felt numb as a zombie watching Jerry hold out his gloved hand, almost as though he wanted to shake. He didn't. He was just signing off.

"Think it over, Cal. Priscilla will call you in an hour or so. Think how you're going to feel, when Rachel is deprogrammed. Because of your relationship with Rachel, you may be able to alleviate this trauma for her and your parents. But you can't come in as a neutral observer. You're either with your family, or you are against them. That's how they feel about it."

Gloomily oppressed, he rummaged in his father's desk. He didn't know what he was looking for and didn't expect to find anything. The drawers were tidily arranged with sundries from a stationery shop. Martin worked on sermons at this desk and took private phone calls here. But his main workplace was the church office. Cal had wanted to search there, but the ring of church keys for emergency use had been taken from its peg on the memo board beside the back door to the kitchen.

He lifted a neat stack of fancy typing paper embossed with Martin's letterhead, a sheet of which he'd received last night. The reminder pinched. He shut the drawer.

On the desk was the Malcolm Muggeridge book, its Byzantine Christ giving no clue—to anything. He had left the book for Martin with a note tucked inside: "This is on loan, in case Jim asks. How do you feel about the beautiful violation of the Second Commandment on the jacket?"

Calvinists used to abhor and strict ones still avoided all but verbal representations of God the Son. Cal's Sunday School books had always shown the Lord with his face turned away, as though Jesus' Godhood was in his face but not his body. The illustrators had had to rely too often upon the benedictory pose of the hands; and the figure's build and posture had to be both manly and meek—pretty tough when the guy had hair down to his shoulders and wore a robe that looked like a long dress. Occasionally, in turned-away profile, a virile but trim beard showed.

Beside the Muggeridge book was an appointments calendar open to December twenty-third. Cal turned pages, scanning the sparse entries back to early in the month. They were all of the call-so-and-so variety. He opened and quickly closed the top drawer of a filing cabinet, glimpsing the crush of manila folders containing neatly handwritten sermons and the typed up copies produced by the church secretary. Martin always preached extemporaneously. He was proud of that, but he was so good at memorization that the best parts of his sermons were delivered verbatim from what he'd written out beforehand and always polished up afterwards. Cal prophesied that his father's first retirement project would be a modest volume of selected sermons.

He glanced despondently at the label of the other cabinet's top file drawer—BOOK AND ARTICLE NOTES. It was crammed with folders containing handwritten notes on every book and journal article Martin had considered worthy of close textual scrutiny. The folders in the bottom file drawer were from his college and seminary years.

My legacy, Cal thought. He switched off the light and stepped into the hall. Although dejected and feeling worn out, he couldn't muster the will to resist his sleuthing compulsion's next command.

His mother's dressing table smelled like her, only stronger. He knew from what. He lifted a bottle of Oil of Olay, wondering for the umpteenth time if Olay were a place, plant, or playful echo of the Spanish bullfighting cheer.

The top of his father's tall bureau was severely uncluttered. In a slim black jewelry case, he examined spare change, keys, buttons, chapstick, tie clasps, cuff links, American-flag lapel pins, all manner of odds and ends meticulously arranged in velvet-lined compartments. None of the objects electrified him with suddenly realized significance. He let the cover fall shut

and opened the bureau's top drawer. The briefs and under-
shirts were individually rolled up and stacked like ammuni-
tion. One of Sarah's standard anecdotes about Martin was
how on their honeymoon he had presented her with a copy of
the United States Army regulations pertaining to the proper
packing of footlockers.

Martin had attained the rank of corporal in the 66th In-
fantry—The Black Panther Division. They arrived late to the
battle in France and almost didn't make it. On Christmas Eve
1944 one of their two troopships was torpedoed within sight
of the lights of Cherbourg harbor. The ship listed badly but
initially didn't appear to be sinking. Another ship from the
same convoy came alongside; the swells slammed their hulls
together and pushed them apart. Often Cal had imagined
himself in his father's boots during the moments before his
leap to the other ship. About eight hundred soldiers of the
66th perished that night, either crushed between the ships or
drowned in the icy waters after the troopship finally sank.

No wonder Martin believed in Providence, and that he was
one of the Elect. His survival that night was a tale of incredible
luck: One absurdly random happenstance after another. And
the final stroke of fortune was that the decimation of the 66th
before it got sent to the Battle of the Bulge meant that the
division would suffer only light casualties during the remaining months of the war. Instead of being sent as reinforcements
into the freezing cold killing ground of the Ardennes, Martin
went out on boring hedgerow patrols in eastern France, where
the 66th kept remnant German forces hemmed in along the

Atlantic Coast, uselessly protecting Hitler's fortress-like submarine bases.

Cal stood at the door of his parents' bedroom, his hand on the light switch. He looked at the dainty dressing table; said, "Good night, Mom"; then, at the manly chest of drawers. "Good night, Dad."

He moped down the dim hall. A compulsion nudged: He turned into Priscilla's former bedroom and switched on the light. Priscilla and Jim had slept in the twin beds that had been pushed together. (Naomi and Ruthie had slept in Rachel's old room, which now had a bunk bed.) He walked around the closet-side of what now served as the Wideman's guest bedroom. He picked up the lavender plastic wastebasket placed beside the night table. In it were a few wadded tissues, which he dismissed with a snort. He puffed his cheeks sighing as he straightened up and for a moment stood musing again on a development in the fundamentalist world that particularly galled him: They had discovered how to "harmonize" female married lust with the Scriptures.

An ex-beauty queen, the wife of a wealthy lawyer, had rocked the born-again subculture with a book preaching that a Christian wife's biblically mandated submission to her husband should be sexy as all get out. Marabel Morgan assured Christian wives that unconditionally worshipping their husbands was the key to earthly happiness. Her first book, *Total Woman*, made the best-seller lists and mainstream talk shows because it was so cheerfully ribald, coaching Christian wives on how to spice up their sex lives—with their husbands only, of course. Putting the children to bed early and seducing hubby by candlelight under the dining room table was one suggestion.

Cal gave the room a final looking over, his fingers on the light switch. His eyes stopped on the closed closet doors. It was stupid but he had to obey, or the still small voice of unreason would pester. He pulled the doors open one at a time—slatted, tripartite wood panels that folded together on tracks. He found nothing to excite his curiosity.

He sat in the rocker—his mother's chair. Gently rocking he let the thoughts come to mind without a conscious purpose. There were cults he considered coercive, such as Jim and Jerry described, but TLF wasn't like them. He wasn't sure that mattered. If what someone like Jim would call "brainwashing" was accomplished without overt physical or psychological coercion; when the force behind indoctrination was entirely psychological and passively submitted to, the black and white of the matter mixed and merged into murky gray. And the whole issue got completely fogged in when you considered that parenting involves indoctrinating children before they have wills of their own, inducing acceptance of certain beliefs with a vast and ancient panoply of mind-manipulation techniques. Love-bombing or withholding love, by turns, for example.

Thinking about Jerry's claim that those who go through deprogrammings afterwards suffer anxiety attacks, nightmares, ulcers, et cetera, he wallowed in a sense of righteous superiority: He had endured all those ills and more—in the course of gradually deprogramming himself.

Nobody has the right...to do unto others what they would not do unto themselves.

That thought reminded Cal that Josh was militantly opposed to deprogrammers. He maintained that even sicko cults had to be included in the Constitutional protection of religious freedom, just as, politically, the lunatics on the right and the left had to be accorded freedom of speech and assembly. When Jack Bristow began to make headlines, in a series of court cases for kidnapping, unlawful imprisonment, and other charges related to deprogrammings, Josh had bitched obsessively about it, insisting that the scofflaw ought to be given a long prison term, along with penalties for the parents who had hired him to deprive their kids of their civil rights. Josh thought sentencing such parents to appropriate community service would suffice.

Cal had generally agreed but with so many nuances that Josh took it as disagreement. Cal thought that the murky gray area had to be painstakingly explored case by case. But who could do it, or should? Who had more right than parents to rush in where judges feared to meddle? But, of course, judicial review only happened when there was a case brought before a court; and that only happened when the deprogramming didn't go off as planned or didn't succeed and the intended victim filed charges.

Remembering those arguments with Josh eased Cal's burden of incipient guilt. Under different circumstances, definitely: He might have gone along with the family on this.

He imagined that hypothetical scenario: He visits an actual commune and talks to Rachel and comes away convinced that her "real" personality was now "buried alive" in a cult personality.

Josh would ask: "Does she want to leave?"

What relevance did that question have if her ostensible will was part and parcel of her captivity?

He saw himself confronting the hypothetical evil cult leader, who looked very much like Mark. And then the guy *was* Mark, for the sake of argument. Mark turned and looked at Rachel, asked her if she wanted to leave—in a soft, mockingly confident voice. Rachel said, "No, of course not, never"—ugly paranoid fear shooting from her eyes.

Thus might a TV drama portray it, Cal thought, and switched back to his internal talk show.

If Josh's brother Elliot became a Moonie and Josh's parents begged him to take part in a deprogramming, would Josh refuse? Cal was certain: Josh would insist he not only wouldn't take part he would try to stop his parents.

You wouldn't try to rescue your brother? Cal thought.

Like you tried to rescue me? the voice of Josh replied. And Cal flashed on Josh's confused, guilt-fraught eyes, just begging to be shown the way, on Derby Day.

He found a cigarette in his hand with a long column of ash, which collapsed when he tried to move it over the ashtray. He tamped out the butt and brushed ashes off his jeans.

He recalled Rachel's face aglow at TLF with the peace that surpasses understanding; thought of the times he had felt that way recently, a contact high, standing in churches with Mexican families who had taken him into their homes. He'd have rather hung a millstone around his neck than mock or question their faith. What did he care what anyone believed? As long as they didn't try to force their beliefs on anyone else, or otherwise oppress and persecute those who didn't share their faith.

He was thinking of Josh again, but it was his own inner voice that said: *Exactly.*

"No, no, forget that," he said. "I realized as soon as Jerry left that I had to make a clear-cut decision. He said some things that really got me thinking."

"Promising to stay neutral isn't good enough, I can tell you that," Priscilla said.

"I know, Jerry told me there was no middle ground—if I wanted to help. Well: I do want to help. I'm not a hundred percent sure it's right, but I'm never that sure about anything. I've decided I have to support the family, for Rachel's sake. Jerry said deprogrammings don't fail. I'm sure Rachel will see the fallacies in Lewten's bullshit. If she's going to be deprogrammed anyway, I may as well help."

"Forgive me, Cal, if you're being sincere, but I don't know whether to believe you," Priscilla said.

"What can I say? Okay, this bothers me, to admit, but...I don't like Mark. I'm worried that she'll marry Mark and have kids, and then... You're right, Pris. I didn't react the way I should have, but partly it's because the religious part of it took my attention from, this being the first time she's been in love and everything. She'll get disillusioned, eventually, with Mark and marriage and then with the cult.

"I can see it now, okay? I sat and thought about it for over an hour and that's what I came to see—so clearly that it hurts. You guys were right not to tell me about this beforehand. I wouldn't have initiated this, all right? But now that it's happening, I want it to succeed as quickly as possible, to get the trauma over with for everybody concerned.

"Pris, you've got to give me the benefit of the doubt here. Take as many precautions as you want, but please, really, you've got to give me a chance to help get through to Rachel, to get her to start thinking and talking."

"Just what all did Jerry tell you?"

"He just...implied that it would go faster if I help out. I mean, it's pretty obvious that she'd try to shut them out, by chanting to herself in tongues. I figure it would create a pretty solid shell, for her to crawl into."

"Why didn't you figure this out before?"

"What do you want? I'm admitting I was wrong. I'm sorry about it, and I want to make up for it if I can."

"I'm not saying I believe you," Priscilla said, "but if you're telling the truth, I'm really sorry, because it's too late. You couldn't have gotten through to her anyway, Cal. We realize now that Rachel is possessed by a demon."

"A *demon*? You can't be serious—"

"An unclean spirit. Mom suspected it all along."

"Demon possession, Pris?"

"Before, we thought you might be able to help, but now... I'm sorry, Cal. I'll give you the benefit of, a lot of doubt, and tell Mom and Dad you changed your mind at the last minute and offered to help. But it's too late now to let you get involved. I don't think there's anything you could have done. It's too bad you didn't decide to help sooner, though, because the experience might have really opened your eyes."

"I didn't see *The Exorcist*," Cal said, "so you'll have to explain it to me: Just how is an exorcism different from deprogramming?"

"Cal, please. There's no point in talking about this anymore. I am exhausted. Please, don't say something now that will make me regret giving you a break. Mom is ready to disown you."

"What a surprise. And Dad isn't?"

Priscilla's voice came a moment late and cracked: "Dad..."—she said the rest while holding back tears—"has always held out hope for you, Cal. His heart aches with sadness and disappointment."

She broke down in barely stifled weeping. He swallowed the lump in his throat and said, "Good night, Pris."

He lifted his lids a crack to check on the fire. He was in the recliner—had it fully extended. He nixed the urge to look at his watch. The last time he checked, it was a few minutes past two. Between midnight and one he had drunk two mugs of warm skim milk with brandy and had taken a hot shower with an icy cold rinse to finish. That woke him up a little too much.

Keeping him awake now was a faintly throbbing pain right about where Hindus locate the eye of spiritual insight. Trying again to slip from consciousness, he had a vision of Rachel sitting in a chair with her hands pressed over her ears, her body curled against the stinging wind of so many words she didn't want to hear.

Charity, he thought, remembering Martin smugly nailing down the letter of Paul's essay on love in First Corinthians thirteen. And tonight: crucifying its spirit.

CHAPTER TEN

Help Thou Mine Unbelief

He suddenly found himself there: Rachel cornered, cowering, fending them off with a mad stare, which she aimed suddenly at him. She recognized him, eyebeams excitedly embracing him with what she knew he knew, which he began to feel, too, seeing it in her: The bliss of an LSD high streamed from her eyes, filling him with oozy sensual panic...

He groaned and bent double but couldn't muster enough force in his legs to lower the recliner's elevated footrest. He flopped back and bounced, throwing himself forward, and the chair snapped into sitting-up position with such force that he was thrown to his feet. He staggered backwards and flopped back into the chair.

He put his face into his hands and rubbed, trying to recollect earlier parts of the dream. He'd had an incoherent shouting match with Jim about demon possession.

He looked at his watch. "Fuck."

He stood up and staggered into motion; ended up in the kitchen, moping on his feet. It was a little after four. Maybe he ought to go down to the police station to make the statement—while those who knew about the case firsthand were still on duty. He wondered what giving a statement would involve. Was he going to dictate while someone typed? Or were they going to give him a pen and some kind of form to fill out?

He decided not to rush it: He'd need a couple hours to make an adequate explanation concise. He tried to psyche himself up for the writing assignment but got sidetracked and then mired in murky review of his dream. That made him decide he was too tired to write a masterpiece of a statement, so the hell with it: Let them type while he talked. Or maybe they could tape it? He'd give them a call, say he wanted to come in ASAP. Like right now. So he could go back to the apartment, to hell with what he told Bob. He'd call them from Evanston.

He went to the phone hanging beside the back door. On the memo board beside it, covering painted flowers below a floridly hand-lettered snippet of Psalms 72—"In his days shall the righteous flourish..."—a fluorescent orange sticker displayed Numbers to Call In Case of Emergency.

He looked at the number for the police—the phone was in his hand—and wondered if maybe he ought to look in the phone book for another number. He wasn't actually reporting an emergency after all.

Then again, maybe he ought to get a little more sleep before trying to talk to anybody about anything.

He let the reins on his eyes go slack and they wandered like horses to the nearest patch of browsable stuff, which happened to be the memo board's letter holder. He'd already sorted through the bills, invitations, and announcements there—after looking for the keys to the church on the peg reserved for them. He hadn't found anything in the letter holder even remotely mysterious, but now he felt his eyes dilating excitedly as he focused on the first envelope's return address. Its top line was printed in large Old English type: Richfield Christian Academy.

He hung up the phone and lifted the envelope. The school was on Rohlwing Road: He remembered it now. He'd driven Sarah and Rachel one summer afternoon to Schaumberg to see little Naomi, not quite a year old and already walking. It was the summer after his freshman year, a Saturday. He'd come back for the weekend so Sarah would quit calling to see how he was; he showed her—healthy, clear of eye, and quick of wit as ever; in fact, he'd looked better than she expected, having gone from hippie to hip for the sake of his job as a door-to-door environmental fund raiser.

Taking Rohlwing Road to Schaumburg wasn't the quickest route, but it was a much more pleasant drive until the suburbs of DuPage County closed in. Before then, while they were still in farmland gone to pasture and going to woods, Sarah got excited, turning in her seat. He had slowed to a crawl while she explained, mainly to Rachel, about the new private Christian school. She told him to turn into the driveway so they could take a closer look. He remembered an impressive tunnel of trees. He'd peered up through the windshield at the sky-chinked canopy of leaves while Sarah and Rachel peered out their side windows across a huge open lawn at a colonial brick building. It was the old county poor house. Sarah had gushed over how nicely the restoration had turned out as they crossed the parking lot behind the school to exit by another tree-lined driveway.

"Dear Rev. & Mrs. Wideman," read the handwritten salutation of the mimeographed typewritten letter from Richfield Christian Academy; the handwriting's homey round clarity contrasted with the headmaster's illegible signature and his stilted prose inviting attendance at a special Christmas program on Sunday night, December twenty-second.

Cal went to the study and got out the street map of Greater Chicago he'd come across in the desk. On its verso, the cartographers had stepped back a few thousand miles to show the suburbs as far west as Wheaton. Richfield was only about fifteen miles from Elmore—over the winding river a couple times, over the East-West tollway, then skirting the Morton Arboretum.

It seemed likely that Martin had been invited to the Christmas program because children of his congregation attended the school. Jim and Pris might have been officially invited, too; they probably knew people connected with the school—friends from Wheaton, perhaps, or Jim's colleagues. And Naomi would be starting kindergarten next fall: Maybe they were thinking of enrolling her there.

Priscilla had said Sunday night was the first time they discussed a deprogramming, after they'd talked to Cal on the phone. Possibly that was true. But Jim, at least, could have been thinking what it would take to pull off a deprogramming—before going to the school that night.

And the way Cal remembered it, the school may have seemed ideal for a deprogramming. No nearby neighbors to notice suspicious comings and goings, and the parking lot was hidden by the building from cars passing on the two-lane blacktop road. There had to be a kitchen, so they could hole up there for days without going out. But if they had to make a quick getaway, within ten minutes they could be speeding east, west, north, or south on an interstate, or simply driving into a garage in any one of a dozen suburbs.

He assumed from what Jerry said that they hadn't gone that far away...yet. When he had tested Priscilla with that inference, she had refused to say—in a way that he took now as confirmation. Jerry had said the situation was going to change today. Obviously, they were going to take her somewhere else.

Jim and Pris had had dinner with Sarah and Martin the previous Sunday after church: They hadn't finished off the bottle of Cold Duck. They had trimmed the tree. They would have spent the afternoon talking about TLF, discussing what they could do. In the evening: They probably all went in the same car to the program at this school.

That would explain why Pris and Jim were at the house later, when he called. If Priscilla was telling the truth, okay: Maybe they didn't discuss deprogramming until after he called; and when they did discuss it, they didn't come to any agreement; they put the idea on hold. Fine, but Jim had probably made up his mind already. And during the socializing after the program at the school, he could have approached a friend connected with the school...

Cal sipped a cup of instant coffee—quickly made from water heated in the microwave oven. He eyeballed his hunch. No doubt about it, this felt like a kind of gnosis: The dark side of his mind saying for certain. While the skeptical side merely admitted the suspicion was not ruled out by anything he knew, although it was sheer guesswork when it came right down to it. He didn't really know if they'd gone to the program at the school. Did he? At the post-caroling gabfest, could he have overheard some tidbit of conversation that planted the seed of an idea that grew into this chain of circumstantial conjecture?

He remembered reading that the human brain takes in about a hundred thousand percepts per second. He must have seen the letter's return address when he first checked out the memo board; his unconscious must have reviewed what he didn't know he knew while he slept, making tentative connections.

It comforted him thus to reason away the possibility of clairvoyance—until he carried the logic further. Was it, then, his unconscious mind's purpose to wake him up with that dream? Were the thoughts that led him to the vicinity of the memo board merely manipulation?

Why did that implacable, impassive, unknown knower within always vanish when he turned his thoughts on it? He remembered catching it off guard one time when he was really ripped on some dynamite hash. Staring at nothing he could remember, he was suddenly aware of that inner other staring right along with him, out the same eyes. And it didn't move when he thought of it. He asked, "Who are you?" And it was gone, seemingly. But he heard a still small voice asking back: "Who wants to know?"

Once past the fringe of Elmore Estates, the dark became darker, without streetlights, without stars, a primal dark swallowing the headlight beams. Occasionally lights outside a distant farm house gave him a twinge of cold comfort.

He didn't want to think about what he would do if he found them at the school. It seemed so improbable...now that he was determined to go there. Ironic doubtfulness had replaced premonitory certitude as soon as he got behind the wheel. No matter: It felt good to be intently focused and in motion instead of tensely emoting in place.

He didn't want to think about it, but he decided he had to. If he found lights on in the school, and his parents' car in the parking lot, what would he do? Would Martin have had his lawyer forewarn the police in Richfield too? After mulling the problem over, he decided he'd let the air out of the tires of their vehicles and call the state cops from a phone booth in Richfield. He'd tell them there was a robbery underway at the school, and then he'd be there to explain the actual situation when they arrived.

If the school was dark and empty, he'd drive on to Schaumberg. He'd ring the bell and try to wring something out of Priscilla while her defenses were down. That scenario turned sour as he envisioned Priscilla just out of bed and angry as hell that he'd woken the girls.

Getting a hunger pang, he remembered the Denny's on Roosevelt Road. He wasn't sure he could handle it: The bleary eyes of strangers exhausted by their dreams and the mundane hauntings of their own unknowable inner others.

A consoling alternative occurred to him: He could go by and wake up Josh. But then he'd have to deal with Josh's mother probably.

Gloomy guilt resurfaced. Mrs. Levinson wouldn't understand; she'd identify with his parents... Maybe he could call Josh first, and then go by and pick him up.

He came out of his daze when he saw streetlights ahead: the little town of Richfield. Meaning that he'd passed the school. He turned around at the first side street and raced back up through the gears.

The school's entrance closer to Richfield was marked by an arrow-shaped sign. He drove slowly past it, rolled down the window, and looked across the flat, elevated lawn—big enough for a couple football fields. The building, defined for him by four illuminated sections of brick wall, looked like a colonial manor house. White window frames showed in the dimmer reaches of the ground-level spotlights; there were two on either side of the entrance: white double doors under a keystone arch.

Fortunately, he wasn't going fast when he turned into the second driveway—he had to jam the brake. The headlights stopped only inches from a heavy chain hanging between metal posts. Centering the chain's sag was a round red reflector, which he'd glimpsed in the nick of time.

The headlights went out when he switched off the ignition: Pitch blackness shocked. He groped the passenger seat for the flashlight. He hesitated to switch it on.

"I know they're not in there," he said. His voice was a comfort. "I know they're probably not in there... Which means, they might be in there, so I have to act as though they are, right? Right."

He put the flashlight in his jacket pocket and got out of the car. He closed the door too softly and it didn't latch. He whispered: "Let's not overdo it, Wideman." He shut it forcefully in slow motion and stood back. The dark gripped.

What the hell: Even if one of them happened to see the flashlight beam, they'd probably think it was a cop coming to check things out. Or Jerry, or somebody else from the church.

He switched on the flashlight and lifted the beam along the ground to the nearest post. Balking, he turned and tossed the beam across the road, spotlighting scraggly weeds poking from a ditch; he raised the beam into rows of stubbled corn stalks. Aloneness pierced and he recognized the desperate visceral confidence that had rescued him from metaphysical shame that night on Cozumel. He turned and followed the beam forward.

It was one spooky place to be at five in the morning. He swung the beam up at the branches: They seemed to stiffen into place when the light hit them and to relax when he drew it away. He stopped and pointed the light like a gun at a tree. "That's right, keep 'em up there, arbol."

That relaxed him so much he decided to do without the flashlight, worried that a Richfield cop might catch him snooping around.

"Yes, sir, Mr. Officer Sir, that's some story all right. Just call my good friend, Safety Officer Ron Cushing over in Elmore. He'll vouch for me."

There was a gap in the phalanx of trees at the edge of the driveway. On the other side of the driveway, a cement walkway went to the front entrance. He drew up close beside a tree and peered around it. He didn't see any windows showing lights on inside the building.

"I tell ya, Mr. Harpuh, there ain't no one heah but us, and I ain't sure you is all heah."

Imitating Paul Newman's imitation of a lunkhead with enlarged adenoids, he said, "Izdatso? Then there's nuthin' to worry about, right?" In his own voice, he said, as he went forward, "Right, except how stupid you're gonna feel in a few minutes."

He cut across a patch of lawn, alternately peering at the ground just ahead and glancing into the dark reaches of the parking lot behind the building. The cold and his momentum encouraged him to accept the obvious: His sleuthing adventure was a story he wouldn't be telling Josh any time soon, and certainly not unless they were stoned.

Giving the corner of the school a wide berth, he strode into the parking lot. He slowed, surprised by how much light there was all of a sudden. All of it seemed accounted for, though, by the spotlights over what was plainly the most-used entrance: Sturdy double doors centering a three-sided projection of the facade that appeared to be a stairwell.

He focused on the turn-around point only moments away; he had only to follow through to free himself of this compulsion. He switched on the flashlight and threw the beam into the parking lot; he glanced behind—and had the breath seized from him. He stopped but didn't turn fully around.

The first three ground-floor windows on the other side of the projecting stairwell-entrance were lit up behind drawn shades. The shades looked like screens and there was a silhouette in the middle one, a man cautiously stepping on a surface well above the floor; a man whose build and manner of moving Cal recognized at once. It took him a few seconds to believe it: The man was his father.

With a clanking thunk, one of the doors burst open and a gangly guy with curly dark hair and dorky black glasses strode briskly into the spotlights and through, glancing straight at Cal for a moment and then bowing his blankly preoccupied face as he stuck his hands into his jacket pockets.

Snapping from stupefaction, Cal switched off the flashlight. Its beam, aimed at the asphalt, must have been blocked from view by his body. He scuttled away, deeper into the parking lot, and glimpsed a parked car. He passed some distance in front of it and started to angle away when he saw another car two parking spaces from the first. He changed course and ducked around the side of the second car.

It was his parents' Buick. He crab-walked toward the front end and peeked over the bumper. The guy looked up and slowed down, getting his bearings; he veered toward the first car. Cal primed himself to dash into the dark—away from the school. Maybe the guy would think he was a thwarted thief.

His heart took off sprinting without him.

A car door opened. He put his nose close to the pavement behind the tire: Light spilling from the driver's side of the other car showed a cowboy boot tilted on its pointy toe. He heard the glove compartment lid slammed shut. The feet came down; the cowboy boots scraped. He heard the front seat flopped forward; the boots shuffled, then took a couple steps backward and the door slammed shut.

Against the distant light from the school he saw the boots moving toward the front of the other car. He got to his haunches, his heart revved to run all out. Carefully he put the flashlight in his jacket pocket, listening hard. He heard the other car's passenger door opened; when it didn't close right away, he realized the guy might search the Buick next. He thought to zip up the jacket pocket as far as he could, to hold the flashlight snugly. He was at this, fumblingly, hampered by his gloves, when the car door shut.

He tightened his crouch and leaned his shoulder against the tire. The steps he heard said the guy was coming around the front of the Buick. Indecision paralyzed him; he was afraid to look and flashed on moments of peak suspense in games of hide-and-seek. Just as he was about to explode into a sprint, he heard the slick boot soles scraping from sudden acceleration.

He almost laughed: Trying to skedaddle, the guy had slipped. With shaky bravura, his voice getting farther away, the guy said, "Hey, you. I saw you. You better get outta here right now."

The voice of a dweeb. Cal crept forward. The guy was a good ways off and nervously poised to run.

Cal switched the flashlight on and located the tire's valve. Using a key, he started letting the air out. He was interrupted by the distant but again instantly familiar clanking thunk of a school door opened from inside by a violent push on its horizontal metal bar.

He saw a short stocky guy walking rapidly through the light.

The tall guy ran toward him and yelled, "Melissa!" And Cal looked again, squinting.

She yelled back, "Dintcha find it?"

"There's someone messing around by the car."

"Wha-a-at? Well, why didn't you stop him?"

The dweeb stopped and turned halfway around, glancing toward the cars. "I think he ran off," he said, as Melissa caught up to him. She passed him without breaking stride. "He better have, if he knows what's good for him."

Cal stifled the panicky urge directing him to flatten one tire at least before she stopped him. He didn't want to be caught in a cowardly act by Melissa. He stood up and composed himself for the encounter with Priscilla's first and only college room-mate.

The first time he met her, Missy had read his mind. "They put me with Prissy to keep the guys away from her. I'm like her watchdog." She had cackled merrily at his flummoxed expression.

He swung the beam up at her. She flinched and marched into it, squinting. She was wearing hiking boots, jeans, and a down vest over a sweater—no gloves and nothing over her ears, but she looked overheated.

"Okay, guy, who are you and whaddaya want?"

Cal lowered the light; he'd taken a position out in front of the first car.

When she was at Wheaton she'd always had the same plain ugly swept-back permanent; she'd switched to a natural short style—no fuss, no bother. Her face struck him as being much more attractive than he remembered, maybe because she'd about eliminated the make-up. All in all, even without a uniform, she looked exactly like what she was: a bossy nurse.

"Oh, it's you." She stopped. "I hear you wanted to be a neutral observer. I didn't think Prissy would fall for that crap. Well, here you are. Observe all you want, just make damn sure you stay out of the way."

"I thought you were in Africa."

"I came back. You mind stepping aside, please?"

He looked over his shoulder at the car and moved out of her way.

"Thank you."

As she opened the door on the passenger side, the dweeb said, "I already looked. It's not there."

"It's here," she said, reaching under the front seat.

She shut the door. He aimed the flashlight at what she had in hand—a classic black doctor's bag. She rolled past the dweeb, saying, "Come on, Jeff, ignore him."

Jeff took a few hesitant steps sideways and backwards, then whirled and hurried to catch up. Cal was stunned. He walked calmly after them. Jeff leaned down; Missy said something to him. Jeff straightened and they both took off running.

Cal almost laughed then realized they intended to lock him out. Did he care? He could do what he'd planned: Let the air out of their tires and call the state police.

He watched them. What if the state police already knew? As for the flat tires, they could call Pris or Jerry to come with another car. He snapped into a jog; sensing that he still had a chance, he sprinted all out.

He was glad he'd worn his tennis shoes. Jeff was an ungainly loper but so long-legged he was a shoo-in for first place. Missy was surprisingly swift given her short legs. Jeff opened the door and leaned out on the bar from inside; he yelled, "Hurry up!" Cal foresaw a neck-and-neck and, if Jeff shut the door on him, possibly a broken-neck finish.

Jeff back-stepped and Missy charged through. Jeff made a fakey feeble attempt to push the door shut, stumbling back an instant before Cal slammed the door aside with his hands. He caromed into Missy; the collision kept him from falling and she absorbed the blow with mincing steps.

"I'm sorry," Jeff said, after shutting the door. "I was afraid he might get hurt."

Cal put his hands on his knees to facilitate huffing. Catching Missy's disgruntled glance at Jeff, he asked, "Who's this?"

"Jeff Krimmer. He was deprogrammed from, the same cult last year. He can tell you, things about it, that might open your eyes."

Pulling off his gloves, Cal glanced at Jeff.

Looking ashamed but angrily sincere, Jeff said, "The leaders are hypocritical egomaniacs, many of them... Some are just bullies, intellectually. And there's a lot of hanky-panky goes on."

"Is that so?" Cal said, pulling off his knit cap.

"He can tell you the nasty details later," Missy said. She glanced toward the brightly lit portion of hallway adjacent to the vestibule. "We have an extremely delicate situation here, Cal. Rachel is either possessed by a demon or they've programmed her to go psychotic if someone tries to get her to think for herself. All night she's been catatonic or raving in that phony tongues language they teach them. Jeff will tell you: It's how they control people. We need help and we know where to get it, but we have to move her. All I ask is that you do like you suggested—observe and say what you want to us, but don't try to interfere. You can't help her. She's too far gone."

"I haven't made an agreement with anybody to stay neutral," he said. "Priscilla didn't tell me you were here. Nobody did."

He stopped short of explaining himself but stared hard at her, as though letting her read his mind.

She said, "This is no time to pull your smart aleck know-it-all schtick. Demon or no demon, Rachel is having a psychotic episode. I have worked as a psychiatric nurse. I know what I'm talking about and I'm telling you: If you try to interfere at this point you might just send Rachel permanently over the edge."

She glanced at Jeff and then at the doctor's bag still clutched in her hand.

"What do you have in there?"

"Medicine," she said, already turning her back on him. Jeff caught up with her.

Cal followed with less urgency, fixing dumbly on Jeff's navy pea jacket—the sleeves were way too short. Mutt and Jeff turned left into the first of two intersecting hallways. Cal had his wind back but not his will. He didn't feel capable of interfering. He could make things difficult for them, sure; but maybe worse for Rachel and without forcing them to stop.

The hallway from the vestibule went to the front entrance, and he could see a lobby with an open doorway on one side—an office. There would be a phone. He considered calling Bob to ask what he should do. He could suggest that he just follow them when they left here.

In the intersection of the first hallway of classrooms, he stopped and studied the light spilling from the first doorway to the left, from which his mother's voice came: "Please, Rachel, please let us help you... We only want..."

He surmised that they were going to give her a shot, a tranquilizer. How crazy could she be acting?

His mother's pathetic pleading drew him closer: "Oh, Rachel, let us help you, please, darling, you're exhausted, you need to rest, please, sweetheart..."

He remembered his dream the instant he stepped into the doorway. Shoved into the corner across the room was a gray metal teacher's desk; children's desks were jammed together around it, forming a lower platform. Rachel was on her knees on the teacher's desk, her back to the corner of the room, her eyes fervently shut. She clutched a Bible just under her chin. Her face, slightly uplifted, was sickly pale; the hair at her temples was sopping and streaky flat where pushed back around her ears; her lips were puffy and cracked and the tip of her tongue protruded.

Hoarsely, Sarah's voice ground to a halt. Jeff hurried from the corner of the room opposite Rachel. Sarah hastily took a plastic glass of water from him, looking past him at Missy.

Missy stood before a table in the corner, filling a syringe; she pulled the needle from a small bottle, squirted, and capped it with a plastic sleeve.

Sarah started up the broken record again. Cal stepped deeper into the room. Jim leaned over the little desks to the side of the big one, his left elbow touching the blackboard. He had glanced back at Cal a few times; he looked nearly as sweaty, wrung out, and desperate as Rachel.

Martin stood on the platform of desks, slumped against the wall between the room's middle window and the one nearest Rachel. His head was bowed and his eyes were closed. His hands hung limply.

Watching Missy approach the lower platform of student desks, Jim's focus narrowed hungrily. He licked his lips and hissed at Jeff, motioning frantically. Jeff rushed to Missy with a chair and helped her up. As she steadied herself on a student desk, Jim whisper-yelled, "Marty!"

Martin's left hand lifted to his brow a moment. Grimly, he stood up straight. Seeing Cal, he gaped; shot an alarmed look at Jim. Jim wagged his head and motioned for him to move in on Rachel.

As if detecting Martin's shaky step closer, Rachel leveled her face; her eyes popped open and zeroed in on Jim—looking at him as though he were the next rapist.

Sarah moved closer to Jim along the edge of the platform, pleading more urgently; Rachel looked furiously defiant, and deaf. Sarah became distraught: Her words tumbled and tears gushed down her cheeks. Missy waved Jeff over; he approached her, saying, "Mrs. Wideman, please... Mrs. Wideman." He touched her shoulder and she snapped forward, sobbing into her hands. Jeff put his hands on her trembling shoulders and turned her around. She straightened and violently hugged him around the waist. He limped off to the other end of the room with her sobbing into his ribs.

Jim signaled and Martin again took a cautious step. Some of the student desks were wobbly, but it appeared to Cal that Martin's unsteadiness was due more to shaky legs.

Cal moved so he had a clear, only slightly oblique line of sight into Rachel's eyes over Jim's shoulder. It was no longer déjà vu: He saw the shocking contrast between her eyes as he'd seen them in his dream, radiating the pure ecstatic joy of a good trip, and her eyes as they were now—holding out like a shield this shockingly fierce aggressiveness that contained a haughty challenge and hateful anticipation.

Her tongue had withdrawn, but her mouth was still open, her chin thrust out: She looked as though she were primed for a savage struggle. Still on her knees on the teacher's desk, she put her right hand out to the wall and got to her feet. Without releasing her eye-hold on Jim, she backed up against the wall and jerked her arms stiffly out, holding the Bible aimed at him. Maniacal animosity peaked in her eyes and flipped into exaltation—she squeezed her eyes shut and threw her head back. Her chapped lips and puffy tongue began to move. The revolting blather that came forth was hoarsely high-pitched.

Missy signaled Martin and they each stiffened into another step toward Rachel. Cal lunged forward, shouting, "LEAVE HER ALONE!"

Their response befuddled him: Martin and Missy impatiently glanced at him; Jim tossed him a nervous glare. Rachel went right on babbling, from deeper in her throat where there was still a bit of moisture. "She needs water," he said forcefully. "Let me give her a drink. Let me talk to her."

"We poisoned the water," Missy hissed at him. "She needs this needle. Now help us instead of acting like a perfect ass."

The temptation to obey seized him. He shook it off: Rachel needed the water and she'd take it from him. He went over to the table in the corner; there was a pitcher of water on it, but no glass. He looked at Jeff and Sarah, sitting across the room before a stack of molded plastic chairs. Sarah was still profusely crying, daubing with a handkerchief. Jeff had the plastic glass in his hand; he startled when he saw Cal approaching but noticed Cal's focus and eagerly held out the glass.

Turning from the table after filling the glass, Cal noted that Missy was conferring with Jim over by the door. They were going to give him a chance to make contact. Why not? If he managed to calm her down, it'd be a cinch to get the needle into her. He pictured himself wrestling the syringe from Missy and holding them at bay with it.

He used the chair Missy had used to climb onto the student desks. Martin was again slumped against the wall, staring dazedly down: From the looks of it, he'd been running his fingers through his hair for hours. The sleeves of his pin-striped oxford shirt were sloppily rolled up to the elbows. Cal finally realized why his eyes looked so vulnerable: He wasn't wearing his glasses.

Rachel's voice had become nearly inaudible, harshly soft. Though her organs of speech were still going through the motions, haltingly, the sounds were mostly in her throat.

When Cal got within three small steps of the teacher's desk, Rachel tensed, throat sounds clogging. She'd brought the Bible in close to her chest; she thrust it out again and pivoted till it was aimed at Cal, her eyes still fervently closed.

"Rachel? Rachel, it's me—Cal."

Her eyes stayed tightly shut. He repeated himself, louder. Her eyelids twitched.

"I'm going to take you back to Mark," he said.

Her eyelids flew open. Concentric rings of energy pulsed from her eyes. He forced himself to remain openly staring back, letting her search, trying to tell her with feeling-thoughts that he knew what she'd been experiencing, that he'd been there, and he was here now to stop all this.

"I had nothing to do with this, Rache, believe me. I would have stopped it, if I'd known... They lied to me, too. I'm going to take you back to Mark and Annie and Bob and the rest. But first, you need this water. It's just water. Look, I'll take a drink. See? It's just water. You need it, Rache. Your lips hurt, your mouth is all dry."

The message in her eyes underwent a heartening transformation, a melting metamorphosis from bewilderment to awe. She looked at the translucent red plastic glass he held out as he stepped closer. Her arms retracted, bringing the Bible to her chest.

"It's just water. Take it... Here, let me hold the Bible."

He put his left hand out and gingerly took hold of the hardcover Bible; she lowered it reflexively but still clutched it tightly. The back of his hand pressed into her breast. He let go of the Bible.

"Okay, here, I'll hold the glass," he said, slowly lifting it toward her mouth.

A rush of joyful trust filled her eyes and she parted her crusted lips.

"Don't talk, here, take some water, just sip, slowly." He tilted the brim, placed it against her lower lip, tilted more, straining his neck, moving in closer over her face to watch with sweet release as the water touched and her tongue numbly responded.

More spilled back out than went down her throat. He paused and poured again, his own tongue getting a tingle as she began to gulp. With surprising firmness she pulled the glass from his hand. Her eyes thankfully closed as she lifted her head back, draining the glass. He so forgot himself that, remembering his audience, he grinned and blushed as he glanced around.

Jim was at the door urgently whispering to Jeff. Jeff did not look eager to obey but compliantly hurried off down the hall. Martin vacantly watched Missy; she was back on the desks, apparently waiting for Cal to take his eyes off her so she could give Martin a message. Cal looked for the syringe: It wasn't in her hand.

"Good job, Cal," she said. "Why don't you help us get her down now. She needs to sleep. We have a bed fixed up in the school nurse's office."

He responded with a mockingly stupefied glower. She blushed angrily and stuck her hands in her vest's side pockets. Jim approached carefully along the blackboard.

"Hey, Cal, come on," Missy said. "She's been like this from the start. It's their fault. They did this to her."

Cal backstepped to the wall, next to Rachel; her eyes were shut—but ecstatically now. He looked at Martin, at Missy, at Jim. What had made these normally reasonable mild-mannered people go violently nuts?

Hoarsely, but with shockingly normal sweetness, Rachel said, "Thank you," and held out the glass. The energy in her eyes had flattened out; the radiating rings were gone. She still looked dazzled by an afterglow of exhausted joy.

Cal took the glass. Jim stepped closer and casually leaned over the student desks, stretching out his hand, wiggling his fingers, "Here, I'll get her more water."

Cal took a step and the hand he started to hold out flinched. He flung the glass at Jim's face. Jim swatted it away and it bounced around on the desks.

"Nice try, Jim."

"Come on, Cal. We don't want to get physical with you. I'm asking you to please get down from there before someone gets hurt."

Cal glanced again at each of them in turn. "Don't any of you understand? It's over. You tried and your efforts have failed." He looked squarely at Jim. "If you're lucky, Rachel won't press charges. I will press charges if you so much as lay a finger on me."

He saw the strategy in a flash: He would grip Rachel's wrist with both his hands and cling so hard they'd have to use illegal force—assault and battery—to pry him loose. "Rachel?" he said, intending to explain this plan.

She was flipping pages in the Bible, her eyes avid. "Oh, Cal, I can do it now, I can show them. It's in here, First Corinthians, the reason they can't understand."

Martin, Jim, and Missy traded suspicious looks.

"Marty, we're going to have to get a little rough," Jim said.

Cal looked pleadingly at Martin. "Come on, Dad. Let's call it quits before someone gets seriously hurt."

Martin slightly nodded in slow motion at Jim.

"I'm not going to fight you guys," Cal said. "I'm going to hang onto Rachel though. You'll have to assault me to make me let go, and I *will* press charges."

Jim sidled over to the chair next to the platform of desks. Cal edged in front of Rachel. Missy took her hands from her vest pockets and put them out in front of her hips, fingers spread like a gunslinger's.

Cal's right hand went to the butt of the flashlight sticking from his jacket pocket; he thought about waving it like a bludgeon to hold them off. He considered swinging it in earnest. It was self-defense, after all. He'd hit at their arms and backs, not their thick skulls.

"Here it is," Rachel said, "Here it is, I found it..."

Jim was getting up on the platform. Missy moved closer to Martin, urging him forward. Rachel shouted:

"GLOR-y, GLOR-y!"

"Hallelujah," Cal muttered, abandoning the flashlight idea. He zipped up his jacket while staring at Jim and squared off, lifting his hands out like a wrestler.

"But we are all," Rachel read, her voice rasping; Cal could feel her swallow; "...with open face, beholding as in a glass, the GLOR-y of the LORD...are changed, into, THE SAME IMAGE, from GLOR-y to GLOR-y, by the SPIRIT OF THE LORD." Her voice had become a laryngitic screech.

"She's doing real damage to her vocal cords," Jim said, planting himself one desktop nearer. "Tell her to stop, for her own good. You can hear that she's doing damage to her voice."

"*But the natural man,*" Rachel continued, her voice nearly gone, "*receiveth not the things of the Spirit, for they are foolishness unto him, neither can he know them, because they are spiritually discerned.*"

Martin and Jim were only two desktops away from the teacher's desk and eyeing each other.

"*Christ in YOU,*" Rachel cried, in a squeaky raspy whisper, "*the hope of glory!*"

Cal saw his father's eyes swivel involuntarily toward the door; Jim looked, too, and Cal lunged at him, both hands hitting him solidly in the chest. Jim stumbled backwards; Cal caromed, twisting away as he fell headlong to one side. Jim stumbled and crashed, knocking over a couple desks on the edge of the platform. Cal scrambled to his feet.

Missy stepped between Cal and Rachel, throwing up her arms like a basketball player on defense. Jeff, back from his errand, stood just inside the door; she yelled at him: "Help Marty hold her!"

Cal made the mistake of glancing at his father and Missy rushed him, grabbing his right arm at the wrist and bicep and whirling, stumbling with him over Jim, who was moaning about his ankle.

As Cal staggered back to his feet, he saw Martin lunge for Rachel. She twisted away, ducked when his other arm came around at her, and backpedaled to the opposite end of the teacher's desk, glancing over her shoulder at the lower level of student desks as though it were an abyss. She faced her father defiantly; he moved toward her. She clumsily cocked the Bible and pitched it.

The book hit Martin smack in the face. He let out a truncated moaning yell, stumbling backward, and when his hand came away from his face blood was streaming from his nose.

Rachel's hands went to her mouth and then moved out toward Martin—but hung in the air a moment helplessly and came back to her face. Missy stumbled over to Cal and grabbed his arm. She looked to see why he'd gone limp and let him go. Martin backed toward the corner, bowing over his blood, gape-mouthed.

"Head back, put your head way up and hold it back," Missy commanded. "Where's your handkerchief?" Martin shook his head. "Jeff, my bag!" Missy yelled, looking for him. He hadn't moved at her last command, but he reacted to this one, hurrying across the room to the table.

Jim sat up, groaning that his ankle was broken as he unlaced his shoe. Cal caught a vicious glance from him and had the distinct feeling Jim was exaggerating his injury to excuse himself from further struggle.

Cal grabbed Rachel's arm and got her down off the platform. At the door, she balked: "Where's Mom?"

He only then noticed. "Not here," he said, "come on."

He stopped in the intersection of the two hallways. Rachel didn't recognize the word *parka*; but *coat* she understood. She shook her head.

"I—I don't know."

"Forget it," he said.

"Oh-h!" she cried and put her hands hard over her eyes. Tremblingly, she said, "The office, the nurse's office—where I woke up and—Ohhh..."

"Don't think about it. What happened? Did they drug you with something?"

"I felt crazy. Missy and Jim... I saw the devil in them."

Jeff came hurrying down the hall. "Your mother's out that way, waiting in the car." He stopped—at a safe distance. Edging around, he said, "Maybe you should go out the front."

"We need her parka," Cal said.

Jeff thought, said, "I'll get it," and moved briskly past them toward the front of the building.

"Come on, Rache," Cal said, following him.

She was looking toward the doors to the parking lot. "I have to see her, Cal, I have to tell her...that I forgive her, that I still love her."

"She's too upset now. You can do it later, you can call her."

She looked at him blankly; he held out his hand. "Come on." She shook her head and looked at the floor. He stepped tentatively, she relaxed, and he began to walk faster; she caught up and they fell into step.

Jeff had disappeared. They looked down the intersecting hallway off the front lobby. Jeff stepped out of a room, holding the parka. "It was in the nurse's office."

While Rachel put it on, Cal stuck his hand out to Jeff. "Thanks for not shutting the door on me."

Jeff blushed and limply shook hands. "I'm sorry," he said, glancing warily at Rachel, "about...everything."

"Listen," Cal said, "would you tell our mother that Rachel will call her in the next few days? Tell her she's not going to hold this against them."

"All right," Jeff said, swallowing such embarrassment that Cal knew he'd never do it.

As they stepped outside, he pulled the flashlight from his pocket—and saw that they didn't need it. The trees were stark black thickets against the lavender-gray sky.

As they hurried across the frosty grass, Rachel looked up and asked, "How did you find out—about this place?"

He squelched the urge to wisecrack. She glanced again.

"I'm not sure how, exactly. I'll tell you about it in the car."

After he dropped her off at the TLF house in Lake Forest, Cal joined the southbound rush hour traffic on Sheridan Road, which was light to start but quickly slowed to crawl. He had plenty of free time to throw glances at the Bahai Temple as he passed it in slow motion. He was exhausted physically and yet keyed up mentally. He fell into autopilot mode as he recalled the last time he had taken LSD.

The Nabobs weren't a tight group sophomore year. Hank and Injun Joe lived at the other end of campus from Cal, Josh, and Kevin. Brought together every day except Sunday by their jobs in the dorm cafeteria, they maintained their special rapport, but they rarely socialized as a group anymore.

One night near the end of spring quarter, while they were sitting around a table in the cafeteria enjoying the post-work gabfest of the entire crew, the hip young food service manager asked them about tripping. The Nabobs regaled him with hilarious tales of yore.

Nostalgic camaraderie carried the five of them back to Hank and Joe's room; they'd stayed in the same dorm, but the dorm hadn't stayed the same. McCullough Hall had gone from freak zoo in the spring of 1971 to premed mausoleum that fall—obviously a conspiracy of the Registrar to take more second-rate but straight. Disgust for the super-competitive career-obsessed assholes prevailing in the freshman class catalyzed a consensus as the Nabobs passed around a joint.

Almost a year had passed since their last trip together. Each of them had tripped at least once since then: Cal with Tamara, Josh with Kevin, and Hank with Joe. They all agreed that their recreational tripping days were over, but they were happy to have the memories, and they valued their fraternal bond born of numerous shared psychedelic adventures. They were each a little afraid, but they were all willing to drop acid again if they all did it together.

The following Saturday, early in the morning, they dropped in Josh and Kevin's room. They lounged around, smoking and joking to keep primal dread at bay. Alarmed by how fast he was coming up, Cal woozily stood and wandered across the hall to his garret room and kept on going—out the door and down the wobbly fire escape their landlady did not want them using except in an emergency, which he felt this was.

He sat down under the magnificent tall old tree that had graced his late night solitary gazing all that school year; a branch, on windy nights, had tapped on the roof right over his bed. He'd never bothered to find out what kind of tree it was. He sat down in its shade as on the first day of creation, enchanted by the birds dipping, darting, flitting, flying away and back, making their usual joyful racket, which threatened to stop his heart with unbearable gladness.

Hank appeared on the fire escape and came down; then Injun Joe, Josh, and Kevin. They sat down or sprawled around Cal; he sat cross-legged, smoking a cigarette and secretly rejoicing in the mundane miracle of the grass underneath them: Innumerable tiny tongues of biochemical flame praising the outpouring of the sun's holy light.

He repressed the urge to point out the obvious. He sensed them sensing that he had something to say, their evasive glances gravitating toward him.

He let the joy go goofy all over his face. "You can bury me but you can't kill me," he said, tearing out handfuls of cool succulent grass and tossing them into the air.

His brothers in Dionysus laughed and babbled for several minutes about feeling exactly the same way.

CHAPTER ELEVEN

The Wise of Heart

CAL WOKE TO THE ringing phone. The darkness confounded him. He remembered the strange bed. The phone rang again and more of his memory arrived. He wrenched and rolled on the buoyant mattress, lifting the receiver as it rang for the third time.

"Josh's Funeral Home. Where's the body?"

"Who are you?" Josh asked.

"Who wants to know?"

"I asked you first."

"Fuck off."

"That's what I've been doing all day. What have you been doing?"

"Sleeping. I guess. What time is it?"

"You don't sound good. Don't tell me: The peace talks failed, you found my stash, and you've been hitting the water-pipe all day."

"I wish. It's a long story. I'll tell you on Sunday. What time's your mom serving lunch?"

"Ah, come on, tell me now. But just the one-minute version."

"It's way too heavy to get into over the phone."

"I guess that means they didn't hug and make up. Sorry to hear it. Anyway, show up around eleven so we can get our exercise done by lunchtime, after which we'll settle down to drink beer and watch football all afternoon. My Mom gave my Dad a big new TV. As an un-Christmas present."

"Sounds good. Popcorn?"

"You bet. Listen, do me a favor and bring my headband, if you can find it. I think it's in the closet somewhere. The weatherman says it's going to get warm enough to play b-ball without gloves, so don't think you're going to escape your usual drubbing."

He was shaking Tabasco sauce into a bowl of chicken noodle soup when the phone rang again. He debated whether to let it ring. After all, it wasn't his phone. He got up and walked to the bedroom.

"Josh's joint, Cal speaking."

"Hi, Cal."

"Oh. Hey, Rache. What's up? You feeling all right now?"

"Yeah, I feel okay. How about you? Did you get some sleep?"

"I had a little trouble this morning," he said, "but, heh, once I finally conked out..."

"It really helps if you eat something. We just ate," she said. "I only slept a few hours this afternoon, but I feel almost back to normal...emotionally, anyway. I still feel kind of wasted, physically."

He hesitated to mention that he'd just sat down to a meal himself, and she went on: "I wouldn't have called, so soon, but...I'm worried that Dad's nose might be broken."

"No, I don't think so. It was just a nosebleed. His nose will be severely out of joint for a while, but other than that..."

"There was so much blood though."

"Nosebleeds always look a lot worse than they are. I'm sure it's nothing serious."

He read her pause as prefacing the real reason for the call. He swallowed to assess the extent of the sore spot in his throat. He aimed killing vibes at the germs.

"I feel kind of bad," she said, "about the way things turned out. I mean, not that I'm not grateful, for being rescued. Maybe the real good that came out of it is...that you felt God's power at work. But God wouldn't have had to send you to rescue me if my faith had been stronger."

"Oh, Rachel..."

"It's okay, I'm not, you know, looking for sympathy or anything. But I did let God down. I've asked forgiveness and I've grown. I can see that I'd really begun to get a big head about, thinking I had so much spirit power, but when it came time to put my money where my mouth was and really manifest—under pressure—I chickened out."

He shut his eyes, put his hand over the mouthpiece for a moment, and sighed deeply. "Rachel, it wouldn't have mattered how much spirit power you showed them. They were convinced you were possessed by an unclean spirit. Don't you remember when the Pharisees said that Jesus' power came from Satan?"

"Well," she said, with a hint of comfort-taking in her voice, "that's about what Mark and the others are saying. But I still feel bad about not manifesting the operation of the spirit they would have had to understand at least a little bit—prophecy. I didn't start prophesying until after you gave me that drink of water. I did manifest tongues and faith and discerning of spirits, but without prophecy there was no way I could show them that I know the Word in a new way that, that makes more sense than their way, but that you can't really see if your mind isn't renewed, by spirit power. But even if you can't totally accept it, my way, our way, at least you can see that it makes sense."

Cal rolled his eyes. "But they weren't going to listen and respect your beliefs," he said. "They were going to twist anything you said and demean you for believing it."

"I know," she said, "but if I'd been able to prophesy and debate with them, at least then they'd have to think about it, and maybe have their consciences bother them."

(He resisted the urge to suggest again that she ought to press charges, if only so she could magnanimously drop them. In the car she had explained that when she went into the house she only saw Sarah; while they were talking, somebody—probably Jim, she thought—had grabbed her and pressed an ether-soaked cloth over her nose and mouth. When she came to, on a cot in the nurse's office at the school, she vomited into a bedpan held by Missy. Cal had not told her what he suspected: that it was Martin who had knocked her out with the ether.)

"I guess, the only reason I really care that I didn't prophesy," she said, "is because I thought that I might get through to Mom, at least. Oh, Cal, I still feel so awful that she did this to me." She sounded near tears; her voice firmed up quickly, though, as she went on.

"She made me feel crazy when she looked at me. I was so afraid, because all I could see in their eyes was—it really was like 'a veil upon their hearts.' I could see it in their eyes, this veil of ignorance and fear. I didn't see how I could get through, with words... I thought if I could pray in the spirit hard enough, the veil might be lifted from their hearts, from Mother's heart at least.

"But then when I was praying I got caught up in the spirit of *agapao*... Oh, Cal, it was so intense, I just can't describe how incredibly knowing and beautiful and free I felt. I'd never experienced it so fully before. I really was 'in the heavenlies,' like Paul says. But every time I'd look at them, I just saw that veil of fear and hatred. And it just seemed more and more hopeless, if they couldn't see that Satan was in *them*, not in me.

"Satan had everything turned around in their minds and I just—it just seemed so hopeless I didn't know what else to do but to go on praying that God would remove the veil from their hearts. But it went on for so long. Satan began to make me really scared about what they might do to me. And then all of a sudden you were there, and when I looked into your eyes and I didn't see the veil, I knew God had sent you.

"But I thought, you know, that you had come to believe, or that you'd just realized that you still did, because of your visit the other night, the things you heard and read, and everything. When you were there, it was like I, I felt like I was seeing right into your heart... And what I saw was that you knew what I was feeling. And so, it gave me strength. That's when I began to prophesy. Even though it was too late...

"I realize now that you couldn't have known what I was feeling completely, because...if you don't believe, the closest you can come to it is *phileo*...not *agapao*. But that's good, because it's ordinary brotherly love that leads us to want to experience the best form of love, the spiritual love of God in the renewed mind...

"Cal? Say something."

He took his time, said, "Something."

"Please, Cal, don't. Tell me what you're really thinking. Right now."

"Right now, Rache, I am not thinking anything. I'm just listening."

"Cal... I love you. I wish...I wish we could believe the same thing. I wish we all could."

"I do, too, Rache. And I love you no matter what you believe or what I believe or what anybody believes... There's something I wanted to ask you. I take it TLF doesn't believe in Hades."

"Hades? Oh, yeah. I mean, no, we don't. All the stuff we learned about hell and the Lake of Fire is either misunderstood or added on. The Bible rightly divided doesn't teach any of that; it teaches that if you aren't born again in the Spirit, you just cease to exist when you die. It's spirit that keeps on living eternally and only believers have spirits. When we die, our spirits are asleep in the Lord. It's like suspended animation. And then when Jesus returns we will be awakened in our completely spiritualized bodies, in the resurrection."

"Now there's an eschatology I can live with," Cal said.

"Hell's really a perverted idea," she said. "It always bothered me. It just seemed so inconsistent with the love of Christ."

"Well, then, we have that belief in common," Cal said.

"I wish it was more."

"Maybe someday it will be. As they say in Mexico, about nearly everything, *Who knows?* Thanks a lot for calling, Rache. I'll call Pris if you want me to, to make sure Dad's nose isn't broken."

"Would you?"

"No, wait, what am I saying? I don't wanna talk to Pris. I'll call Jerry Edwards. How's that? Tonight or tomorrow sometime."

"All right. I'd feel better, to know Dad's all right."

"Why don't you write them a letter, telling them what you just told me...but in a way, that's for them, right? Telling them that you forgive them. And then, just give them time. Okay?"

"All right. I'd like to tell them....even if they burn the letter. I hope Mom will read it, though."

"I think she will," he said. "All you can do is try. So, listen, I gotta go. I'll call you tomorrow night. Don't worry about Dad. I'm sure he's all right."

"I hope so. All right. Good night."

"Good night, Rache. Talk to you tomorrow."

He sat on the edge of the bed, staring at the dusty clump of hair on the floor, letting the semi-pathos dissipate. Then he felt a hunger pang, and remembered his now tepid soup.

❖

"Hello, may I speak with Jerry?"

The woman who'd answered—presumably Sally Edwards—said, "May I ask who's calling, please."

"Cal Wideman."

"Oh. Let me see if he's able to come to the phone. He was in the shower."

A couple minutes later the line clicked and Jerry said, "Hello, Cal. If this is a request to convey a message to your parents, I'm sorry but I must refuse, under the circumstances. I'm sure you can understand the position I'm in."

Cal needed a moment.

"Are you there?" Jerry asked.

"I don't understand the position you're talking about, Jerry. But I didn't call to ask you to deliver a message. I just wanted to find out if Martin's—, if his nose is okay, not broken or anything."

"Oh. I see. No, his nose is not broken."

"I didn't think it was. Rachel was worried about it."

"Well. I suppose I can tell you, what you will be learning soon anyway, from Sam Williamson."

"Who?"

"Your father's attorney."

"You've got to be kidding."

"I'm afraid not. I did warn you that opposing your parents in this matter would have serious repercussions. You are no longer welcome in their home, and since you have quite a lot of clothes and books there still..."

"Happy to have them donated to next year's white elephant sale, Jerry. Or dropped off at the Salvation Army."

"I believe your mother plans to have all of it hauled to the dump. Martin thought it only fair to offer you the opportunity, since they are your things...

"Oh, and I should tell you that they had the locks changed. You'll have to arrange a time with Sam Williamson, for getting whatever you want. He'll be in touch with you."

Cal did not speak, for fear that Jerry would hear the tears in his eyes.

"I realize that you followed the dictates of your conscience," Jerry said. "I think you were wrong and that you'll come to realize that, someday."

Cal let the tears flow and snuffled proudly.

"I'm sorry," Jerry said, "I thought, last night, that you understood what was at stake."

Breathing deeply, Cal got his voice back. "You know, Jerry? Many parents, even though they aren't Christians, are able to love their children *unconditionally*. My parents can't do that. But I should have known. After all, their God can't even do that."

He gently placed the handset into its cradle before Jerry could respond.

❖

Josh walked down the driveway, arm hooking the basketball to his side. "You made it," he said.

"Of course I made it," Cal said, tossing him a thick black headband bearing the Chicago Bulls logo. "Why wouldn't I make it?" He shut the door and jogged past the front of the car into the street.

Josh passed him the ball and donned the headband. Cal set the ball to spinning on the tip of his index finger.

"You look like the cat that swallowed the cannabis," Josh said. "What's the story?"

Cal pulled the ball to his chest. "Not yet." He bounced a pass, with English. Josh lunged but only got a hand on it. The ball skittered into the street. Cal ran after it.

"Not yet?" Josh called after him.

"There is a time for every purpose under heaven," Cal said, walking back.

Josh put on a mocking expression, then grumpily frowned. Cal shot a pass straight at his beer belly. Josh skipped backwards and doubled over as he caught it. He held the ball lovingly with both hands, closer to his left shoulder, as he grinned menacingly. "So... Ve haf vays of makink you talk, Herr Videmann."

He did a slow-motion windup and fake-hurled, letting the ball slip off his hand behind him. Cal cringed. Josh whirled and snatched the ball on the bounce and sharply passed it. Cal jumped into catching position and bobbled it against his chest.

"You gotta stay on your toes if you wanna play in this league, boy," Josh said. "So enough curiosity-teasing already. Come on, what happened?"

"I've submitted an application to the Peace Corps," Cal said while dribbling the ball back and forth in front of Josh while trying to stay on his tippy toes.

"You lie," Josh said, feinting like he was going to try to steal the ball.

"I'm not lying. I'm not even kidding. Did you know they're now part of this big agency Nixon created called ACTION?"

"Actually," Josh said, "I did know that. It's also the bureaucracy mothership for domestic volunteer programs, like VISTA."

"Not sure what my chances are, as an English major. But they have openings for English teachers and translators."

Josh grimaced and slapped at the ball, knocking it away. Cal was quicker going after it and ended up with a half-step break. He didn't get the timing of the last step right, but the ball hit the rim off the backboard and went in.

They settled into an easy-going game, not keeping score, rarely really trying to stop a shot. Occasionally one would reward an especially good shot by letting the shooter go again.

After about ten minutes of this, Josh pulled in a rebound and made the time-out T with his hands. He set the ball down and sat on it. Frowning hard, he said, "So: This is serious."

Cal grinned. He sat down cross-legged.

Josh said, "I think you ought to go for that paralegal job."

"I don't think the guy would hire me now," Cal said. "Tell your granddad I'm interested in something short-term; almost anything if the pay is good. If the Peace Corps takes me, I have to attend some kind of orientation here in the States, a last chance for them to decide if they really want me, and vice versa. If neither side backs out at that point, then I'm off to pre-service training *in-country*, as they say. They don't have any projects in Mexico, so I told them any other Spanish-speaking country would be fine with me."

"I think you ought to go to law school," Josh said. "Preferably one I could get into the following year, so you could give me all your notes and make sure I pass with minimal booking."

"I'd rather get a master's in journalism...maybe," Cal said. "I have three years to think about it. If all goes according to plan."

"Three years? I thought it was only two."

"Several months of waiting to hear if I've been accepted, several more months of training, a two-year assignment, and then at least a few months to recuperate, right?"

Giving him a long hard look, Josh was finally convinced. He shook his head disgustedly. "I bet your parents are happy. It's almost like being a missionary."

"Almost," Cal said, standing up. "Come on, let's play." Josh flipped him the ball and he sauntered to the street, dribbling.

He turned around and crouched slightly, looking like he wanted to see some serious defense.

Josh did not oblige; he stood a few feet in front of the basket, aping apathy as he watched Cal's slow progress against an invisible quick little guard who kept poking his hand at the ball. Cal feinted suddenly and made his move: driving from the edge of the driveway straight toward the hoop. Josh lazily raised his hands. Cal stopped, leaping up and back, launching a picture-perfect jump shot. The ball hit the forward part of the rim and bounced down right at Josh's face as he was nonchalantly turning around. Ducking, he swatted it away. Cal walked after it.

"You can't do this to me, you know," Josh called.

Cal broke into a jog, and called back, "Why not?"

"Because..."

He picked up the ball and energetically strode into the neighboring lawn.

"Hey, where you think you're going?" Josh called. "Guatemala's this way."

He got into position for a two-handed shot from about thirty feet away, his sight line parallel to the face of the backboard.

"How much you give me if I make this?"

Josh frowned and lowered his face, crossed his arms and glanced at the basket. He raised his voice: "Five million eight hundred fifty-six thousand, seven hundred thirteen dollars...and ninety-seven cents."

"Is that all? How much you give me if I miss?"

"As many beers as you can drink without laughing so much at your own stupid puns that you embarrass my mom."

"Okay, you're on."

"Your chances of making this shot are about the same as your chances of getting into the Peace Corps. Especially if you listed me as a reference."

Cal lowered the ball. "Now, just what are you going to tell them?"

"I can't let you do this to me."

"You forget everything you learned in college? The trip gets to be a drag unless you think of some excuse to get yourself moving so things can happen. You gotta keep on truckin', man."

Josh rolled his eyes. "Hurry up and shoot, you turkey."

Cal planted his feet and without taking aim crouched and launched a two-handed push shot. The ball had enough loft, looked like it might just have a chance... It hit the far inner side of the rim and bounced high, looking for a nanosecond like it just might drop through the net.

It nicked the rim and bounced a short ways down the driveway and off the opposite edge from Cal, onto the lawn.

"You had me worried there," Josh said.

Walking away, Cal said, "Hold on. This is all part of the same shot."

He scurried in a wide circle and came in on the ball, crouching. Grabbing it, he did a slow-motion somersault, flinging with both hands as he came up.

The ball almost hit the bottom of the backboard. Cal cringed and Josh cowered in response to the banging and clattering in the garage. A bicycle fell over.

"You turkey," Josh said, and leaned into a shuffling jog.

Cal lowered his back to the ground, ludicrously disappointed. He arched his neck and scanned until he found the barely brighter spot in the dismal gray sky. Shutting his eyes, he imagined the tropic sun he hoped to be living under—someday, maybe. He listened to the ball bouncing inside the garage and then outside on the driveway. When the bouncing stayed in one place, he raised himself to his elbows.

Josh languidly dribbled, alternating hands, his head bowed, eyes fixed on the ball. A tenuous smirk presaged the embarrassment in his voice. "I'm going to be really pissed off if you actually join the Peace Corps. If you do that, I will probably get to feeling, sooner than I had planned, that I ought to give up my underachiever's dream job and become a professional benevolent person."

Cal kept his eyes on the ball. "It's hopeless, man. We're all programmed."

"Speak for yourself, gaper. Time for a beer." Pivoting on one foot, Josh launched a hook shot. The ball dropped cleanly through the net.

Cal yelled, "All right!" and Josh threw his fist into the air. As he jogged into the garage, he scooped up the ball and flipped it around his hip without looking back. It skittered across the driveway, softly bounced on the grass, slowing to a smooth roll right up alongside Cal's left leg. With insouciantly reflexive, and thus, perfect timing, he raised his hand and stopped it.

He lay down and set the ball on his chest; felt his heart bouncing under it.

All part of the same shot.

He mused in the spirit until the door in the garage slammed shut. He sat up, blinking frantically, lest Josh see, and he be tempted to interpret.

Acknowledgments

Nancy Cavallaro—scientist, teacher, gardener, yoga practitioner, bird watcher, music lover, artist, and chef—has been the love of my life for over 50 years and my wife for nearly that long. An incorrigible optimist, she supported me emotionally and financially throughout the writing and rewriting and not-writing of early versions of this book, a period spanning most of the 1980s.

I am grateful to my late parents for encouraging me to write this story. Ruth and Merritt Dayton enthusiastically shared books and author recommendations and tirelessly answered my questions about their faith journey from free will fundamentalism to the most conservative Reformed Protestant theology. Indeed, it was their wholehearted embrace of double predestination, when they were in their fifties, that inspired me to start imagining Cal Wideman and his family. I should add, though, that if Cal's parents had been like mine, the family drama at the heart of this story would never have happened.

Finally, I must acknowledge a debt of gratitude to three comrades in the love of literature who agreed to respond to early drafts: Daniel Margulis, who gave me engaging and thoughtful feedback on longer and longer manuscripts over several years; the late Patricia Wilcox, a mentor and friend whose feisty affirmations revived my creative spirit when I was ready to give up; and the novelist and professor John E. Vernon, who showed incredible generosity in answering Patricia's plea to help me. John read my thousand-page typescript during his break from university teaching one summer. His response was a master class in uncompromising but sympathetic critique. His incisive evaluation led me to sever two complicated fictional worlds that had become competitively entangled. I took his advice and focused on the story I had started out writing, the one I knew best. The other story I had to abandon was a surrealistic tale about a hopeless love affair that Cal left behind in Mexico City. Fortunately, I have not been able to find any surviving copies. It's doubtful I'd have enough years left to finish that story.

About the Author

At the Imagine Museum in St. Pete

David Dayton worked for thirty years as a writer, editor, teacher, and researcher in higher education and government. He specialized in business and technical writing, information design, and usability testing. After retiring in September 2019, he revived an earlier career focused on creative writing. In 1979, Copper Beech Press published his first poetry collection, *The Lost Body of Childhood*, which you can read for free online or purchase at Google Play Books. From 1979 to 1990, he ran Alembic Press, which published eleven books of poetry and literary prose by others. In April 2023, he published his second book of poems, *The Bus to San Simón*, under a new Alembic Press imprint, Boca Ciega Books. His current main writing project is a family history and memoir. Explore all his published writing, audio and video recordings, and drafts of new work at daytonwriting.com.

www.ingramcontent.com/pod-product-compliance
Lightning Source LLC
Chambersburg PA
CBHW071524260626
47170CB00002B/489